THESE FATES THAT BIND US

EVENING STAR SAGA: BOOK ONE

RACHEL TORK

To anyone who has been told they're "too much".
Burn brighter.

Note (Trigger Warnings)

This book is meant for adult audiences and contains sensitive content including:
explicit sex scenes, explicit language, sexual assault (brief on-page),
references to abuse by a family member, and (on-page) physical abuse

ONE

Light fractured in my eyes as the intoxicating pull of the vodka shots I'd taken earlier dragged me further into a haze. Deeper and deeper I fell, until I became one with the beat of the music and the flashing neon glow around me. Down so far into the silky depths of numbness that I forgot my name, my purpose, and even my body.

That was until Lil shouted from a few feet away, "Aster!"

I slammed into a very hard body just as her slurred warning reached my ears. I looked up, my gaze locking with that of the stranger I'd nearly toppled over.

Through the blur of the colored lights and my drunken haze, the stranger's amber eyes lit up in what I could only decipher as amusement. His wavy, silver hair was pulled back in a casual bun, a few loose strands framing his face. I giggled, starting to reach out to touch one of those loose pieces. His hair almost looked like starlight taking corporeal form. Maybe he was starlight…

"Hey, woah, woah, Aster!" Lil stumbled over. "Let's not just go petting random strangers."

I didn't even have the sense in me to glare at her. In fact, my expression was probably something between blank and ridiculously ditzy.

Around us, the club was packed. The dance floor was writhing with scantily clad bodies and the marble-topped bar was flooded with patrons, a few even sitting on the counter. Neon lights in the shapes of flowers hung from the tall ceiling—very appropriate for a venue in the Seelie Court. I wondered idly what Unseelie Court clubs looked like. If you asked someone here, they'd probably say that anything to do with our rival court was full of shadows and ill-intentions. As if those things weren't rampant here too.

"Is that what you were trying to do?" a voice floated over, cutting through my hazy, wandering thoughts. "*Pet* me?"

I raised my gaze back to the silver-haired stranger I'd bumped into. Fae, by the delicate point of his ears. Or at least half. Sometimes it was hard to tell.

I must have stared a second too long at his ears because he chuckled. He then brushed a strand of my hair back before tracing a thumb up my own slanted ear.

"Yes, love, I'm just like you," he said.

I think Lil's mouth might have popped open. The stranger smiled slyly at me, dragging his hand from my face, before disappearing. About a minute later, the music floating around us began to quicken. But it wasn't the typi-cal, bass heavy beat of the club music that had been playing only a moment ago. This music was undeniably Fae.

A few patrons—shifters, sirens, and maybe even a human or two—groaned. They knew they'd never be able to keep up with the quick, odd rhythm that was faerie music. Lil glanced around nervously, but at that moment, the stranger reappeared in front of me.

"If the ears didn't convince you, maybe this will," he said.

He hardly paused before sweeping me into his arms and moving to the music. I stumbled a bit before catching up with him. His hands found my waist, his touch featherlight. The movement on his part gave me some more confidence; or perhaps that was from the last spiked seltzer I'd chugged with Lil only minutes ago, finally kicking in.

My hands reached up to twine in the loose strands of his hair. It was silky beneath my fingers and I laughed softly.

"What's that?" he murmured, leaning close to my ear.

"I didn't say anything," I replied breathlessly.

Something flickered in those amber eyes as I spoke to him for the first time. It was gone in the breath of a moment as the song began to fade out. Seconds later, the pulsing beat of the usual club music replaced its melodic chaos. Still, I did not let go of the beautiful stranger.

His broad hands trailed up my back and I couldn't help the soft sigh that escaped me. His hands tightened for just a moment, then he let me go. I stumbled back at the sudden loss of a steady presence. He gave me one last half-smile and turned to leave.

"Wait!" I called after him.

He slowly faced me again, a dark brow raised.

"What's your name?" I asked, my words slurred.

A shadow curled up around his ear and my eyes widened at the sight of it. His long legs ate up the distance between us, until he was back, standing inches away from me again. Goddess, this man smelled good, like a strange combination of night air and sweet, tangy citrus.

"You don't want to know my name, love," he breathed.

I shivered at the hush of air tickling the shell of my ear. A low rumble escaped him, and just before he left, he tugged on my earlobe with his teeth.

I gasped, but by the time I recovered, he was gone, almost as if he'd never been there at all. Blinking several times, I slowly turned to face Lil.

"Holy fucking goddess above," Lil said, her voice low and serious—well, until a giggle escaped her, and she gushed. "Aster, that was pretty much the hottest thing I've ever seen happen in this club. Or maybe anywhere. Watching you two had *me* turned on."

I swatted at her as a shifter migrated through the crowd, making his way over to us.

"Was that your boyfriend?" he asked once he approached me.

I glanced at Lil, snorting. "No, wolf boy. But neither are you."

The shifter looked offended, and then snarled, "Presumptuous much?"

I rolled my eyes, pointing to my ears and Lil's. "We're Fae, pretty boy. We can smell the wolf all over you."

The shifter groaned. "It's dark so I didn't see your ears… never mind."

He began to shuffle away, but Lil called after him, "Do you know who he was? The man my friend just danced with?"

The shifter's grin was devious and he let out a low chuckle.

"If you don't know who that was… well, it seems to me

that you're already in too deep," he said with a glance in my direction.

Then he was gone, lost in the crowd. Lil and I looked at each other for a moment before guffawing at the shifter's ridiculous warning. The butterfly clips in Lil's violet curls caught the silvery light above. As our laughter died down, I watched the sparkling reflections, mesmerized.

Lil followed my vacant stare and sighed. "Alright, party girl. Let's go home. I'll call a taxi."

"We could walk. Taxis are expensive," I said as Lil dragged me through the still pulsing crowd.

"Don't worry, I'll pay," she replied.

We shoved open the doors, spilling out into the cool night air. I started to protest against Lil's offer, but she shushed me with a finger to the mouth. I nipped at it and she yelped, pulling her hand back.

"I just got these done!" she exclaimed, waving around her freshly painted pink nails. "You'll chip them!"

I grinned stupidly, flashing my own nails. Painted black and chipped. My usual.

Lil groaned as she waved down a taxi. "We can't all pull off your effortless, goth pixie look," my best friend said.

Indeed, she was much more polished than I was. A short metallic gold dress molded to her curvy body like a second skin. Matching heels wrapped up her calves and her violet hair was shining and lush, even after a night of dancing and drinking. Whereas me… well, I embodied the look of a rebellious teen, even though we were far past sixteen. Chunky leather ankle boots weighed down my feet, while ripped fishnet tights covered up most of my lanky legs, ending in shorts that barely covered my ass. The look

5

was completed with an old t-shirt ripped at my midriff and silver bangles in my ears.

Lil and I were polar opposites, but that was why we worked. We'd even dated for a short time as teenagers before deciding we were better as friends. It wasn't that I didn't love her, and I would never stop thinking she was sexy as hell. But being friends had always felt more effortless for us.

"C'mon, you sons of bitches!" Lil screeched as another taxi passed us by. "What absolute assholes!" she snarled, waving her hands.

Few club goers were around, yet the taxis still ignored us.

"Come on!" I shouted as another sped off.

Lil turned to me, her round cheeks pink with anger. But her eyes were tired and defeated.

"I just want to go home and eat leftover pizza," she whined, wrapping her arms around herself.

"Can't you just call Raven?" I asked.

Lil shrugged. "My mom's been weird about me hanging out with him lately. I don't want to stress her out any more than she already is."

"Lil, he's your brother," I reminded her.

Well, half-brother. Before Lil had been born, her mom had an affair with a faerie from the Unseelie Court. Lil's dad stayed, but he and her mom's relationship had been slowly crumbling ever since. Divorce was definitely in the cards at this point. Maybe keeping Lil from seeing Raven too much was her mom's way of trying to keep her marriage together.

"And besides," I added, "it's not like the Unseelie Fae are inherently evil. The whole thing is dumb."

6

Lil shot me a look as we both began to shiver in our thin clothes. It was a look that said, *You should know better than anyone why it matters.*

I ignored it, just as I ignored the burning beginning to flare in my chest.

Shut it down, shut it down, shut it down, I pleaded silently with myself.

The burning subsided and I sucked in a sharp breath of the cool air, steadying myself. Lil glanced at me worriedly, then sighed and relented, "Alright, I'll call Raven. I don't know where he is though, it could take a while."

I snorted and slumped down on the curb. "Better to wait a little while than stay out here all night."

Lil didn't protest and lifted her cell to her ear. With my excellent Fae hearing, I could hear nearly every ripple of the dial tone. My ears pricked as Raven's deep voice answered, "What, Lil?"

She scoffed into the phone and explained our situation. After a moment, Raven sighed and replied begrudgingly, "Alright, alright. Be there in twenty."

She cut the call immediately as he agreed, running a hand through her curls as she stumbled down next to me on the curb. I glanced sidelong at her and she gave me a loopy grin, before reaching over and tugging my hair out of its ponytail. It tumbled down my back, dark as a starless night. Lil seemed to admire it for a moment before murmuring, "Better."

I rolled my eyes. "You're drunk."

She raised a perfectly sculpted brow and said, "So are you."

We sat in silence for a minute or so as a few shifters tumbled out of the club. Finally, she broke it and said, "Are we gonna talk about that mega-hot stranger you danced with in there?"

A smile played on my lips. My mind was still clouded and my memories of what happened inside the club even hazier. But I knew I would never forget that face. I'd probably never see him again, the amber-eyed stranger. Even as some strange instinct snarled at my senses to go hunt him down. He was just another pretty... well, beautiful, distraction.

They all were.

Fae, an odd shifter here or there, and sometimes humans too. Men and women alike, they filled my bed, or the space between the bathroom stalls of clubs and bars. What they didn't know is that they were all nothing but placeholders, trying to make up for the permanent, gaping hole in my heart. Lil shone light into that space, but it had never been quite enough. It wasn't her fault. I didn't think anyone or anything ever would be.

"Aster, you're drifting," Lil's voice brought me back down to earth.

I snapped my head in her direction and muttered, "Sorry."

She smiled gently, though her grin quickly turned feral and I sighed through my nose.

"I'll probably never see him again, so wipe that expression off your face," I said.

Lil laid her head on my shoulder.

"I don't know, Aster. I don't think I've seen you look at anyone quite like that. Not even Jude."

I flinched at my ex-boyfriend's name. Jude Ever had been everything I thought I'd wanted when I was eighteen —tall, handsome, and just kind enough to soften my frigid heart a fraction. Until he'd cheated on me the night of my nineteenth birthday. Two days after I'd finally told him…

It didn't matter what I'd told him. It never would. And I would never let myself fall like that for someone again. I'd had enough heartbreak in my life.

"All the more reason to stay away," I said, trying to sound as sarcastic as possible. But I knew Lil caught the edge to my voice. She knew me too well.

"Aster, sweetie…" she began, lifting her head to look at me.

But I shakily shot to my feet as Raven's maroon convertible rolled up in front of us.

"Hello, ladies," he purred as Lil got to her feet too. He flashed a secret, special smile just at me.

Raven was handsome in the way that scared most mothers. Long dark hair, sparkling green eyes, and a deliciously muscled frame. I knew he held a flame for me. He had since I was thirteen and he was fifteen, when Lil had first learned of his existence. But Lil was my best friend, the only person who I truly trusted. I wasn't about to hurt our relationship by shattering Raven's heart. Because I knew that's what would happen if I let him get close. And whether Lil liked to admit it or not, she cared about her brother.

Lil climbed into the car, nearly flashing me as she hauled herself into the backseat. I slapped her butt and she squealed before landing on the seat with a dull thud. My long legs easily swung over and she scowled at me as I sat down.

"I wish I was tall," she pouted as Raven started to pull away from the club.

"Nah, you're cute and petite," I replied, shouting over the wind as our speed picked up.

Raven snorted and Lil stuck her tongue out at him.

"You two don't seem too overly wasted," he said. "Weird that the taxis weren't picking you up."

"You should've seen us forty minutes ago," I shouted back.

Raven rolled his eyes, shaking his head. But there was real concern in his expression as he glanced back at me in the rearview mirror. Since I'd graduated from the Seelie Court University, nights like these had become all the more common. Without the pressures of school to keep me in check, I'd fully succumbed to life's baser pleasures: alcohol and sex.

Not that I hadn't in college. But I'd also been hell-bent on graduating and excelling in my studies. It pissed my uncle off—especially since I'd majored in astrology, an area of study usually reserved for Unseelie Fae. It was a miracle he hadn't removed the option from the university curriculum altogether. But I'd graduated six months ago with honors, successfully irritating him even more.

Except that, once the charade was over, and I began my job as a receptionist for one of the museums of our court, purpose began to leach out of my life. I filled the empty spot of school with tequila shots and hookups. And who was Raven to judge? He had a long list of ex-girlfriends and a love for whiskey. How were my habits any worse than his?

Lil seemed to sense the slight tension in the air and yelled to Raven, "Aster met a hot Fae dude at the club!"

Raven's face lifted in false surprise. "Oh?" he mused. "And where is he? Or have you already completed your conquest, Aster?"

I narrowed my eyes at him, but Lil answered for me before I could shoot back a retort.

"That's the weirdest part!" she gushed. "They danced to some strange faerie party music that he somehow got the DJ to play, and then he bit her ear and left."

Raven's expression darkened a fraction before he asked, "Did his teeth come out?"

I snorted. "Of course not."

Faerie's sharp canines came out for two reasons. One, they were going to kill you, or two, they wanted to claim you, potentially as a mate.

Raven looked relieved, and even playfully asked, "Well, what did he look like? Lemme guess—dark hair, green eyes, maybe a few tattoos?"

I opened my mouth, but Lil beat me to it again.

"No! Totally the opposite of her usual type actually. He had these gorgeous honey-amber eyes, like flecked with gold or something. And his hair was white, well, no silver. I don't know, it was like—"

"Starlight," I cut in. My cheeks warmed as I realized how ridiculous that sounded.

Raven turned into our neighborhood, suddenly quiet. I glanced at Lil and she shrugged. A minute or two passed before we reached our apartment. Once the car was off, Raven turned, his face serious.

"Did you notice anything else about him?" he urged.

I narrowed my eyes and asked, "What do you mean?"

He took a deep breath and then went on. "Any other defining features? Or maybe a strange magical signature? I know you were probably drunk out of your mind, but was there anything else at all?"

I started to say no, but the memory of that shadowy

aura that had seemed to surround the stranger, just before he'd left, flashed through my mind. Raven caught onto my hesitation and looked at me expectantly.

"He…" I took a quick breath. "He might have been Unseelie. I thought I saw some shadow magic, maybe."

Raven nodded and Lil cocked her head.

"Why are you acting like you know who she's talking about?" she asked.

Raven looked me directly in the eye as he replied darkly, "Because I'm fairly certain I do. The person you're describing…. Aster, I think you danced with the King of the Unseelie Court."

CHAPTER

TWO

"WELL, *SHIT*," Lil swore loudly.

Phantom wings flared from Raven's back as he got out of the car. As far as I understood, the wings were a trait that sometimes manifested in Unseelie Fae. Though, I'd never seen his wings become fully corporeal, maybe due to his half-Seelie heritage. I'd never asked him about it.

But I'd heard rumors that Nox Ether, the King of the Unseelie Court, had wings—enormous, claw-tipped wings, straight from the worst of nightmares. And the beautiful man I'd danced with tonight, could that have somehow been him? Raven couldn't be right.

Could he?

There was no way. I was sure the King had better things to do than hang out in Seelie Court night clubs.

But a creeping feeling snarled at my sense that, just maybe, Raven wasn't so far off in his claims. The stranger *had* refused to give me his name.

If it truly had been him, he wasn't what I would've expected, I'd give him that. Everyone in the Seelie Court always talked about how terrifying Nox Ether was. The Night King, darkness given form, Shadow Walker; there were many names for him. I wondered if he really *was* a Shadow Walker—faeries who had sold their souls to demons in exchange for night-shifting abilities and lethal killing power. I wasn't even sure I believed in Shadow Walkers. Demons had long been gone from our world...

"Aster."

Raven's stern voice startled me out of my hazy thoughts. Goddess, I was so tired. The last thing I wanted to do was be scolded or, even worse, worry about kings and their agendas. But I climbed clumsily out of the backseat of the car along with Lil, and then faced Raven.

"I'll try to avoid dancing with kings in the future, alright?" I muttered wearily.

He ignored my weak attempt at a joke, shaking his head. He looked off into the distance and muttered, "What the hell was he doing there?"

"Maybe he just likes club music," I sighed.

Again, those phantom wings flared behind Raven as he began to pace around the parking lot, grumbling something indiscernible under his breath. Lil and I stood there watching him, until she sighed then walked towards him, touching his arm.

He jerked, but paused his pacing for a moment. The dim yellow light cast by the streetlamps above us stretched harsh shadows across his face, making him look older than he was.

"Raven, we're tired," Lil pushed. "Come back tomorrow, have dinner with us. We'll talk about it then."

He ignored his sister, looking back at me, as he said very softly, "Your uncle cannot know about this."

A cold feeling whooshed over my entire body, my skin raising with goosebumps. My body had long learned to be afraid at the mere mention of my uncle.

"I know," I hissed. "You don't think I don't know that?"

Raven shook his head. "Not just for your sake but… if he found out King Nox was on Seelie lands, mingling with citizens for that matter, we could have a problem larger than—"

He cut himself off.

Because we all knew what the "less-than-large" problem was—what Uncle Calum, the King of the Seelie Court, would do to me if he found out just who I'd danced with tonight. We all knew I didn't need to cover up any more bruises.

It was a large part of the reason I went by the alias, Aster Quiin, and not my true name, Asteria Fairwae. Uncle Calum was just supposed to have been regent until I was old enough to rule. It had been in my father's will; I was to be the next in line for the throne upon his death.

But my uncle had quickly made it clear to his advisors and small council that I would be unfit to ever rule and that he had no intention of letting me. So, I made a deal with him. Dangerous for the twelve-year-old I was at the time we'd made the agreement, but worth it.

I would live as a citizen of the court; go to school, work, dance at clubs, get rip-roaring drunk. I would be normal, boring even. And he would allow it, as long as I did not contest his rule. Giving up a crown I'd never wanted for a life away from him had seemed like a fair trade at the time, and I still thought it was. Besides, it wasn't like I could challenge his claim at this point and win. He was powerful, like most faeries in our family.

Except for me, apparently. I had never exhibited any extraordinary magic, had never shown any of the potential of my bloodline.

Lies... a voice clawed at my mind, a beast begging for release. I shoved it away like I always did.

My face must have become stony, because Raven grimaced and reached out to touch my arm. "Aster, I'm sorry, you know I didn't mean..." he trailed off.

I reigned in a flinch as his fingers brushed my forearm and muttered, "It's fine."

"You're sure?"

I forced a smile to my lips and said, "Yeah. But Lil's right, we'll discuss this more tomorrow. None of us are thinking straight, and I have to be at work at eight-thirty in the morning."

Raven stepped back, finally conceding.

"Does seven work?" he asked. "I'll pay for the pizza."

I knew he was offering a token to go along with his apology. But I nodded and said, "Sounds great."

"See you then," he replied with a genuine smile. Then, he glanced at Lil and said softly, "Call if you need anything, okay? Either of you."

She yawned and sighed, "Alright. Night, Raven."

He tipped his head and I didn't look back at him as I stumbled to the front door of our building. Lil grabbed my hand to keep me from tumbling to the ground as we stepped into the too-bright hallway. The fluorescents were messing with my vision. Or maybe that was just the lingering effects of the last seltzer I'd consumed only a couple hours ago. I fumbled with the keys, then pushed open the door to our little apartment.

"I'm gonna shower," I said absentmindedly. My mind

was a little hazy and I needed to clear it. Plus, I knew there was no way I'd have the motivation to get up and shower in the morning before work. It was now or never.

Lil nodded, yawning again as she slumped over on the couch, the blue velvet fabric contrasting with the purple of her hair. Our apartment was small but neat—Lil saw to that. Gently worn second-hand furniture, bought at half price, or given to us by friends, filled the space. Soft glowing lights were strung around the living room, along with a few colored lanterns. The kitchen was tiny, but we ate out enough that it didn't matter. Our bathrooms had dated pink tile flooring, but Lil somehow made even that work. The only space that wasn't exactly organized or clean was my bedroom.

I lazily snapped on my bedside lamp with a swish of my finger—faerie magic at its finest—and began pulling off my collection of earrings and rings. Once that was done, and the jewelry lay scattered across my cluttered vanity, I stripped down to nothing but my skin and walked to the bathroom. I rubbed at my eyes, starting the water.

Goddess, my head already hurt. Mercifully, the water warmed up quickly and I stepped under the stream, then stayed there for a long, long while. Except that the longer I stood under the water, the more my mind wandered, and unwanted thoughts began to stream in.

The truth was, whether I wanted to admit it or not, Raven was right. What I had done tonight was dangerous. Especially if the Unseelie king ever realized who I was.

The true, chosen heir to the throne of the Seelie Court.

Even the notion of the title in my own mind made me cringe. I didn't want anything to do with it all and, yet I wasn't clueless. Tension between the two faerie courts had been stirring for decades, if not centuries. Despite how little I paid attention to politics, I knew it was coming to a tipping point. Who knew what would happen when it did. War?

I shivered at the idea, even under the scalding water.

It was probably fine. Whatever the Night King's business in a Seelie Court club was, it likely had nothing to do with me. I had just looked like an average twenty-two-year-old party girl who was trying to wash away the pressing weight of her adult responsibilities with club beats and vodka.

I really, really needed to chill about the whole thing. And I probably would have if it wasn't for the strange, nagging sense that I was wrong, continuing to tap on my mind. I ignored it as I toweled off and hastily brushed my teeth. I dressed in underwear and an old t-shirt before climbing into bed, my hair still wet.

Once my head hit the pillow, I was asleep in less than a minute.

.✦.

"Asteria, run!" my mother screamed.

She had been holding me only moments ago, my tiny child body cradled against her thin chest. My mother had always been a fine-boned woman. I'd never thought about it, not until that night when I heard those bird-like bones snapping like twigs.

"Not my baby, please," she sobbed as a dark, towering presence drew nearer.

It looked like a man but… not. I eyed it as it began to encircle my body, encasing me. I stared at the shadows, both in terror and curiosity, as they swirled all around me.

From a few feet away, my mother screamed, "NO!"

The shadow limbs slithered past me and snapped another bone as my mother cried out in pain. That was when I began to realize something was very, very wrong.

"Mamma, Mamma!" I shrieked.

I heard my father's roar from down the hall, just as I felt the dark presence enter me. It was like swallowing oily water and I choked on it. My mother screamed again, just as my father reached her. He held his hand out to pull me away from the shadows, but the presence lunged at him. He clawed at his throat and I watched in horror as my mother's eyes rolled back in her head. My own vision was beginning to blur and shift and—

There was a blinding flash of white light.

I was encased in darkness and shadow, so the celestial blaze didn't touch me. It took my parents before they even had the chance to scream.

When I opened my eyes I was so, so tired. I only wanted to curl up and sleep. But I was just awake enough to hear my uncle's strangled whisper, laced with unending rage.

"What have you done, Asteria?"

THREE

I woke up from the dream in a cold sweat, the echo of my uncle's voice still in my head. Lil was shaking my shoulders gently and she shouted, "Girl, it's eight!"

Her voice was much too loud for my pounding head and I groaned, "Well, fuuuck."

She stood back, hands on her hips. "Did you have another dream?" she asked.

I blinked and muttered, "Let me wake up before the interrogation starts, will you?"

Lil rolled her eyes. "Aster, have you ever thought about trying talk therapy?"

"Have you ever thought about sticking a red-hot iron up your ass?"

Lil smothered a laugh and said, "It wouldn't be *that* bad."

I dragged myself out of bed, swatting at her.

"Let me get ready," I rasped.

"Fine," she said, drawing the word out into a whine.

"But don't think this is the last time we're talking about this. My co-worker, Asha, says it's done her wonders."

"I'm pretty sure Asha also smokes her weight in gillroot every night," I grumbled.

Lil sighed loudly and slammed the door to my bedroom behind her, definitely on purpose.

"Asshole!" I shouted, wincing at the volume of my own voice.

Lil didn't reply and I let out another little groan before swapping my oversized t-shirt for my usual work attire: black dress pants, a white button up, and heeled boots. I pulled on all my rings and earrings then gathered my raven-dark hair into a ponytail, trying to flatten my bangs so they weren't sticking up off my forehead. After brushing my teeth and swiping on a quick layer of makeup, I hurried out of my bedroom. Lil was waiting with a cup of to-go coffee in her hand.

"You know I love you," I said sweetly, taking the coffee from her and grabbing my bag off the hook on the wall next to the door.

She flared her nostrils and said, "I deserve an award for living with you. But"—she patted my arm—"I love you too, asshole."

I grinned at her then headed for the door, shouting, "See ya later!"

"Be safe!" she called back.

"You know it," I said, quietly enough that she probably couldn't hear it.

Once I made it down the single flight of rickety stairs that led to the ground level and out onto the sidewalk, I half-ran to the bus stop. Even then, I barely caught it.

The inside of the bus was crowded and I found myself

wedged between a Fae man wearing way too much peppery-smelling cologne and a shifter who kept trying to sniff me. The Fae man looked venomously at the shifter, sticking his too-big nose up in the air. I reigned in a rolling of my eyes at the display.

Some of the Fae, probably including this guy, thought it would be better to close our court's borders again—to just kick out the non-faeries then go back to being merry little forest sprites. But we'd sealed our fate during the war that ended the second Long Night our world had endured; an age, a few centuries ago, when demons ruled and everyone was subjected to their wrath. But Fae, shifters, sirens, humans… we'd all finally united and sent the demons back to their realm, wherever that was. And once it was over, everyone signed a treaty, an agreement that we would always aid each other in times of unrest and keep our lands open for free travel. Many—most—had flocked to the two faerie courts if they could afford it. So now, our once purely Fae lands were a hodge-podge of Beings. I really didn't give a shit, but some fairies thought it was time we returned to the old ways. My uncle being one of them.

I pushed him quickly from my mind as the bus halted and I grabbed onto the rail to keep from flying forward. The faerie next to me ran his eyes over me, once then twice.

"Your stop?" he asked as I pushed forward through the crowded aisle.

This time, I did actually roll my eyes, turning back briefly to say to him, "Obviously. And a pro-tip: lighten up on the perfume. I think you just about made us all high off the fumes."

Rage slid over his features at the insult and I offered him a final, sly smile before stepping off the bus. My boots clicked on the sidewalk as I hurried towards the pristine glass doors of the history museum where I worked. As soon as I entered, my boss, Miriam, clicked her tongue and said, "You're nearly late."

"Sorry," I replied, trying to sound sincere.

I set my travel mug down on my desk and sank into the office chair behind the receptionist desk. Miriam narrowed her eyes at me and sniffed delicately. I raised a brow.

"Yes?"

She sighed and said, "You smell of alcohol."

I shook my head. "No way. I showered last night and brushed my teeth twice this morning."

That was a lie, sort of. I had only brushed my teeth once and very quickly. But Miriam didn't need to know that.

She shrugged and said, "If you fill your veins with it every night, maybe the stench doesn't go away." Then she turned and walked towards her office, humming some weird little sea shanty.

Miriam was a siren in the most traditional of senses. In fact, I wouldn't be surprised if she actually spent her free time luring men to sea and drowning them.

With a click, she shut her office door, leaving me alone in the empty lobby. I bit the inside of my cheek and quelled the burst of anger stirring in me at her insult. Once it was carefully tucked away, I pulled out a stack of files from the filing cabinet below the desk and began the monotonous task of digitizing old records. Since the museum wasn't very busy this time of year, Miriam had me work on other tasks to keep occupied. "Idle hands create idle minds," or something stupid like that was her favorite expression..

For an hour or so it was mostly quiet and I became

surprisingly engrossed in an ancient looking folder of records titled: *Evening Star*. The first page briefly detailed a strange type of magic that had surfaced once, centuries ago. The record dated back to just before the second Long Night ended.

The file went on to state that the demons were banished by a powerful Being... Fae maybe? It was difficult to decipher, what with the fading ink and the fact that the whole thing was in the old language, something that had fallen out of favor once the treaty had been signed. I'd only partially mastered it during my time at the Seelie Court University. From what I could gather, the power itself could only be translated as "starlight."

I had only encountered something remotely close to the magic described here once before. But I was positive that the similarities were just a coincidence.

Faerie magic was typically divided into three categories: elemental magic (mostly Seelie Court), shadow magic (exclusively Unseelie Court), and healing magic (both). All faeries had a varying amount of basic, lower tier magic; the sort that allowed us to open doors without touching them or extinguish candles without blowing on them. Party tricks, really. Though, I had known a guy at school who could sketch full portraits without touching the pen or paper. He'd once drawn Jude and I...

I sucked in a deep breath, trying to settle my suddenly whirring mind.

Okay, collect the facts, I told myself calmly.

Except that the facts about this strange power were just as unsettling as any speculations. A power that could wipe out an entire horde of demonic forces? That kind of magic could be devastating in the wrong hands. There was also the small notion stirring in the corner of my mind, slyly whispering that maybe I already knew what this kind of magic could do. But that was ridiculous. I had no "starlight" magic. Whatever the power described in the document truly entailed, it was long gone, lost to the centuries.

I flicked through another page of the file, half-deciphering descriptions of the final days before the Long Night ended. It seemed there had been a victory... but not? I wasn't sure how to translate that particular section. Moving on, I read the next section. My eyes skimmed over the name of a demon prince, or king, or something along those lines.

Abaddon.

The name alone sent shivers through me. Names like that held their own sort of power. And not the good kind.

"Excuse me?"

I jumped, dropping the folder in my hand. It landed with a *plop* on the dusty linoleum floor under the desk. I leaned down and snatched it, quickly setting it back on the desk before looking up.

A woman stood in front of me, and I recognized from her scent that she was human. She seemed tired, her hair slightly mussed and her eyes heavy. But though she appeared a little frazzled, she wore a pleasant, happy smile.

Next to her, two children tugged at the hem of her shirt. One of them, a little girl with a bushy mane of brown hair, looked up at me, beaming. Something in my heart tore at itself at the innocence in her expression. But I set the feelings aside and cleared my throat.

"Apologies, how can I help you?"

The woman smiled slightly, her attention wandering for

a moment to the little boy who was currently meandering off towards Miriam's office.

"Colin!" the woman called. "Come back so we can buy our tickets!"

"But, Mamma—"

"Uh-uh, come on!" The woman cut him off.

He pouted but trudged back to his mother and sister. The woman looked back at me and chuckled before she said, "I'm sorry."

I pasted a smile onto my face and said, "No worries at all."

She smiled too and told me, "I'd like one adult day pass and… is it free for children here?"

"How old are they?" I asked, glancing at the children milling around below her.

"Well, Lina is seven and Colin is four," she replied distractedly as Colin began to wander again.

I nodded and said to her, "They have free admission. One adult ticket is eleven tabs."

The woman dug in her overflowing purse for a moment before pulling out the money. I rang her up and gave her the tickets. All the while, the little girl, Lina, stared at me.

When her mother began to try and pull her away, Lina stopped short, pointing at me.

"What is it, darling?" the woman asked her daughter.

Lina looked intently at her mother. She nodded, conceding, and leaned down to listen as Lina whispered in her ear. The woman's eyes widened slightly and she straightened, looking at me. Something had changed in her expression—she almost looked alarmed.

"My daughter has begun to exhibit the abilities of Sight," she explained to me. "We're not sure if she's a mage or an oracle, but she just told me... well, Lina, sweetie, do you want to tell her?"

Lina nodded and walked over to my side of the desk.

"Come here," she rasped, gesturing to herself.

Feeling uneasy, I stood from my chair and walked over to her. She pointed to herself again and I leaned down so she could whisper in my ear.

"Your soul's match will be the reckoning," she breathed.

She pulled back, her eyes still bright and curious despite the ominous words she'd just spoken to me. Her mother looked at me warily as her daughter returned to her side.

"Enjoy your day," I managed to say and the woman only nodded.

They headed off into the museum and I retook my place in the office chair.

If that wasn't strange, I didn't know what was. First, the record, now this? And what did the girl mean about my "soul's match?" She couldn't mean a mate, could she? If so, I didn't want them, whoever they were. Especially if they were going to be the "reckoning," whatever that meant.

I groaned inwardly, sitting back in my chair. Of course, I just had to meet a freaky little oracle today. Humans who were born with magic, especially shadow magic like that, were rare enough that it almost didn't feel like a coincidence. The goddess definitely had it out for me today, I knew that much.

The rest of my shift dragged on as slowly as it possibly could have. A few patrons came in and bought tickets, but mostly I just continued to pore over the record, doing the best I could to enter half-accurate translations into the computer and organize them into files on the desktop. When five o'clock finally rolled around, I pushed back my chair from the edge of the desk, stretching my aching legs in front of me. Sitting all day didn't exactly do wonders for my joints, especially since I always forgot to get up and walk around every once in a while.

I closed the file I'd been working on and logged off of the computer. Once I had my empty travel mug and bag in hand, I headed over to Miriam's office. I rapped lightly on the fogged glass door and a few seconds later, it opened.

"I'm going," I told her, as I did every day.

Months ago, when I'd first started working here, Miriam insisted I let her know when I was leaving after each workday finished. It had resulted in me sometimes having to track her down within the museum to say "goodbye."

"Fine, don't be late tomorrow," she clipped before shutting the door right in my face.

I rolled my eyes and turned, heading for the exit, leaving Miriam to close shop and lock up. I was happy to let her do it; I didn't want to be there any longer than I needed to.

There had been a time I'd been excited about this job. Just before I'd started, Miriam had confided in me that she'd studied astrology too and could be a sort of mentor to me on the side of the museum work. Obviously, that hadn't panned out at all. Our personalities ended up being too different. She was uptight and meticulous, whereas I was lax and messy. Now, it was just a boring day job, supplying me with funds to pay my half of the rent and buy takeout.

When I finally did step outside and away from Miriam, I relaxed, the mid-spring air warming my face.

I pulled out my phone and texted Lil: *Raven still good for pizza tonight?*

Seconds later, she responded: *Please hurry. I just got home and he's sitting on our couch like a creep. I should've never given him a key.*

I laughed softly. Apparently, Raven was eager for our pizza night. I had to admit, I was too. Whenever the three of us got together, it felt like old times, when we used to crowd around Lil's shitty laptop and watch movies in Raven's old bedroom. Nights like these gave me a sense of nostalgia for a time when I used to naively think my life was only going to get better, that I had already been through the worst of it—that I couldn't possibly get played any more bad cards.

It made me a little sad too, but that wasn't anything a few shots couldn't fix.

The bus was crowded again, though no one tried to sniff me or flirt with me (or both), which was a big plus. Once I got off at my stop, the sun was beginning to sink into the horizon, casting a red-orange hue across the cityscape.

I walked the short distance from the bus stop to Lil's and my apartment, actually enjoying the short commute for once. We were in that comfortable spot between the icy chill of winter and the blazing hot of summer. I had many bitter-sweet memories from this time. Spring had been my mother's favorite season.

When I arrived at our unit, I opened the door cautiously, peeking my head inside. Unsurprisingly, Raven and Lil were already bickering.

"Aster, thank the goddess," Lil said as soon as she saw me. "Please tell Raven that pineapple on pizza is disgusting and that I'm not letting him bring it into our home."

I shut the door and pulled my boots off, smiling slightly

as I said, "Lil, when are you going to remember I actually *like* pineapple on pizza?"

"What?" she exclaimed. "But you never order it!"

I chuckled and replied, "Yeah, baby girl, because you don't like it and I'm a good friend."

Raven smirked and quipped, "Told you, Lil."

Grinning as I headed into my bedroom, I called, "I'm changing, please decide on something—or I'll eat you both!"

I shut the door before Lil could gripe at me more about the pineapple situation. I stripped down and rinsed off quickly in the shower, then threw on a faded t-shirt that proudly proclaimed the name of my favorite punk band as a teenager. All but one of the members were Unseelie, so I tended not to wear the shirt in public spaces. The whole court divide problem was so, so stupid, but I also didn't want to get harassed.

Once I'd shimmied into a pair of worn, comfy sweatpants, I opened the door to find Lil pouting on the couch.

"You win," she said in greeting.

I raised a brow. "Why didn't you just order another pizza without pineapple."

She rolled her eyes and muttered, "I did. But I'll eat all of mine tonight and then the leftovers will be covered in that stupid fruit."

I sat down heavily next to her and patted her hand. "I think you'll survive," I said. "Where's Raven?"

"Bathroom," she sighed, just as he emerged back into the living room.

"Pizza should be here in twenty," Raven said to me.

"Good, I'm starving," I said, kicking my feet up on the coffee table.

Raven smiled, though it fell slightly as he began to say, "So, I was wondering if we could talk about—"

"Food first," I cut him off. "Then you can lecture me."

Raven lifted up his hands, the material of his leather jacket groaning. "Fair enough," he conceded.

"Can we watch TV in the meantime?" Lil asked.

"This is your apartment," Raven pointed out.

Lil narrowed her eyes at him and said, "I'm trying to be a good host."

"What about the new siren dating show?" I asked, trying to diffuse the mounting tension between them.

"Ugh, that show is borderline unethical," Lil said. "I swear most of the siren contestants just glamour all the non-sirens so they'll do what they want."

"Oh, they definitely do," Raven added with a deep chuckle. "That's why it's good."

I leaned forward and snatched the remote, turning on the show before Lil could stop me. Of course, a whopping five minutes later, she was completely sucked into it, staring at the screen, her green eyes bright and focused. Just as we made it to the end of the first episode, a knock sounded on our door and Lil shot up, shouting, "Pizza!"

She pranced over to the door, Raven following close behind her, ever the attentive brother. As soon as she went to pay, he slipped his hand past her, handing tabs to the delivery girl.

"Raven, seriously?" Lil said, looking back and scowling at him.

The delivery girl looked nervously at Raven, though her expression grew dreamy the longer she stared at him.

"I'll take those," Raven said to the girl and she handed him the pizza boxes, transfixed.

I rolled my eyes as Lil shut the door and said, "That girl was eye-fucking you, Raven."

He shrugged, setting the pizza down on the coffee table in front of our couch.

"Not my type," he replied, a little too quietly.

Lil's gaze shot to mine. I knew what she was thinking. That *I* was Raven's type. But that wasn't happening and she knew it. We all did. He'd tried enough and I'd gently rejected him each time. That of course didn't stop him from dating other people by any means. But it had given a slight awkward edge to conversations about our love lives when he was around.

"Well, I'm going to eat," I proclaimed, opening up one of the pizza boxes.

Less than a minute later, we were all stuffing our faces. Lil made a happy sighing noise as she bit into her slice of pepperoni and sausage.

"Do you and Mr. Pizza need a room?" I snorted.

She swatted me, her mouth still full. Raven made a face, though his expression quickly turned serious as he said to me, "Aster, have you ever met the Night King before last night?"

I swallowed hard and replied, "No."

"Never at a function with your uncle or…?"

"My uncle has never taken me to a 'function' and I think you know that," I said flatly.

Raven ran a hand through his hair. "I just wanted to make sure that King Nox had no reason to be interested in you, beyond you being a hot girl in a club."

Lil raised a brow at the words: *hot girl*. But I ignored it, saying, "Raven, he had no idea who I was."

"You're sure?"

"I'm sure."

Raven sighed and picked up another piece of pizza, taking a bite and chewing thoughtfully. Eventually, he muttered, "Maybe it was just a coincidence."

"It had to be," I insisted, ignoring the nagging feeling that it somehow wasn't.

Raven smiled at me, one of his big, dazzling grins, then patted me on the head with a large hand.

"The three of us should hang out more often," he said.

I smiled back, though it was a little sad as I replied, "We used to."

"I know," Raven said, looking down at his feet.

Lil rolled her eyes. "It's not as if it's on purpose. We used to all *live* together. Now, we have jobs and stupid adult responsibilities. They get in the way."

"They do," I chuckled. Then with a sigh, I added, "I was always so eager to graduate from university, but now that we have…" I trailed off and shook my head.

Raven nodded and said, "I felt like that too. You'll get used to it with time, though."

I nodded, knowing all too well he was right.

One could get used to anything with time.

CHAPTER
FOUR

RAVEN STAYED for about an hour longer before heading out, giving us each a chaste peck on the cheek before he left. He lived in a one-bedroom apartment on the other side of our territory. A territory that had once been made up of rolling hills, lush forests, and fields of flowers—or so I was told. After the second Long Night, when we faeries opened up the borders of the courts to all the other Beings, modernization began to replace the old ways of our kind. Now, our court was made up of brick buildings, paved streets, and modern technology. I assumed the Unseelie territory was similar, though I'd of course never been there.

"Aster," Lil waved a hand in front of my face. "Earth to Aster!"

I swatted her hand away and said, "I hear you."

She laughed, the sound like a tinkling bell, and asked, "What were you thinking about?"

I raised a brow. "Do you really want to know?"

"Maybe?"

"I was thinking about the modernization of our court and—"

"Ugh, boring!" Lil groaned. "I swear, you should've been a history major."

I shrugged. "Maybe. But that would've pleased my uncle, so there was no way."

Lil's face twisted into a mixture of pity and anger as I mentioned Uncle Calum. Well, King Calum to her.

"It's fine," I said quickly. "You don't have to freak out every time I talk about him."

Lil's brows knit together and she shook her head, saying, "How could I not?"

I had nothing to say in reply to that. If I were her, I'd feel the same.

When I was seven, only months after my parents died, my uncle had shoved me into the care of Lil's family. Later, I found out it was his way of punishing her mother for having Raven. For having an Unseelie bastard, as he put it. But little did my uncle know, he'd just made the best possible choice for me. I think he started to eventually realize that too, but it had been too late. Lil and I were already joined at the hip and her mother fiercely protective of me. But while I lived there, once a month, I'd see my uncle. And once a month, no one could protect me. I'd come back covered in bruises, and sometimes a cut under my eye.

Lil's mother was a healer and did her best to make sure the wounds from the beatings never stuck around or hurt me more than they had to. Still, she never said a word against my uncle, probably terrified of what would happen to her or her children if she did. And then there were the

35

wounds she couldn't do anything about. Abuse she didn't even know occurred. Lil was the only one who I'd ever told.

Once I moved into the dorms of Seelie University, I finally evaded those visits. I wished I could say that once I stopped seeing my uncle, I stopped hurting. I hated the ugly emotions that persisted. They made me feel weak. But years of enduring him had turned into years of trying to unravel trauma.

"Would you think about seeing someone?" Lil finally asked after a moment of silence.

I shook my head. "I can't, Lil. What if the therapist asks who my abuser was?"

"Then you tell them," she said flatly.

I smiled sadly and said, "You're being very idealistic if you think that'd lead me anywhere but deep trouble."

She screwed her eyes shut momentarily, took a breath, then opened them and asked, "Do you want to cuddle and watch TV?"

A relieved smile broke across my face and I replied, "As long as I get to pick the show."

She didn't even complain, just took my hand, and began arranging a nest of blankets for us on the couch. Once we were situated, I turned on the dating show from earlier and we fell into a comfortable, still silence, the only noise coming from the cheesy music of the show.

Around two in the morning, Lil fell asleep against my shoulder, snoring softly. I flicked her nose and she startled.

"Bedtime," I whispered in her ear and she groaned.

"I don't want to move," she muttered. "I'm tired."

"C'mon, let's get you into bed. You need your beauty sleep," I said, smiling as she made another low whining noise.

I helped her off the couch and then tucked her into her perfectly made bed. I dragged myself into my own room before climbing into the mussed-up sheets. As soon as I shut my eyes, I drifted off.

✦

I was standing on a bridge of light. It was familiar and somehow, I knew that I'd been here before. I turned and a woosh of cool night air hit my face. I realized it was coming from the other side of the bridge, where the glimmering light faded off into swirling shadows. I felt drawn to that darkness, so much so that I took a step towards it.

And then, I realized exactly when I'd been here.

Almost every night, for years. And each time, I forgot it all as soon as the morning came. Over and over, in a cycle that never ended. A sort of innate part of me knew that I had little time here, so I tentatively made my way closer to the shadows. But as soon as I got close enough to touch them, they began to move and corporealize into the figure of a person—a man.

Just before his face became visible, I heard a voice whisper into my ear, "Not yet, love. I want you to be awake when you remember my face for the first time."

The bridge fell out from beneath me and the dream faded into wisps of nothing.

✦

I woke up with a start. Glancing over at my alarm clock, I realized I was awake nearly an hour earlier than I needed to be, which was weird for me. Really weird.

I snuggled back into the covers and closed my eyes, trying to go back to sleep. But something... something tugged at the edges of my consciousness, keeping me awake. I groaned and sat up in bed, staring at the blank, white wall, trying to figure out what the heck was keeping me from my precious final hour of sleep. Nothing came to me. Not for a while, at least. In fact, my alarm went off just before I realized what I was forgetting.

I swore loudly, slamming my palm against the top of the clock to silence it. Then I got up, threw on my work clothes and some makeup, then walked swiftly out into the living room. Lil was unsurprisingly already up and sipping on a steaming mug of coffee. She liked to call morning her "special me time." I didn't get it, but, hey, whatever made her happy.

As soon as I emerged, wide-awake and bouncing on my feet, she looked at me like I had a horn growing out of the side of my head.

"So... perky this morning," she said.

I shrugged, trying to act nonchalant as I perched on the couch next to her, bouncing my leg.

"Yes?" she ventured, and I realized I was kind of staring in her general area.

"I wanted to ask," I cleared my throat. "What do you know about dream magic?"

Lil's brows raised and she paused before replying, "Well, it's an Unseelie Court thing, or at least that's what Raven told me. In fact, I think he told both of us. Why are you asking?"

I pressed my lips into a line, shrugging. I did know dream magic belonged to the Unseelie Court—a twisted form of shadow magic. But I'd wanted someone to confirm my suspicions just in case I was wrong. I had hoped I would be.

Lil scrutinized me, then questioned, "Wait. Do you think someone was in your dream?"

"I don't know," I replied honestly. "I think… I think I've been having the same dream for a while now. But this is the first time I remembered it when I woke up. I think it was because I finally recognized who spoke."

"Someone actually *spoke* to you? What did they say?" Lil demanded.

"I don't remember," I said carefully. "But I think it matters a lot more who I heard than what they said."

Lil sat still, waiting.

"I think I heard the Unseelie king," I finally admitted.

Lil didn't move nor react at first. Then, her expression clouded as she said, "You think you've been having this dream for a while? As in, you think the Night King has been in your dreams for a while?"

I exhaled. "I don't know for sure. It's hard to remember and it only gets foggier the longer I try to focus on the specifics of the dream."

Lil glanced at her worn leather watch, one her father had given to her when she was fifteen, and said, "We both have to go, or we'll be late for work. But we're not done talking about this, alright? I'll see if Raven can come over again tonight. He knows way more about Unseelie magic than I do, so maybe he can clear this up."

"Okay," I sighed.

She reached over and squeezed my hand as she said, "We'll figure it out. No need to be scared."

I gave her a tight smile and replied, "I know."

What I didn't mention to her was that Nox Ether being in my dreams didn't scare me. It was the notion that I might not remember him again when the next morning came.

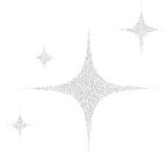

CHAPTER
FIVE

THE BUS WAS MERCIFULLY LESS crowded today when I boarded. Unfortunately, the experience was instantly ruined, because the same faerie who I'd told off about his perfume was there, right in the spot I wanted.

"Hello, again," he said with a wide smirk.

I resisted snapping at him with a snarky retort, instead giving him a somewhat pleasant smile and replying, "Hi."

Somehow, he took my mildly civil interaction as flirting, leaning in close to me as the bus started to move forward.

"How old are you?" he asked, a gleam in his muddy-browneyes.

Um, *ew*.

"Not interested, sorry," I shot back coolly, turning away from him.

Except the dickhead didn't take the rejection well and decided to play with a strand of my ponytail as he whispered creepily in my ear, "Playing hard to get, huh?"

I whirled and some of my hair ripped off in his greedy fingers.

"I said I'm not interested."

He narrowed his eyes and demanded, "Do you have a boyfriend or a mate?"

"No, and you're not going to be either of those things," I said.

"How about we talk about it over dinner—"

"Leave me alone," I snarled as the bus stopped.

He backed up, but his gaze wasn't on me anymore. Instead, his eyes were pinned on a spot just behind me. I turned to see what he was looking at and nearly stumbled back myself.

Nox Ether stood in the aisle of the bus I took to work every day.

"W-what are you doing here?" the man behind me asked the King of the Unseelie Court. "You're not supposed to be here."

The King cocked his head as the bus began to move and said in a low voice, "I'll go where I wish."

The man behind me tapped on my shoulder and hissed, "Do you know the Night King or something?"

"I believe she said she wasn't interested," Nox said.

The hand on my shoulder dropped as Nox approached me, his long-fingered hands skimming the railings.

"What are you doing here?" I demanded.

He raised a brow. "Not happy to see me?"

I huffed out a short breath and said, "He's right you know. You shouldn't be here and you shouldn't be talking to me either."

"And why is that?"

I flared my nostrils, staring him down. He didn't move from his spot next to me. I stood, stubbornly silent, until we got to my stop outside the museum. I hoped he wouldn't follow me off the bus but... nope. He trailed after me, earning us both a few wary looks from the other passengers as we stepped off the bus and onto the bustling sidewalk.

"I have work," I stated irritably.

"Oh, really?" he said. "I thought you were just taking a day to go and stare at dusty old relics."

I narrowed my eyes and demanded, "How do you know I work here? How did you know I'd be on that bus, for that matter?"

He chuckled and replied, "I'm a king, love."

A non-answer if there ever was one. But what I knew he really meant to say was, *I have eyes everywhere who answer to me. Finding you was easy.*

Stalker much.

"Well, I have to go," I said. "And you are not following me inside. My boss will flip if I walk in with you."

To my surprise, he shrugged, said, "Understood," and then walked away to the other side of the street.

I shook my head, confused but glad to be rid of him. Sort of. There was of course that wild, curious side of me that wanted to see just what he tasted like... felt like. Especially after our night in the club. But rational, sane-minded Aster reminded me that this was a *king*. And not just any king; my uncle's rival. My rival, really.

My enemy even.

I stepped inside, Miriam not in sight. On my desk, she had left a fresh stack of paper files to digitize, neatly piled next to the computer. I reigned in a sigh as I looked at them, then headed for her office. Normally, I wouldn't brave facing her this early, but she had a coffee maker and I had a need for the life-giving stuff at the moment.

I knocked on her door and called, "Miriam, do you mind if I grab a cup of coffee?"

I heard the sound of her shuffling over, then the door opened as she clipped out, "Fine. But be quick about it, I have a call to take in five minutes."

"Got it, I'll be in and out," I muttered.

I retrieved my coffee quickly, thanking the goddess Miriam had good taste. I hated cheap coffee. Once I was out of her office and settled behind my desk, I began to flick through the files.

Just as I became engrossed in one about ancient weapons, I heard a familiar voice drawl, "Good morning."

I jumped in my seat, nearly spilling the coffee all over the papers on the desk around me. It only got worse when I looked up and my gaze locked with that of a pair of familiar amber eyes.

This time, our third time meeting face to face, I really took a moment to notice him.

Nox Ether's wavy silver-white hair was tamed into a loose bun, framing his sharp, but symmetric features. He wore a fitted black shirt, unbuttoned slightly at the top, along with tailored pants of the same color. I swallowed and his mouth quirked up slightly, his half-grin feline. He knew very well that I'd been checking him out.

"What are you doing here?"

The words were out of my mouth before I could stop them, in a harsher tone than I'd intended. His dark eyebrows shot up and he laughed softly.

"You didn't think you'd get rid of me that easily, did you?" he said.

I cleared my throat, adjusting the papers around me.

When I looked back up, he was still there, waiting. He inclined his head past me, towards the exhibits.

"I'd like a tour," he stated, his hands sliding into his pockets.

"I'm a receptionist, not a tour guide, so no," I replied coolly.

Then I watched as his gaze slid over to where Miriam's office door was currently opening. This was about to get really interesting.

Miriam's eyes widened into saucers as she beheld the King of the Unseelie Court standing in her lobby. She gaped like a fish for a moment before gathering her wits about her, running a hand through her dyed blonde hair, and breathily asking, "Your Majesty, how can I be of assistance?"

I nearly rolled my eyes. Nox Ether wasn't our king, so there was no need to address him as such. We didn't exactly respect him in our court. He seemed to share my line of thought because he smiled and said, "Mr. Ether is fine. No need for titles at the moment."

Miriam pursed her lips and nodded.

"Mr. Ether… what can I do for you?"

His eyes flicked back to me, the gold flecks within them flashing in the sunlight streaming in through the tall windows. Though strangely, the light seemed to shy away from the rest of him.

"I'd like a tour of the museum."

Miriam smiled and said, "Of course, of course. Just give me one moment—"

"With Ms. Quiin," he inclined his head in my direction, cutting Miriam off.

Shock flickered across Miriam's face, but to her credit,

she recovered quickly and explained, "Aster is just our receptionist. I don't know if she'd be comfortable with a tour quite yet."

Right, Miriam. Speak for me. But still, she wasn't wrong. I wasn't comfortable, but not because I didn't know my way around the museum. On the contrary, I knew the exhibits like the back of my own hand. What was uncomfortable was the way Nox Ether was looking at me. And the worst part about it was the fact that there was a wild, unchecked part of me that wanted to bask under the weight of his stare forever.

Nox smiled, though his tone was slightly cooler this time as he replied, "I'm sure Ms. Quiin will be able to manage."

Miriam's expression fell, but she nodded and relented, "Very well. I'll watch the front desk while you're giving Mr. Ether his tour, Aster."

She shot me a look that said something along the lines of, *Don't you dare screw this up.*

I ignored her, taking a deep breath and standing from my seat. Nox watched me with a predatory gaze as I walked out from behind the desk and breezed past him.

"Follow me," I said, adding, "please," just for Miriam's sake.

Nox fell into step close behind me. We walked in a tense silence to the first exhibit: a painted depiction of the second Long Night, along with a shining sword sitting in a glass box. Rubies glimmered on the hilt of the weapon, taunting us like the eyes of some great beast. I ignored them, just as I ignored the goosebumps that were beginning to trail up my arms.

"Legend is that this is the very weapon that aided in sending the demon horde back to the depths of Hell, swaying the tide of the war," I drawled, glancing at the painting briefly.

It was mostly made up of whorls of dark colors, flecked with shining slits of yellow—demon eyes. There were splashes of dark maroon near the bottom, which I assumed to be blood. And mixed in were the agonized, terrified faces of faeries, humans, sirens, and shifters. There were even children woven in, their tiny expressions twisted into various states of agony and fear.

As I looked at the painting, Nox examined the blade, and something shadowy flickered in his bright eyes.

"Well, legend seems to be correct for once," he murmured.

"How would you know?"

Goddess, I needed to learn to shut my mouth.

But Nox merely gave me a small smile and said, "I've lived a long time, love."

I wanted to push, to ask if he was really *that* old. But it seemed rude, so I didn't, and we moved onto the next exhibit. It was another painting, this time of a faerie circle, in which the Fae depicted were dancing, drinking, and fucking. Sometimes all three at once.

"A depiction of a time when our kind were little more than beasts," I said dryly.

Nox glanced at me and asked, "Why do you say that?"

I shrugged. "They're more creatures of the forest than civilized Beings in this."

He stepped a little closer to me, crossing his arms across his chest. Even through the dark shirt, I could tell he was corded with muscle, though he wasn't quite as huge as Raven. He wore another smirk, tilting one side of his full mouth up. I realized I was staring again and swore internally. Why did this man have to be so damn pretty? As he spoke, I averted my eyes quickly.

"Do you of all people really think that submitting to our true nature is a bad thing?" he asked.

I choked back a retort, instead saying evenly, "Just because I like to go to clubs doesn't mean I think we should rut around like animals again."

Nox chuckled darkly and leaned in as he asked, "And did you do any rutting the other night?"

My nostrils flared and I replied, "That is absolutely none of your business. But no, I just went home."

I swore I saw relief flash across his features, though I was probably imagining it.

"Let's go to the next exhibit," he said after a beat.

We did, wandering from painting, to sculpture, to artifact. Nox was quiet for the most part, letting me jabber about the history behind each exhibit. Every once in a while he made some remark, though it always seemed to be more to himself than to me.

About an hour later, I sighed, "That's it. The grand tour."

Nox smiled and bowed slightly. I looked at him in confusion as he rose up and explained, "It's a gesture of thanks or respect in my court."

"Oh," I replied lamely.

He circled around me, his eyes not leaving mine as he mused, "I think you'd like my court."

"Maybe," I said. "But I'm never going there, so it's kind of a moot point."

There was something hungry in his expression for the briefest of moments, but it disappeared quickly before he replied, "Don't talk in absolutes, love. You should know by now that anything is a possibility at all times."

"Sure, stalker," I retorted.

He raised a brow. "Stalker?"

I chewed on my bottom lip, suddenly realizing who I'd just so nonchalantly insulted. Nox seemed to notice my sudden hesitation, because he cocked his head and said, "Don't stop on my behalf. I like being challenged by you."

"You do?"

He nodded, then asked quietly, "Does your boss know?"

"Know what?"

Nox pulled a hand out of his pocket and brushed back a stray strand of silvery hair from his face. I resisted the sudden urge to run my fingers through his hair like I had the other night in the club. His eyes flashed, as if he was remembering that moment too.

"I mean," he began, "does your boss know just who she's ordering around?"

I blinked and quickly said, "I don't know what you mean."

He took a step closer and then murmured in my ear, "Lying doesn't suit you, princess."

I jerked back, stepping away from him. "You're mistaken," I whispered hoarsely.

But the truth was already written all over my panicked face.

Nox raised a brow. "Why hide?"

"That's none of your damn business," I said.

"How old are you?"

Coming from him, the question wasn't creepy. Because he wasn't asking it to see if I was old enough for him to get in my pants. He was asking because of the crown… my crown, which I was supposed to have taken by now.

Still, I replied coldly, "Also none of your business."

He waited and I finally said through clenched teeth, "Twenty-two."

Nox stared at me and he asked, "Then why haven't you taken your uncle's place? You're well of age, and he was only supposed to be regent."

I kept my mouth shut and he muttered, "Unless there's something stopping you."

When I said nothing in return, he took a short breath and reached into his pocket, pulling out a smooth, milky-white stone. A moonstone. I was pretty sure Raven had one.

"I have to get back," Nox said to me, not bothering to explain where "back" was. "But if you decide you don't want to work as a receptionist anymore, just put your lips to this."

I glared at him. "I suppose you want me to think of you while I make out with your stone."

He raised a brow and said, "You're not wrong."

"I'm not taking it. I don't need help from a king, especially an Unseelie one."

He chuckled and said, "I don't believe for one moment that you care about our courts' divide."

Before I could even react, the stone was shoved into my hand, his lips brushing my cheek. A second later, he was gone in a whirl of shadows.

So, he was a Shadow Walker. Interesting.

Interesting and dangerous.

CHAPTER
SIX

THE REST of the workday crawled by slowly, as usual. A few patrons came in here and there, but just as I had yesterday, I spent most of my shift poring over more records and staring at my computer screen. Not to mention, my strange encounter with the Night King kept replaying itself over again in my head.

Finally, when five o'clock hit, I let out a loud sigh and logged off my computer. I called out to Miriam in her office, "I'm going!"

But just as I was about to leave, Miriam said my name, stopping me. I turned, to find her leaning against the doorway, her arms crossed and her face stony.

"Aster, I don't want any trouble," she said sternly. "You won't be bringing in more trouble, will you? Because I have a reputation to uphold."

I mustered a forced smile. "Of course, I know. No trouble, I promise."

She cocked her head at me, her hair beginning to fall

out of the tightly coiled bun she'd put it up in halfway through the day.

"What did he want? The king?" She asked.

I shrugged. "Just a tour."

"Strange. Even stranger that he wanted you to give it to him," she said. "Almost as if you know each other."

I shook my head. "We don't. I promise, Miriam. No trouble."

She narrowed her eyes briefly at me and for a moment I was almost afraid she was going to try and force the answer from me by using a glamour. It wouldn't work; my faerie magic was too strong. And besides, it was illegal for sirens to glamour other citizens, unless it was sanctioned by the crown or the authorities. A *lot* of sirens worked for my uncle in the Investigation Bureau; their brand of magic was good for interrogations. Thankfully, Miriam only nodded and stepped back, letting me go.

I quickly walked past her and shoved open the door, stepping out into the fading early-evening light. Around me, the street was bustling and busy; everyone else was getting out of work too. They hurried to parking garages or bus stops, everyone intent on getting home.

In the past ten or so years, our court had become a single-mouthed beast. The beast being the crown, also being my uncle. Everyone, from faeries to sirens, worked hard to sustain the royals' lavish habits and ways of life. Though, as I'd gotten older, it had become more and more apparent that, while being the lords and ladies of the royal court, Fae held most of the more prominent positions in the corporate world.

I wondered if it was that way in the Unseelie Court too.

Our courts hardly interacted, and a magical veil of sorts

separated them. The Veil was probably a large part of the reason war hadn't yet broken out between us. I'd heard that its magic was tied to that of the Unseelie ruler, which of course was currently Nox.

I realized I'd been standing in front of the museum for far too long to look normal, and I'd caught the attention of a few shifters who were meandering down the sidewalk towards me.

"Oy, pretty girl! Anything goin' on in that head of yours?" one of them cajoled.

I ignored the catcalls—it was typically the best way to deal with them—and headed for the bus stop. Thankfully, no one followed me and I just made the bus. Another plus was that, though it was crowded, it was free of creepy perfume faerie. The ride home was quick and I spent it staring at the buildings as we whizzed past. Our court, though modern, had maintained a sort of quaintness, with a landscape of red-brick buildings and plenty of greenery.

Once the bus arrived at my stop, I stepped off and headed for my apartment. By the time I got there, I was exhausted and my feet ached from my heeled boots. As I opened the door, I called out Lil's name, but there was no response. I flicked on the entry hall light and noticed the note on the kitchen counter.

Hey, Aster. I won't be home until later. Sorry—I know we had plans, but my mom insisted both Raven and I come over to her house tonight. Weird, I know. Anyways, there's leftover mac and cheese in the fridge if you want it. See you later.

—Lil

I sighed loudly at nothing and no one. I had been looking forward to talking to Raven about the dreams I'd been having and hopefully finding some answers. I rubbed my eyes, probably smearing mascara all over my face. It didn't matter. I was staying in tonight, with the deafening silence as my only companion.

Food was currently priority number one. Miriam didn't give me a lunch break, which was basically legal torture. Not to mention I was notoriously bad at remembering to eat breakfast, and I hardly ever got up early enough to do so. Consequently, each night when I got home I stuffed my face with as much food as my stomach could handle.

I shoved the entirety of the leftover mac and cheese in the microwave and watched it spin round and round. A questionable smell emitted from it, though it wasn't enough to dissuade me. A crack sounded through the air just as the microwave beeped, and a prickling sensation began to tease the back of my neck.

Someone was here.

I whirled around and my heart caught in my throat. Standing just a few feet away in front of me was my uncle. He smiled coldly as he saw the panic blooming on my face. My eyes followed every movement of his, though I was frozen in place by an old fear. He ran a hand through his short, dark-blonde hair. Surprisingly, he wasn't wearing his crown, but he was clad in some sort of fancy gold-threaded tunic. His cloudy, ice-blue eyes—my blue eyes—assessed the apartment around us.

"You could bathe in riches and feast on wondrous food each night, yet you stay here, in this hovel, eating whatever that is," he mused, looking at the still-beeping microwave.

I hit the stop button on the microwave, trying to hide the shaking of my hand. Then, I gritted my teeth and asked, "What do you want, Calum?"

His amused expression darkened. "You will address me as 'My king' or 'Your Majesty,' Aster," he growled.

"I could say the same to you," I sneered. "Or am I unworthy of your stupid titles?"

He paused, his body becoming unnaturally still. I knew I'd made a big mistake by insulting him. That was always a mistake—my uncle was a proud, vain man.

Seconds later, a large hand collided with my face and I stumbled back, pain shooting needles and daggers through my nose. My uncle was breathing heavily as he leaned in, trailing a hand from my waist to my breasts. His touch was light but bleeding with possession. He knew he could do whatever he wanted to me and I wouldn't stop him. I couldn't.

"Did you think," he began, "that I would not know what you were up to?"

I tried to school my face into neutrality as I whispered back, "I don't know what you mean."

He struck me again, this time harder, and I both heard and felt my nose crunch. I gripped the counter to keep from falling to the ground as stars blinked in and out in my vision.

"I have eyes everywhere, Aster," he growled. "Your boss, for one, reported a strange occurrence this morning between her young receptionist and Nox Ether," he spat out the Unseelie king's name like a curse.

"He just wanted a tour," I managed to say as I felt the warmth of blood begin to trickle from my nose.

"Oh? And was that tour more or less invigorating than your little dalliance in the club the other night?" my uncle seethed.

My heart just might have stopped. He knew about the

club… he was watching me that closely. And all I could think to say was, "I didn't know. I didn't know it was him."

My uncle laughed cruelly. "And I'm supposed to believe that? Believe me, Aster, I know you're a whore, but this is much too far."

I flinched at the word—*whore*.

I had full control over my desires and each time I used my body to fulfill them, it was my choice. Judging me for that, judging anyone for that, was archaic. But the Fae, especially the men, were assholes and possessive to a fault. My uncle was no different.

I began to shake, hating the fear and helplessness that I knew he could practically taste. Everything could be taken away if I didn't bow under the weight of his power. I'd be swept into the tall, haunted walls of the palace a few miles from here and then never see the light of day again. And he knew it. He bathed in my fear and the control he held over me.

"If I see you with another Unseelie bastard again, especially the king, I swear I will not hesitate to take you back home."

"The palace isn't my home," I said.

His gaze once again flicked around the apartment as he laughed.

"Your parents would be disappointed in you."

The insult shouldn't have hit me so hard, but it did, nearly knocking the breath from my lungs. A moment later, he strode out the front door, slamming it behind him. I heard a crack in the hall as he flitted away.

I sank down on the tiled floor, still clutching my bleeding nose. Despair began to quicken my breath and cloud my rational thought. I had no way out. I would be his forever, and the freedom I thought I'd gained in the last few years—all of it was an illusion.

My breath came in ragged gasps, only sharpening the pain in my nose and my split lip. My pain didn't matter, nothing did. As my heart hammered in my chest and my hands began to shake, I felt for the moonstone, pulling it out of my pocket. I stared at it and then, in a moment of pure, unrationalized panic, I pressed it to my lips. I thought of Nox; the citrusy smell of him, his gold-flecked eyes, the silver of his hair catching in the glow of the flashing club lights…

Almost immediately, the subtle darkness in the corner of the kitchen began to ripple as a form started to appear. First, there were just shadows, then the form became solid. My heartbeat kicked up impossibly faster and I already began to regret my rash decision. But it was too late. Nox stood in front of me, his brow furrowed in confusion as he slowly approached me.

"Why are you on the floor—"

He cut himself off as his gaze skirted over the blood trickling from my nose and the bruise no doubt already forming on my cheek. Shadows coiled tightly around him and his body became completely still.

"Nox?" I whispered.

He unfroze and crouched down, his eyes burning with rage.

"Who did this to you?" he asked roughly, as if it was an effort for him to stay in control.

I wiped at the blood below my nose, wincing as I replied, "No one that matters."

I could already tell he wasn't going to let it go.

"A boyfriend?" he pushed. "Someone you brought home?"

I gritted my teeth and said, "No. Nothing like that."

His brow furrowed, and then his nose twitched. As the realization crossed his face, horror flooded me. Of course. I was sure he'd encountered my uncle at least a few times before. And now he was picking up his distinct, lingering scent in my apartment. Not to mention it was probably all over me too.

His nostrils flared and he moved to stand, but I grabbed his wrist.

"Leave it."

I don't know what compelled me to bark an order at a king, at a Shadow Walker no less. But somehow, I knew if I didn't, he would track my uncle down and do something he'd regret later. Protective, insufferable faeries, all of them.

Nox dragged his gaze back to me and asked quietly, "How often does this happen?"

I didn't know how he guessed this wasn't a one-time occurrence, but I was in no state to dance around the truth. So, I simply replied, "Less than it used to."

"The bastard," he growled.

I laughed softly, though it hurt. "He said the same about you a few minutes ago."

My hand was still on his wrist and I slid it away as he closed his eyes briefly, then muttered, "He's aware, then?"

"That you've been stalking me? Yeah, he knows."

Nox ignored the comment and stood up. I went to follow him, but he stopped me with a gentle touch to my shoulder and asked, "Where are your washcloths?"

I licked my bloodied lips nervously, then replied, "Second drawer to the left of the sink."

He opened the drawer and picked up a clean dish towel, wetting it under the sink faucet, and then crouched back down in front of me. I winced as he cleaned the blood off my face.

"Sorry," he said softly.

"I can do that, you know," I said.

"I know."

He finished, then said, "Your nose is slightly broken. I can fix it, but it'll hurt."

"You're a healer?" I asked.

He nodded, his gaze sliding over my face distractedly as he said, "From my mother's side. Let me heal it."

"Alright," I said heavily. "But be quick about it."

He nodded and I braced myself. One of his hands cupped the back of my neck, while the other lightly touched my tender nose.

"Were you aware," he began and I gasped as I felt my bones crunch and reset, "that I know your friend's brother?"

Dizzy, I shook my head and managed to gasp, "Raven?"

"Yes, he grew up in my court actually. We have always had a place for bastards cast out by their Seelie families."

I took a shaky breath. "He never told me."

Nox smiled slightly—a sad smile—as he said, "We all have our secrets."

My mother's scream.

Blinding white light.

"What have you done, Asteria?"

I shook off the long-buried memory and rasped, "Yes, we do."

Nox stood, offering a hand. I accepted it and then he helped me over to the couch. I was still wincing from my nose when he reached a hand towards my face as I sat down. I flinched away from his sudden touch and he paused.

"I can make it hurt even less," he told me.

"How?"

He smiled slightly. "Like I said earlier today, I've lived for a long time and I've picked up some less... common healing techniques over the years."

His hand was still poised and I relented, "Alright."

Gently, his fingers skimmed my cheek, whispering across my mouth for a quick second. My gaze flicked to his, but he was already concentrating on whatever the hell he was doing to my nose.

His magic felt warm, almost uncomfortably hot, at first. Then, it became soothing and cool. I felt a little sleepy by the time he pulled his hand back.

"Sorry," I said. "I might have made you a tad too relaxed."

I yawned and said, "You don't say."

"You can sleep if you want."

I snorted and my nose didn't even hurt as I did so.

"If you think I'm lying unconscious and prone with you in my apartment, dream on, little king," I said.

He narrowed his eyes and said, "Two things, love. First of all, that is definitely not my thing. The first time I make you come, you're going to remember every second of it."

Make me... *what?*

"And second," he went on, not missing a beat. "I am not little."

I was majorly unsure of how to respond to either of those things. And he was just staring at me. Eventually, I said, "I have a question. But first," I groaned as I adjusted, "first I need you to go to the cabinet next to the fridge and get me my bottle of whiskey."

"*Your* bottle of whiskey?" he mused.

"Yes," I hissed. "*Mine.* Lil knows not to touch it. It's my comfort bottle."

"And how many comfort bottles have you run through this past year?" Nox asked with a smile, though there was a slight edge to his tone.

"Just get me the damn whiskey," I snarled.

He put his hands up and said nothing more as went back to the kitchen and retrieved the bottle. After I'd had a long drag of it and Nox was seated next to me—now a cushion away—I finally spoke again.

"Two questions."

He nodded and reasoned, "Then I get two as well."

I rolled my eyes. "What is this, a schoolyard game?"

Nox didn't respond, and I knew he wasn't going to budge, so I sighed loudly before asking my first question, "Why were you in the club that night and why did you pretend you didn't know who I was?"

"That's two already, just so you're aware," he cautioned.

I rolled my eyes. "Fine. Three for three then."

He shrugged and stretched his long legs out on the coffee table. The King of the Unseelie Court was lounging on my coffee table. It was absurd, really.

"I was at the club that night for reasons I cannot yet disclose to you. It was for… court business. That's all I can tell you for now. I hope I can say more soon, but—"

"You don't trust me," I cut in.

He shook his head. "Not necessarily true. But I want to make sure you're fully aware of other elements of the situation before I tell you my reasoning."

Cryptic, elegantly crafted words. We were faeries after all. But I waited for the other answer anyway.

He hesitated, then said, "I do admit, I knew who you were immediately. But not from your face or even your scent. I picked up on your power right away and knew you were no ordinary faerie girl. Only those born of certain bloodlines have that kind of power. Or, if they're a fluke, they push their way to power. And then there's your eyes. I'd know those eyes anywhere. I hate... hated those eyes. Anyways, I put two and two together quite quickly. Someone with your power who had Calum Fairwae's eyes. You had to be the missing Seelie princess."

"No one thinks I'm missing," I cut in. "They just think I'm living a sheltered, pretty life in that palace on the hill."

Nox shook his head and said, "No, they do. Your uncle wasn't exactly forthcoming about the details of the accident." He paused as I flinched.

Of course, Calum didn't want anyone to know. Neither did I. But I didn't say that. Instead, I said as evenly as I could, "The accident that killed my parents. I'm quite aware. Continue."

He looked like he wanted to say more about it, but instead he pushed on, "Some believe you're truly dead. Most, I think. After all, you're well past the minimum age to rule. Why wouldn't you have stepped forward by now, especially when your uncle is such a tyrant?"

Guilt slammed into me all of the sudden and I looked away. So, this is what he thought of me. Weak and selfish. A child.

"I can see what you're thinking," Nox said softly. "It's written all over your face. But I don't think you're weak. I think you're the victim of an abusive situation and you've done what you need to in order to survive."

"Still weak," I muttered.

"If you take too much stake in what others believe about you, you'll never overcome your fears, Asteria," Nox said.

I snapped my gaze to his as he said my full name. No one, not even my uncle called me Asteria. Asteria was some long-forgotten part of me, one that I did not want to bring back to the surface.

"I have one more question. Then you ask yours, and I want you to leave," I said coldly.

Nox said nothing, seeming to notice the shift in my tone.

"If you're a Shadow Walker, why am I not already dead at the hands of some demon?" I asked.

Nox leaned forward in his seat, narrowing his eyes as he replied, "I'm not a Shadow Walker. At least not in the way that you understand the word to mean."

"Then what are you?"

He stood, cracking his fingers, and said, "Along with being an excellent healer, my mother was half-wraith. Her abilities, and mine, appear to be very similar to those whose craft deals with demons. The discrimination they've faced is partially why wraiths went into hiding for so long. Some even still."

"Oh," was all I could think to say.

In my pocket, my phone buzzed. I ignored it at first, but then Nox said, "You can answer that if you want."

"It's probably just Lil," I said under my breath, pulling my phone from my pocket and reading the message: *Things are complicated here. Won't be home till tomorrow morning. Sorry.*

My heart sank and it must have shown in my expression because Nox asked, "What is it?"

I shook my head. "Nothing, it's… it's fine. Lil just won't be home until tomorrow."

"So, you'll be alone here?"

I raised a brow. "Um, yeah."

He sighed, sitting back down as he said, "This couch is comfortable enough, I suppose."

It took me a moment to process exactly what he meant by that. When I realized he actually intended to sleep over, I said, "I'm good. Like really, I'm fine. I don't need a babysitter."

He glanced at me. "And if your uncle comes back?"

"If that's a possibility, then you should definitely leave," I replied.

Nox only sighed again, before he said, "Question number one."

"Nox, I need you to leave."

"You promised an even trade. Three for three. I'm only claiming what's mine."

I rolled my eyes. "Fine."

"Why do you work at a museum?"

"Really?" I said. "That's what you want to know?"

He shrugged. "It's an odd choice."

I cleared my throat and said, "Well, uh, I majored in astrology. Most people don't know this, but Miriam did too, back when she was at the university. I only agreed to work for her because she offered to help me continue building my knowledge base during down times."

"And has she done that?"

I snorted. "Goddess, no. But I need the money and a job's a job."

Nox cocked his head to the side and asked, "Your uncle doesn't provide you financial support, at the very least?"

I shook my head.

"What about helping you fund your schooling?"

"I got a full-ride scholarship."

"So, he hasn't spent a single tab on you?"

I sighed. "Nope. And I like it that way. I don't want to be in his debt."

Nox cracked his knuckles and then leaned forward as he said, "First of all, that's ridiculous. Second of all, next question."

I waited, worrying my bottom lip as he stared at me, his expression contemplative. Finally, he asked, "Do you actually not have a boyfriend?"

I choked out a laugh and said, "Seriously?"

Nox didn't even smile as he nodded and said, "Completely."

"Um, no, I don't."

"Good."

I narrowed my eyes at him and said, "Why do you ask?"

"Just checking."

"Checking for what?"

He only sat back again and said, "Question number three. Why did you ask me what my name was in the club?"

"Why didn't you give it to me?" I immediately shot back.

"My turn for questions, not yours, love."

I rolled my eyes. "Fine. I don't know… I was drunk out of my mind and I suppose you intrigued me."

"Intrigued," he echoed, letting the word roll over his tongue as if he was tasting it.

I said nothing. He didn't either, not for a few tense

seconds. I glanced at him, daring him to speak first. He simply raised a dark brow at me. Eventually, I gave up and asked, "If you're going to refuse to leave, do you want to do something?"

He furrowed his brow. "Do something?"

"Yeah," I said. "You know, pass the time. Hang out…" I trailed off, wincing internally. I had actually just proposed to the Night King of the Unseelie Court that we "hang out" together. As if he typically engaged in such menial activities.

But to my surprise, Nox only nodded and asked, "What would you do if I wasn't here?"

I thought about it for a second, then answered, "Probably watch a TV show or a movie."

"What do you like to watch?"

I shrugged. "You're the guest, you pick."

He flicked his fingers, causing the remote to float into the air towards him. I resisted commenting on it; instead, I walked over to the microwave and added thirty seconds. As my mac and cheese reheated again, Nox wrinkled his nose.

"What is that smell?" he asked.

"My dinner."

"No."

The microwave beeped and I stopped it, ignoring him. Just as I was about to carefully pull the hot carton out, my nerve endings went haywire, goosebumps trailing up my arm. I knew Nox was there before I even turned.

"Is there a problem?" I asked.

He nodded. "You aren't eating old, twice-reheated mac and cheese. What restaurants do you like?"

"No, you are not taking me out—"

"There's this wonderful thing called takeout, love," he cut in.

I stared at my now crusted-over mac and cheese sitting pitifully in the dirty microwave and finally relented, "Fine. There's a ramen place about half a mile away."

Nox pulled his phone from his back pocket and began to tap on the glowing screen.

"What kind do you want?" he asked.

"Vegetarian."

He glanced up from his phone. "Do you not eat meat?"

"I do, sometimes."

It was odd how enthralled the Unseelie King seemed with my simple quirks and requests. He nodded, pausing for a moment, as if to catalog the information, before finishing up the order.

"There," he said with a final tap on the phone screen. "It'll be here in thirty minutes."

"Okay... thanks," I said, a little awkwardly.

"No need," he said. "It was simply an emergency intervention."

I scowled and shot back, "I would have been perfectly happy with my leftovers."

"And perfectly deceased."

"It was a *day* old. I think I would have been fine."

Nox shook his head and skirted past me, plucking the poor mac and cheese container out of the microwave, before tossing it in the trash. He looked mildly satisfied as it landed with a loud *thunk* at the bottom of the bin.

"Happy now?" I said.

"Mhmm," he hummed. "And I know what movie we're watching."

He walked back over to my couch and it didn't fail to

register that he looked completely comfortable here, as if it were his own home. As if he were not used to luxury and finery in a palace many miles away from here.

He sank into the cushions of my couch and glanced over at me. "Coming?"

I stared at him for a moment before I said, "I don't know you. You don't know me. Why are you acting like we're friends?"

"Are we not?"

"I think we might still be in the 'stranger' or at the very least the 'acquaintance' phase."

He didn't say anything, simply patting the cushion next to him. Once I tentatively walked over and sat down, he turned to me and asked, "How do I become your friend?"

I pursed my lips, but replied, "Well, what we're doing now works for starters, I suppose."

He lifted a hand, and before I could even register what he was doing, he brushed his thumb over my lower lip and murmured, "Good."

His touch lingered for a moment, as did his gaze on my mouth. At that moment, my brain decided to remember his comment from earlier, about making me come. I felt a flush creep up my neck, but then he lowered his hand and said, "I'll start the movie."

I nodded, admittedly a little breathless. This time, he manually reached for the remote and turned the TV on. After a few clicks, the beginning credits to what appeared to be a war drama were flashing across the screen.

"Seriously?" I asked. "A war movie?"

"It's my favorite film."

"Ever?"

"Ever."

I sighed and sank back on the couch, ignoring the urge to curl up against him, like we were a couple of teenagers in our parent's basement. Just as the intro song faded out, a sorrowful mix of strings and drums, the doorbell rang.

I glanced at Nox. "How did you know my apartment's unit number?"

"Raven," he replied distractedly, his eyes on the screen.

"You know Raven well, then?" I ventured.

"The food, love."

I narrowed my eyes at him but he didn't seem inclined to explain further. Giving up, I stood, and walked to the front door, unlatching the chain. When I opened it, a young shifter, probably around sixteen, said, "Are you, uh, 'Intrigued Astrologer?'"

I stifled an incredulous laugh and replied, "Yeah, sure."

I took the bag and said, "I'll tip you on the app, okay?"

The kid nodded, chewing on his lip, and glancing very obviously at my chest as he said, "Thanks. Hey, are you—"

"Sorry, dude, not interested. And I'm assuming you're underage, so it wouldn't work out anyways."

"Can I at least have your number?"

I heard Nox get up from the couch, and I quickly said, "Nope," before shutting the door in the poor kid's face.

I turned. "You can't be seen here," I snapped.

"I know," he replied. "But I wanted to be on standby, just in case.'

"I can handle myself. Besides, he was a kid," I said, rolling my eyes.

"He was an alpha. Someday he'll likely be his pack's leader and—he likely doesn't know it yet—but if he really wanted to try and claim you, he might have shifted without meaning to. And you would have been directly in his path when he did."

"And how the hell did you know he was an alpha?"

Nox took the bag from me and replied, "Power gives off a certain vibration, even a certain smell. You'll learn to identify it with time. Now, let's eat."

The king sauntered back to the couch as he opened the bag. He then carefully pulled out the large plastic bowls that held the ramen.

"Forks?"

I shook off the disbelief that kept overcoming me at his actions and said, "Um, yeah."

I grabbed clean silverware and a couple of paper towels. Then, I joined him on the couch just as he un-paused the movie. We ate in silence, the sounds and colors of the war film filling it. Very quickly, I realized it was less about a war and more about a couple torn apart because of it—star-crossed lovers in a way.

As I finished my food, I glanced sideways at Nox, who was watching the screen intently, his ramen long ago demolished.

"I didn't peg you as a romantic," I said.

Just as I finished saying it, a large explosion bloomed across the screen. I jumped, then, realizing where the lead character had been only moments ago.

I exclaimed, "No way! Did they just kill him off?"

"Watch, love," Nox said patiently.

I looked back at the screen. And that was when I realized that the explosion had occurred right next to the infirmary, where the girl was working as a nurse. Though they hadn't been aware of it, we as the viewers knew that the couple had been close the entire time. And it seemed, as the camera panned out to show the man rushing towards the burning remnants of the makeshift hospital, he had just realized it. He screamed his lover's name, sinking to his knees near the wreckage. That was when I saw the enemy soldiers creeping closer, near the edges of the screen.

"No way…" I whispered, my voice trailing off.

A gunshot went off and the man on his knees collapsed to the ground. He died with a smile on his face, blood trickling from his mouth. I stared at the TV in disbelief as the credits rolled in.

"Are you *kidding* me?" I said. "They both die?"

Nox glanced at me. "Yes, but in the end, he got to be with her."

"Yeah, but c'mon! No happy ending?"

"Is that not a happy ending?"

I raised a brow, shooting him an incredulous look as I said, "You really need to rethink your idea of happy endings."

His expression shuttered, just for a moment, and I caught a flicker of what I thought might be sadness on his face.

"What?" I asked.

He smiled, quickly recovering from whatever had just bothered him and said, "Nothing, love. You should go get some sleep."

I glanced at the clock. It was nearly one in the morning and I had work tomorrow. I nodded and gathered the empty food containers and bags then tossed them in the trash before setting the forks in the sink to wash later. Nox was stretching out on the couch, though it was too small and he looked rather uncomfortable.

"You sure you'll be okay there?" I asked.

"I'll be fine. One request, though."

"Yeah?"

"A blanket, perhaps?"

I cleared my throat. "Right, yeah, of course. I'll be right back."

I disappeared into my room and grabbed a fluffy purple throw blanket. When I emerged back into the living room to hand it to Nox, his eyes were already closed.

"Nox?"

He opened his eyes and took the blanket. "Thank you, love."

"Okay, well... if you need anything, I'll be in my room. Also, you should probably leave early, before Lil gets back."

"Embarrassed?" he asked with a cocky half-grin.

"No," I replied. "But Lil would probably have a heart attack if she walked in and saw you sleeping on our couch without warning."

"Understood. Goodnight, Asteria."

I bit my lip and said, "Goodnight, then."

Quickly, I walked to my room, shutting the door behind me, and then changed into a t-shirt and sweatpants. I hardly realized how exhausted I was until I crawled into bed.

But I tossed and turned for nearly an hour before falling asleep.

CHAPTER
SEVEN

My mother cried out in agony.
Bright, burning light blinded me.
My uncle hissed… "What have you done?"
I could smell my own blood as it trickled down my face.
A hand slipped under my untucked shirt.
And I screamed and screamed and screamed through it all.

·✦

"Asteria," a voice said firmly.

I gasped, thrashing wildly in the gentle grip that held my shoulders down.

"Look at me, love," the voice commanded.

I forced my eyes open, terror still pulsing through me as I met Nox's amber irises in the near dark of my bedroom.

"You're alright," he said. "You're safe, I promise."

I nodded, swallowing hard. He ran a hand through his

hair and I swore I saw the gold flecks in his eyes begin to glow softly as we stared at each.

"I'll let you sleep," he said after a few seconds, moving to stand from the bed.

But I grabbed his hand, and before I could even think about it, I said, "Stay."

He paused, looking me over slowly, then asked, "You're sure?"

"Just for a little while."

"Alright," he said softly.

Nox scooted back on the bed with me and tentatively wrapped his arms around my still-trembling body. He began to stroke my hair. When a few minutes passed and I still didn't stop shaking, he began to hum. At first I didn't recognize the song, but then I realized it was an old faerie lullaby. I swore I remembered my mother teaching it to me once when I was very small. I drifted in and out as he continued to hum the song. My hand somehow ended up on his chest and I could feel it rumbling as he finished the lullaby.

"Nox?"

"Sleep, love," he said in reply.

"Why did you stay here with me tonight?"

He didn't answer for a long while, and I wondered if he'd fallen asleep. When he finally did reply, I was drifting off again.

But I was just awake enough to hear him murmur, "Because I would've wanted someone to do the same for me."

I was walking across a bridge of light. This time, I remembered it.

I remembered him.

As I stepped forward, the luminescent bridge began to meld into shadow and dark, cool stone. A light breeze blew past my face, ruffling my long, unbound hair. I breathed it in and it smelled pleasantly of cool air and the sweet oranges my mother and I sometimes used to pick from our scraggly tree in the back garden.

"Asteria."

I whipped my head around as someone said my name. It came from the darkness on the other side of the bridge. And sure enough, a few moments later, he walked into the light.

"Nox?" I ventured.

He smiled, his face softer and more unguarded than I'd ever seen it in waking as he replied, "Yes, love?"

"What is this place?"

His expression faltered, then he shook his head. "I can't tell you, not yet. But I'll see you soon, I promise."

I opened my mouth to tell him something, but he was already being swallowed up by the shadows, and the words I was about to speak flew from my mind. Moments later, I felt my own strange pull, tugging me back to the blinding light on the other side of the bridge. Before I could resist, it encased me completely and I was no more.

When I woke up to my ringing alarm, Nox was gone.

I almost assumed I'd dreamt the whole thing up, except that there was a short note next to the moonstone on my bedside table that read:

Call on me whenever you wish. I'll always make time for you.

I stared at the words, a little confused. Nox was... intense. And protective of me in a way that I wasn't sure I quite understood, at least not yet. It was all very strange.

As I pulled myself up and out of bed, I realized I hadn't even thought to ask him about the dream bridge. Then again, maybe it was unwise to do so. Shadow Walker or not, he was still dangerous and I didn't want to catch his attention any more than I already had.

Right?

Right.

✦

Just as I'd finished with my quick shower and was heading into the living room, I heard the lock to the front door click. My head whipped around as the door swung open, a part of me expecting it to be Nox again. Thankfully, this time, it was just Lil. Though, her expression grew angry as she looked at me.

Right, the bruises. I'd noticed them in the mirror this morning and I kicked myself for not asking Nox to heal them along with my nose. I wasn't entirely sure why he didn't. Though, quickly I realized why, as wrath filled Lil's eyes. He'd wanted her to see, because he knew that otherwise, I'd probably forgo telling her anything had happened at all.

Faerie asshole.

Lil quickly shut the door behind her, chucking off her wedges and rushing over to me.

"I thought we were rid of that monster," she hissed as she examined my bruises.

"Apparently not," I sighed. "I'm fine though. It was just the usual. Threats and a couple punches. I can take them."

"You shouldn't have to," she said. Then she looked me dead in the eye and asked, "Did he try to do anything else to hurt you?"

I swallowed, understanding what she meant. I shook my head and mumbled, "He hasn't... it hasn't happened since the start of university."

Uncle Calum owned me. All of me, including my body. And as soon as I "matured" enough for him, he made sure I knew it. I tried not to think of those moments most of all.

"I swear to the goddess, I'd cut his dick off if I had the chance," Lil hissed, adding, "and then his head."

I gave her a look and warned, "Careful, Lil."

She sighed, muttering something about this needing to stop. But even she knew it was futile. She had since we were kids. Standing, she then made her way to the kitchen, calling to me, "I'll get you some ice."

"Thanks," I replied from my spot on the couch.

I watched as she put ice from the freezer tray in a little baggy and wrapped it with a towel. But just as she finished in the kitchen, I heard her audibly sniff.

This was about to get interesting.

"Who was in here?" she asked slowly.

"My uncle," I replied quickly. "Can I have the ice?"

But she didn't buy it, narrowing her eyes and muttering to herself, "Your uncle does *not* smell this good."

I bit the inside of my cheek and she prowled over to me, handing me the ice bag. I pressed it gingerly to my cheek and she sniffed me, once, then again.

"You know, you could just let it go," I said under my breath.

She paused, as if trying to think of something, then her eyes widened.

"Citrus…" she trailed off. "I smelled citrus in the club the other night."

I bit my lip and added, "And night air."

Lil laughed incredulously. "Oh, my goddess, Aster. Are you telling me that the king of the Unseelie Court was in our fucking apartment?"

I just pressed the ice to my other cheek, silent.

Lil shut her eyes briefly. She then looked at me and said sternly, "Aster, it was different when you didn't know it was him. But you can't just… I mean why did he even come here? And how does he know where we live? Shit, have you been seeing him for a while? Were you lying about not knowing him and—"

"Lil," I cut in. "Cool it."

She splayed her hands and shouted, "No way, Aster! This is serious."

I sighed deeply. "I know, I know. But I wasn't lying. I didn't know who he was at the club. He just… visited me at work yesterday morning. I gave him a museum tour."

"Let me get this straight. You gave Nox Ether, King of the Unseelie Court, a museum tour? You're not even a tour guide!" she exclaimed.

I shrugged. "I know. He said he didn't want Miriam to do it and I can't say I blame him."

Lil was nearly shaking at my calm demeanor as she

managed to grit out, "That's why your uncle came, isn't it? To… punish you for associating with his enemy."

"Partially, yeah."

"So, then, your uncle left and Nox Ether just happened to be in the neighborhood? Does he even know who you are?"

For a second, I debated telling her about the moonstone at all. It didn't really matter at this point though; she knew most of it already. So, I pulled it out of my pocket. It glimmered softly in my palm. Lil stared at it for a moment, then murmured, "A moonstone. Raven has one."

"I know. And Nox figured out who I was right away apparently, at the club."

Lil bit her lip and nodded, her eyes still on the stone in my hand.

"Does it mean something?" I asked.

She wrung her hands and replied, "I'm not one hundred percent sure what, but yes. All I could ever get out of Raven was that it was some super-secret way to communicate in the Unseelie Court. But I'm fairly certain they have other magical properties."

"Nox gave it to me at the museum and told me I could use it to summon him. Last night, after my uncle left, I was all alone and my nose wouldn't stop bleeding and I… I just panicked. He was here before I could take it back. And he might have, uh, stayed the night."

Lil's eyes widened. "Are you saying that you two…?"

"No," I said quickly. "No, nothing happened. I think he just didn't want me to be alone after what happened with my uncle."

Lil was watching me carefully. Finally, she said quietly, "This whole situation is quite odd. You've known him for less than a week and he's showing up at your work and handing over Unseelie Court relics. It's even stranger that he figured out who you are so quickly and hasn't said anything to the media or the authorities. Or tried to kidnap you, for that matter."

"I know," I sighed. "And there's something else, I think. He indicated that he might want my help or something along those lines. I don't know, I think he was withholding information, but it seemed like he would tell me if I agreed to work with him or whatever."

"I feel like working for him is a very bad idea," Lil warned. "You don't know him and he doesn't know you. It feels like deceit to me. Or maybe he wants to use you to get to your uncle."

"Somehow, I don't think that's true," I said. "But don't worry. I'm not even considering it."

She didn't look fully convinced, but she finally seemed to settle a bit.

"I have something to tell you as well," she said, wringing her hands.

I looked up at her to see tears were forming in her eyes.

"Lil, what is it?" I urged, my mind swimming with a thousand ugly possibilities.

She sniffed, wiping her eyes. "My mom wants Raven to go back and live in the Unseelie Court. Permanently."

I didn't hesitate before asking, "Why?"

More tears tracked down Lil's round cheeks as she told me, "Well, you know more than anyone that there's been a lot of tension between the two courts. We can all feel it. Anyways, her excuse for essentially exiling him was that she wanted to keep him safe from Seelie Fae who might want to hurt him for his heritage."

"What a load of bullshit," I snapped, and Lil nodded.

"I know," she said. "I think she might be getting pressure from your uncle. And after tonight, well, I assume he definitely doesn't want you in particular seeing Raven."

I stared at the soft glow of the lights above us and said quietly, "Nox told me he knows Raven."

Lil wiped her eyes and said thickly, "Wait, what?"

I nodded. "Yeah, he said that there's a place at the Unseelie Court for bastard-born faeries cast out by their families. Maybe they'll take him in again."

Lil's voice was soft as she said, "I never thought to ask where he was all those years as a kid. I mean, I knew he was in the Unseelie Court, but I didn't know he actually lived at the royal palace itself. It must be how he knew who Nox was, right away the other night."

"Maybe," I said slowly, "maybe I should agree to work with Nox. What if it helps Raven? And that way, maybe I could see him, let him know how you're doing."

Lil brushed a few more tears away and said, "Aster, you can't. Your uncle would kill you if you went into Unseelie territory. Like literally."

I looked away and muttered, "I get the feeling that killing me someday is in the cards no matter what. I'll always be a threat to him."

To everyone.

I ignored the nagging whisper in my head, instead focusing back on my friend. She took my hand and squeezed it.

"You'll have to be careful, whatever you decide to do. And Aster," she said. "Guard your heart with your life. It's worth much more than some man breaking it, Fae king or not."

I smiled, squeezing her hand back. "You don't have to worry about that. I'm closed for business forever in terms of serious relationships. Besides with you of course," I added with a wink.

Lil rolled her eyes and chuckled, "Old news. Besides, I have my eye on the demi-Fae girl who works at the coffee and tea shop close to your work. You know, the one with the blue streaks in her hair?"

I released her hand, patting it as I stood and stretched. "Ask her out," I encouraged.

Lil grinned. "Maybe I will. Are you going to work?"

"Yeah," I said with a yawn.

She shifted on the cushions and told me, "The bruises... They look bad. You should stop by my mom's house before you go."

"Miriam won't like it if I'm late," I answered, standing up from the couch to throw away the ice.

Lil stood too, following me to the kitchen as she said, "Go to my mom's. Miriam will like it even less if you show up to work with a black eye."

I grumbled something like, "Okay, asshole," before dumping out the bag of ice. Lil disappeared into her bedroom for a few minutes. I was waiting at the front door once she emerged.

"You're not coming with me, are you?" I asked. "You'll be late to work too."

"Tsh," Lil quipped. "Killian doesn't really care. I'll just tell him I had lady problems or something and he won't dare inquire further."

I chuckled. "Alright. We should go, though," I said, glancing at my phone.

Shit, I was going to be really late. Nevertheless, Lil was

right; Miriam would flip out if I showed up "unfit" for the job. She was even weird about me not wearing makeup to work.

Lil and I trudged to the bus station and I could feel stares landing on my face as we boarded. Thankfully, it was a quick ride to Lil's parent's house; well, her mom's really. Because of her parent's shaky relationship, her dad had been staying at a friend's apartment for the last couple of months.

Just before we got off, a young-looking human woman peered at me and asked, "Are you okay?"

I raised a brow at her and replied coolly, "Fine. And you?"

She sunk back into herself a bit, stumbling over her words as she said, "I-I'm fine—good. Sorry."

Lil shot me a look and as we headed for the exit, she said to the woman, "Don't mind my friend. She's prickly on a good day."

The woman smiled nervously and before I could add anything else, Lil shoved me off the bus.

"You could at least try to be nice," she scolded me.

I snorted, heading for the cozy townhouse on the corner.

"It was none of her business," I muttered.

Lil sighed. "You know, it's okay to let people care about you, Aster."

"Uh-huh."

She rolled her eyes and knocked on the bright orange door—her mother had insisted on the color a few years ago, despite Lil and I's protests. It swung open and immediately I was greeted with a hiss. Not at me, never at me, but at the marks on my face.

"That monster," Lil's mother said, a soft fire in her green eyes.

But she didn't say any more about it, just guided me inside to begin our usual ritual. I sat down on a cushioned wooden stool in the homey kitchen. She rubbed my skin with some sort of cooling ointment before beginning. The healing magic took seconds for wounds like these, especially with the skill Lil's mom possessed. I felt warmth pass over my cheeks, along with a slight burning sting, and then it was over.

"There," she murmured. "Good as new."

I patted her hand and said, "Thank you, as always. I have to run, I'm already late for work, but I'll see you soon."

She smiled tightly, crinkling the laugh lines on her face; the same face that Lil had. Her mousy brown hair was pulled into a braid and she wore worn jeans and a slightly stained floral blouse. Like Lil, she was kind and soft around the edges. Once, Lil had told me she hated her mother—and sometimes herself—for those traits. But what I hadn't even told her then was that I envied them for being so forgiving, so open.

So, I stuffed my anger over the situation with Raven as I hugged her and then followed Lil back outside to the bus stop. We waited a few minutes in tense silence before the bus came. I knew Lil was thinking. She was always quiet when her mind was working. Once we boarded the bus again, she sat down in an empty single seat near the back and I stood next to her.

"I hate that she's already acting like last night didn't happen," she said as the bus shot forward.

I gave her a tight smile, grabbing onto a rail to keep

from flying forward as I said gently, "I know. We'll figure it out, okay?"

She sighed and fell quiet again. We got to my stop first and I told her, "See you later."

She nodded, a little absentmindedly, muttering, "See you."

I glanced worriedly at her one last time, then deboarded. I hurried onto the street and past the sliding glass doors of the museum. As soon as I entered the lobby, I halted. Miriam was leaning against my desk, her arms crossed over her chest and her face stony.

I cleared my throat and began to apologize, "I'm so sorry, Miriam. I took a tumble last night and I needed to see a healer. I just didn't want to show up to work—"

"With a mark on your pretty little face?" she sneered. "Let me guess. You were out drinking last night and tripped, but you didn't realize how bad it was because you were so wasted. But you didn't want everyone knowing how stupid you are so you carried your vain little self to your friend's healer mother."

I opened my mouth, then closed it. Miriam was well aware of my habits and I'd definitely shown up late a few times because of them. And there was the unfortunate time she'd walked into the same bar as me, just as I climbed on top of one of the tables to "dance." I also couldn't tell her the truth about the bruises, and who they'd come from. Besides, even if I did say someone hit me, why would she care? She'd probably blame it on me all the same.

"Your performance has been exceptionally lackluster these past few months, not to mention the unsavory presence you attracted yesterday," Miriam snapped.

A feral anger stirred in me at her insult. I took a deep breath, trying to quiet the roar beginning to fill my ears.

Not now, not now, not now.

But I could feel the deadly power clawing its way to the surface, fighting to break free at last. Miriam's voice felt far away as she said, "You're fired, Aster. Good luck finding another job without a positive reference from me."

I barely heard her, hardly registering the words as they left her mouth. I shut my eyes tightly. *Stop, please,* I pleaded with the power overcoming me.

"Aster! Did you hear me? Pack up your things, now!"

Like a woosh hollowing out my stomach, it was all gone. I stumbled slightly at the absence of the magic and Miriam scoffed, "Are you drunk right now?"

I didn't answer her. Instead, I focused on my breath, sweeping past her, and swiping the few odd baubles and trinkets of mine from behind the receptionist desk. Once I was done, I began to make my way towards the door. Just a few more steps, one after the other. But suddenly, between one moment and the next, the beast was back again, so soon. I forced myself to walk, to take a breath, to walk.

"You're a disgrace to this court," Miriam said with a sniff.

I turned. This time, I couldn't help it or control it, even knowing what she might see as I faced her. Her eyes widened and it was her turn to stumble back.

"What...what are you?" she whispered in horror; her gaze glued to the otherworldly glow I knew was shining from behind my eyes.

I smiled, showing her every one of my teeth as I said in a voice I didn't quite recognize, "Don't cross me again, Miriam. This is your only warning."

"Please," she bleated, frozen where she stood.

"Count your blessings, siren. I could have you begging for your life," I snarled.

Then I turned, the last licks of my sane mind carrying me out of the lobby and onto the sidewalk outside.

CHAPTER

EIGHT

A DROP of cool rain hit my nose and I gasped softly as my head finally started to clear. The power within me quieted, satisfied enough for now.

It began to rain harder, until it was pounding against me like a drum as I stood on the sidewalk outside the museum. Still, I did not go inside or head home. Instead, I began to walk. For hours, I meandered, circling around the main square where the statue of King Odin, the king who had led our court through the first Long Night, stood. I stared up at him, my ancestor, with a detached sort of feeling in my heart.

I was not mighty like him. I was weak and messy. My uncle was right and always had been. I was unfit to rule. Even if my compliance to him meant a tyrant ruled over our court... I just couldn't do it. I couldn't walk the halls of that palace every day. Halls where my parents had once loved me. Halls where my innocence had been stripped away.

That palace held both dreams and nightmares, neither of which I was willing to face.

Eventually, I left King Odin to stare up at the stormy sky and walked away from the main square. Hardly anyone was out, most people either at work or shut in their homes, away from the pouring rain. I avoided walking past the museum again and ended up near the greenhouses where Lil worked. They gave off a soft glow and I could see figures inside, hurrying past plant beds and in and out of the connected lab building.

Once I'd had enough of staring and envisioning Lil doing her work, I wandered aimlessly and without direction. I was freezing and my clothes were soaking wet by the time I finally circled back around to our apartment. It was nearly dark out and I swore softly as I looked at my phone (which miraculously hadn't died from the water exposure). Lil would already be home and wondering where I was.

The minute I pushed open the front door, her voice immediately rang out, "Where the hell were you? And why are you soaking wet?"

"It's raining, or haven't you noticed," I muttered, then walked straight to my bathroom and began to strip. I turned on the shower to let the water heat up as I did so.

"Asteria Fairwae!" Lil shouted.

I clenched my jaw and turned slowly, wearing only my damp bra and underwear.

"That's not my name anymore," I growled.

From the bathroom doorway, Lil scoffed, exclaiming, "It is! It *is*. You can run from it as much as you want, but you are her and she is you! You can't keep this up forever, Aster. At some point you have to face what you are."

My nostrils flared and I replied in a low tone, "Oh, I see. I'm a 'what' now. A problem to be solved, am I?"

Lil looked up at the ceiling, as if asking the goddess herself for patience, and replied in a quivering voice, "You *know* that's not what I mean. You know that. Don't make me the bad guy here."

"I know you're not the bad guy," I shouted, my control slipping. "I know because it's me. I don't know why you don't just fucking say it!"

When Lil didn't respond I cackled humorlessly. That power within me was rising again, just as it had earlier today. I shut off the shower before even stepping in, breathing heavily. Then I went to my room. I dragged a long-sleeved black dress over my head, pulled on a rain jacket, and grabbed the moonstone from my nightstand, stuffing it in one of the pockets. I was still trembling from the cold, but I ignored the feeling.

"Where are you going?" Lil demanded.

"Out," I replied stiffly, stuffing my feet into a dry pair of boots.

She grabbed my arm and on instinct, I let go of the hold on the magic for just a second, allowing a fraction of my power to shine through. Just enough so that she'd let me go.

"Aster, stop," she pleaded as she released me.

I could already hear the tinge of fear in her voice. She, of all people, knew exactly what I was capable of. She was one of the only ones besides my uncle who knew the details, the true details, of my parent's accident.

I pushed past her and hurried into the hallway. I didn't even bother to turn and see if she was following me as I emerged onto the street.

I knew she wasn't.

After walking for about a mile, I ducked into the first club I saw. Tonight was not a night for remembering. I wanted to forget again, and this was the perfect place to do so.

CHAPTER
NINE

THE BOUNCER at the entrance to the club didn't even stop me, despite the mess I probably looked like. He just gave me a curious once over before pulling back the rope barrier and allowing me inside.

Though it was still early in the night, the club was already packed. Heavy music shook the walls and the flashing lights cast a seductive red hue across the dance floor. I longed to join the writhing throng of bodies, but first I needed to get a drink.

I hadn't even thought to grab my wallet before leaving, so I forced myself to flirt with a musty smelling shifter. He bought me two rounds of shots, eyeing me hungrily all the while. But I wasn't interested in that sort of escape tonight. So, once I'd knocked the vodka back, I gave him the slip and disappeared into the pulsing crowd. I became the beat of the music, wild and unchecked. No one paid me mind; they were all in their own worlds too.

Once the shots began to wear off a little, I stumbled back over to the bar. After a few minutes, I managed to get a couple more drinks from a soft-spoken demi-Fae man with chocolate brown eyes. Eyes that reminded me way too much of Jude. I chugged the drinks and left him at the bar as quickly as I could. About half an hour later, when I stumbled back to win someone else's attention, the bartender shook his head.

"I'm not serving you anymore, sweetheart."

"Why the fuck not?" I slurred.

He swiped a washcloth across a dirty glass and replied, "Because I don't want your blood on my hands. You came in here alone, soaking wet and with no money. You've already flirted your way through more alcohol than even I can handle in an hour and you're barely standing. I'd also venture to guess you don't have a ride. So, I'm going to give you some water and hope you sober up a bit before we close, so that you find yourself home tonight."

I narrowed my eyes and then snarled, "I don't need your help, asshole."

He grimaced, but replied, "Drink some water, kid. Talk off to me for a while if you want. I'll even give you some free food. Just hang around until you've sobered up, alright?"

His expression was sincere, and deep down I knew this was a good man. He was trying to take care of me, like a father would take care of a rebellious daughter. I'd had that once, or at least a taste of it. Tears pricked at my eyes, but they were quickly replaced by burning anger. That felt better.

That felt good.

"Find someone else to coddle," I snapped, flashing a vulgar gesture at him. A few people at the bar stopped their conversations to look at me. I snarled at them too, shouting,

"Show's over!" then turned, stumbling towards the back of the club.

I managed to make my way onto the street without incident. Except now that I was out of the club, the world had become even more disorienting and blurry. Goddess, why were the streetlamps so damn bright? My boots suddenly felt like lead on my feet, weighing them down and making it feel like I was sloshing through still water. I took a couple steps forward and nearly face planted on the sidewalk. As I righted myself, I quickly realized I was not alone.

Four men—Fae—were circling me. They wore dark clothing and three of them had hoods concealing most of their faces.

"Hey there, cutie," one of them sneered.

"What's up, little girl?" another said.

"You look lost."

"You look hungry."

"Oh, she's hungry, am I right, boys?"

That was the leader. I could tell because his hood was down and the others stood slightly behind him. He advanced towards me; his brutally scarred face twisted into a cruel smirk.

"Go away," I said, but my voice came out smaller and less clear than I'd meant it to.

The leader laughed and soon the others joined in too. The next thing I knew, scar-face was pushing me up against a wall. Since when was there a wall behind me? His hands began to trail up my leg, higher and higher, until his fingers were grazing my inner thighs.

"No, stop!" I cried out.

"He wouldn't mind if we had a little fun with you

before we got the job done, would he?" he breathed in my ear.

"Stop, stop," I pleaded.

But it was futile.

And again, I hated my helplessness. I hated it with my whole being. But I wouldn't dig up my power. I refused to reduce even these low lives to nothing but ash. Desperately, I tried to claw and kick, but suddenly their hands were all over me, squeezing my breasts, trailing up my dress, tugging at my hair.

Then I remembered the moonstone I'd somehow thought to put in my pocket before I left. If only I could get it to my lips... I shoved my hand in my jacket pocket.

Please, Nox. Please.

I pleaded silently with him, but nothing happened. Soon my hand was dragged out of my pocket and slammed against the wall. I closed my eyes because I did not want to watch what they were going to do to me.

I'd go somewhere far away. I imagined an orange grove, a pool of sparkling water, my father's booming laugh, and my mother's smile. I could pretend my body wasn't even mine at all. I could ignore the rough hands and the biting teeth. I forced myself to keep my eyes closed, to keep seeing the grove, the water, my parents...

A loud crack cut through the air.

I heard one of the faeries cry out in agony and a rage-filled, feral roar filled the alley. Scar-face was pulled away from me and I collapsed to the filthy ground. I wrapped my arms around my body, hardly conscious.

Through my blurred vision and the rain, I watched as a silver-haired shadow reached into a chest and ripped the heart out of one of my attackers. He held it in his hand, staring at the others; a challenge, should any of them dare to accept it. None of them did. They ran as the shadow tossed the heart to the side.

Shivers began to rack my body as the shadow approached me, becoming a solid body. The blood on his hands had somehow disappeared and he picked me up as if I weighed nothing. I didn't fight his arms as they tightened around me. I just shuddered as the rain began to fall down harder, as if the sky itself was opening up in sorrow. There was a woosh of shadow, a brush of cool air, and then we were no longer in the alleyway.

Warmth cocooned me just as my world went dark.

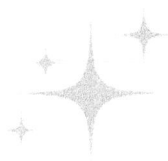

CHAPTER
TEN

WHEN I CAME TO, I was covered in a nest of soft, heavy blankets. I opened my eyes wearily to see an electric fireplace crackling in the corner of the room. Above me, I could see the frame of a large, four poster bed. I tried to lift my head but, goddess, it was pounding. I turned to see that there was a glass of water on the bedside table next to me…

Wait.

A bed. I was in someone else's bed. In someone else's *room*.

I shot up, very quickly realizing I was wearing an oversized t-shirt that was not mine. My dress was gone and I couldn't even tell if I was wearing underwear. Who in the hell decided they could change me? What had happened? I vaguely remembered the club and then there was rain and those faeries who had tried to—

Nope. Not going there, not now.

But there had been something else… a warm, hard

body holding me and the smell of citrus, then a brush of shadow and a cool breeze. And darker, more violent memories; a silver-haired god holding a still-beating heart as my attackers fled the alley.

It had been Nox. I was almost sure of it. He must've heard my call for help through the moonstone and had shown up just in time. But did that mean I was with him now? Was I in the Unseelie Court?

As if on cue, the door to the bedroom opened and Nox entered. I pulled the blankets up to my chest, suddenly feeling very awkward. He said nothing, just placed a few white tablets on the table next to the glass of water, then slumped down into an armchair by the fireplace.

"What are they?" I asked, gesturing to the pills. My voice was raw and hoarse, almost as if I'd been screaming.

Nox didn't look at me as he said, "Painkillers. I'm fairly certain you probably have a massive headache right now. Though, before you take them you should decide if you want to vomit now or later."

My eyes widened as a wave of nausea indeed swept through me. Nox seemed to somehow sense it and stood swiftly to then open a door, letting me bolt inside the apparent bathroom behind it. I found the toilet just in time, flinging open the lid and retching violently. After a moment, hands pulled my hair back. I tried to push him off, but another wave hit me and I no longer had the wits to care what he saw. When the waves of nausea finally began to ebb away, I flushed the toilet, then sank down onto the cool marble tiles.

Nox started to rub his hand down my back in broad, gentle motions. I half-heartedly tried to swat him away, but eventually surrendered to the calming strokes. After a time, when the last of the queasiness had subsided, I asked raspily, "Who dressed me?"

The circling stopped and I peered up at Nox. His expression was hard to read, but his voice was uncharacteristically quiet as he replied, "Not me."

"Who?" I asked.

He glanced back towards the bathroom doorway. I followed his eyes to where Lil stood, nervously clasping, and unclasping her hands.

"Lil?" I whispered.

She smiled sadly and said, "I'm so sorry, Aster. This is all my fault."

"What's all your fault? And how are you here… wherever we are?" I asked, shakily sitting up.

Nox watched me carefully, only looking away to give Lil a slight nod. She cleared her throat and replied, "We're in the Unseelie Court."

"Does he…" I trailed off.

"Your uncle," she finished for me with a nod. "Yeah, he knows you're here."

I suddenly felt a little sick again. Still, I urged her on, "That's not it, is it?"

She bit her lip, looking at Nox, as if wanting him to finish. That was weird. Since when did they know each other?

Nox sat back, not touching me anymore as he said, "The faeries who attacked you were a part of your uncle's inner circle. Spies of a sort, I believe. When I killed one of them and flitted you out of the alleyway, the others went straight to him. Now, he's claiming that I've kidnapped you."

"It's all over the news," Lil added and Nox shot her a look that might have been a warning.

I shook my head, trying to clear it, then glanced at Nox.

"How did Lil get here?" I demanded.

Nox grimaced and replied, "I sent Raven to get her once the news stories started circulating."

"There were already reporters knocking at our door," Lil said. "They all wanted to know about the suddenly not-missing princess. I imagine your uncle told them where I was."

"Well, technically if I've been kidnapped, I'm missing again, aren't I?" I said tiredly.

Lil's mouth kicked to the side in a smile I could tell she was trying to suppress.

"Is he… is Raven here?" I asked, glancing at Nox.

Nox nodded and I swore I saw a flicker of something like irritation in his expression, but he said nothing.

"I want to see him," I said to no one in particular.

Lil nodded, stepping into the bathroom and holding out her hand. "Let's get you dressed and then get some food in you," she said gently.

I took her hand, and we left Nox still sitting on the floor and staring at the bathroom wall.

Lil let me out of the bedroom with the fireplace then down the hall. We passed a large, open living area complete with a huge couch and several armchairs. Another electric fireplace was beneath an enormous flat-screen TV. Before I could get a better look at the kitchen beyond, Lil led me into a smaller, lighter-toned bedroom. She began pulling clothes out of a duffel bag that rested on top of a large set of drawers. My clothes, I realized.

"You packed," I commented.

She sighed, pausing her search for clothes, and said to me, "Of course I did. You can't walk around wearing the Night King's vintage t-shirts all day, can you?"

I glanced down at the oversized shirt I was currently wearing and Lil chuckled softly and said, "Then again, maybe you can. He seemed to like you in it, at least."

"What's up with him? Nox, I mean?" I asked her carefully.

She bit her lip. "You're still on a first name basis with him, huh?"

I glared at her and she glanced at the closed door, before telling me in a hushed tone, "He's super weird, Aster. I mean, yeah, he's hot as hell and definitely powerful, don't get me wrong. But he's been... off. Maybe he doesn't normally act like this, I wouldn't know. But when I arrived, Raven was already here. First of all, they confiscated my phone and yours too. They told me it was so your uncle's spies couldn't track us here, but... I don't know, I still feel weird about it."

"And the other thing was, every time Raven tried to come near you, Nox would stand in front of the bedroom door and stop him. I swear to the goddess, a couple of hours ago, he actually snarled when Raven tried to force his way in. I mean, I know Raven looks a little intimidating, but both he and you know him."

I digested her words as I slipped on a pair of ripped jeans and a clean forest green t-shirt.

"He's just acting like any faerie idiot," I finally said. "They're overprotective at the best of times."

Lil shrugged and said quietly, "I don't know, Aster. Is it

really every day that the *king* of the Unseelie Court rescues some girl from an alley, especially with you being the niece of his enemy? Not to mention, he literally ripped apart one of those assholes. The photos they showed on the news were pretty gnarly."

I sighed and asked, "What are you getting at, Lil?"

She flared her nostrils and simply said, "I just think anything is possible at this point."

I was just about to ask her to explain further when there was a knock at the door.

"Come in!" Lil called, cutting me off before I could speak.

The door swung open to reveal Raven, his face riddled with concern. I got to my feet as fast as I could in my hungover state and rushed into his waiting arms.

"I'm sorry," I whispered into his chest. "This is all my fault and now you can't go home."

"Nah, it's okay," he murmured back, the tenor of his voice rumbling through me. "I never really belonged there anyways."

I pulled back ever so slightly to look into his piercing green eyes. He smiled tightly, tucking a strand of hair behind my ear as he assured me, "It's going to be okay, Aster. We'll figure this mess out, just like we always have."

I forced myself to nod. As I did, I glimpsed Nox over Raven's shoulder. He was standing by a window, watching us closely. His jaw was clenched and a shadow crept up and around his ear. But he said nothing as our gazes met. He looked away first.

I focused back on Raven, suddenly very aware that my hands were still pressed up against his muscled chest. I slipped out of his embrace and he cleared his throat as he stepped back. I glanced back at Lil and asked, "What about your mom?"

Raven answered for her. "Our mother has been loyal to King Calum for years. That hasn't changed."

"What do you mean?" Lil asked, her voice quivering slightly.

Phantom wings flared behind Raven, and Nox took a step closer to where we were in the doorway, his gaze hard. I almost swore I saw the ghost of wings on his back too.

"Mother was the one who tipped off the reporters," Raven said to Lil, his voice hard.

"How do you know that?" Lil inquired sharply.

A muscle feathered in Raven's jaw and he replied, "Because I have eyes in King Calum's court. She was there, early this morning, begging for forgiveness and professing her loyalty despite our so-called 'traitorous' actions."

Lil closed her eyes and muttered, "I didn't think she'd actually go this far."

"Wait," I cut in. "What do you mean, you have 'eyes' in my uncle's court?"

Raven glanced back at Nox who nodded and said, "'Eyes,' meaning spies for me. Because of his unique situation, Raven has helped me infiltrate the Seelie Court for years now."

I opened my mouth to ask just how *exactly* well Nox and Raven knew each other, but Raven spoke before I could, saying, "There's something else," he glanced at me. "Talks of the inner council are in the works. I have... someone there, reporting to me. Apparently, your uncle and his council are planning to publicly declare you unfit to rule."

"Why?" Lil demanded.

I threw back my shoulders and rolled my neck before

answering. "Why not? He has a multitude of reasons to pick from. I've been cowering in hiding for years. I'm a party girl, drunk more than I'm sober. I've had a line of lovers longer than he could probably count, which is unacceptable for a woman of my status. And then there's the fact that one of my best friends is half-Unseelie and oh, yeah, I'm currently kicking it back with the Unseelie King in his…" I trailed off. "What is this? A condo?"

Nox's voice was rough as he clarified, "Penthouse, love."

I chuckled, the sound a little unhinged as I nodded. "Yup, I'm chilling in the Night King's fancy-ass penthouse. He's being kind by doing this, instead of just outright declaring me an enemy of the crown. I'm even more surprised he didn't do that a long time ago. He had plenty of reason to after—"

I cut myself off sharply, remembering I wasn't alone with Lil. She glanced at me and so did Raven. But where her expression was gentle, his was calculating.

"Aster, why would he have reason to declare you an enemy of the crown?" Raven asked slowly. "I mean, Unseelie Court involvement aside."

Nox was looking at me intently from across the room and I met his eyes. I'd never gotten the chance to ask him about the dreams and the bridge between us in them. Maybe it had just been that; a dream. But if not… he knew more about my magic than I wanted him to already.

Finally, I looked back at Raven and shook my head. "It doesn't matter right now."

Raven narrowed his eyes. "We have to be able to trust each other, especially now. If there's something you're not telling us then you need to say it right now. This whole situation is a mess and whether you like it or not, you're right in the middle of it."

I stared at Raven, at the only man I'd truly had any sort of lasting trust in and said nothing. I said nothing because he was absolutely right. I'd dragged them all into the mess that was my life and now they were suffering.

When a minute or so passed and I still hadn't said anything, Raven took a step closer to me and demanded, "When are you going to realize this isn't just about you, Aster?"

"Enough."

Nox's voice cut through the room, sharp as the blade of a sword. Raven turned, glaring at him.

"I don't mean to offend, my King, but what the hell do you know about Aster that I suddenly don't? I've known her for most of her life."

"And that gives you license to be an asshole to her?" Nox asked, his voice low and dangerous as he approached Raven slowly.

I wouldn't want to cross him right now, that was for sure.

But Raven didn't seem to share my sentiment. He ground his teeth and then shouted, "We're walking into what could become war! We need to know everything." He turned back to me. "And if there's something you're withholding, *princess*, you need to say it now."

"She's been through enough in the past twelve hours," Nox snarled.

I wanted to protest at their stupid dominance battle, to tell them not to talk about me like I wasn't in the room. But I was exhausted. And as much as I didn't want to admit it, Nox was right. The last twenty-four hours had been a nightmare and I really just wanted to sleep for a little longer before facing everything.

"Cool it, both of you," Lil said, surprising even me.

Nox looked at her, almost as if he'd forgotten she was there behind me. The gold in his eyes flared, as though fiery beams of light truly lived within his irises. Lil began to shove Raven out of the bedroom, before gently tugging me inside.

"We don't have time for this," Raven said under his breath as he stepped back.

"I think your King can decide what we do and don't have time for, Raven," Lil snapped. "Or would you like to contest him for the title?"

Raven was silent.

"I didn't think so," she said. "And if you'd get your big head out of your ass for two seconds you'd realize that Aster was fucking assaulted last night. And the night before that? Oh yeah, her uncle came to our apartment, threatened her, and then beat the shit out of her. So, you'll excuse me while I give her a few goddess-damned hours to regroup and rest before we face this together. Now get out of my sight."

She slammed the door in his face before he could say another word. But just before it shut, I saw something like devastation on Nox's beautiful face.

"Thanks," I muttered, sitting back on the bed.

Lil nodded. "I've always got your back, no matter what. But you already know that."

"I'm sorry," I began, "about last night. I didn't mean it, I was just scared and—"

"Shh," she cut me off gently. "I know. I know and it's alright, I promise. Let's just get you into bed, okay?"

I nodded, unable and unwilling to fight her on this. She folded back the covers and I climbed under and let her tuck me in. Just before I drifted off I murmured, "Love you, Lil."

"I love you too, Aster," she whispered, with a kiss to my brow.

CHAPTER
ELEVEN

I WAS BACK on the dream bridge, staring across at the whirling shadows. I stood there for a long moment, waiting. I knew he would come. Sure enough, Nox emerged out of the darkness, the shadows trailing him like a cape of his power. As he met my gaze, a memory slammed into me, a memory that was somehow both his and mine.

It was a day away from my eighteenth birthday. I had visited my uncle a few hours earlier and I sat on my bed, nursing a bloody nose. He'd tried something new this time. As punishment for being particularly disobedient, he'd given me eight lashes. My back ached, but I refused to let Lil or her mom see them, to see how weak I was—to see that I would let him whip me like an animal. My faerie blood would heal them soon enough. As my nose finally dried up, I curled up on my creaky twin bed. I wanted to think of my mother, of our afternoons spent in the garden, tending to flower beds, and picking oranges from the lower branches of our tree. But each time I tried to lean into the sweet, happy memories, her scream echoed through my mind.

My fault, my fault, my fault...

I drifted off, thinking it over and over again, until it was a mantra in my head.

That night, I dreamt of darkness. But not the terrible, monstrous kind. No, this darkness reminded me of a lullaby my mother sang to me as I drifted off to sleep under the stars. I swore I smelled our tree of orange blossoms as I awoke the next morning.

I blinked, stumbling back on the bridge. Then I whispered, "It was you, wasn't it? You sent me the dream that night?"

From his spot in the shadows, Nox didn't deny nor confirm my statement. He just walked closer to me, until he was nearly on my side of the bridge. I met his eyes and without thinking, reached out a hand. As soon as my hand came into view, I realized it was luminescent. The light to his dark aura.

But just as I touched him, he began to fade away.

"Wait!" I called.

"Come find me," he whispered before the shadows swallowed him up completely.

.✦.

I jolted awake with a short gasp. Lil stirred beside me, and the room around us was dark. I must have slept through the rest of the day and into the night.

As I carefully crawled out of the bed, I replayed the dream I'd just had over in my mind. Was it real? Were *all* the dreams real? Or maybe they were simply manifestations of my own longing for someone to understand me. Either way, I was thirsty, so going to the kitchen seemed like a pretty good idea.

I carefully pushed open the bedroom door, silent on its hinges as I padded out on bare feet, then closed it. The kitchen was huge and made up of granite countertops and steel appliances. Fancy enough that I knew very well that this apartment... I'm sorry, this *penthouse*... wasn't cheap. Only the best for a king, I supposed.

I searched the dark-wood cabinets for a glass. But as I looked, a half-full bottle of amber liquid caught my eye. Before I could think too much about it, I snatched it then sank down on the ground next to the dishwasher. I took a swig, though I nearly choked on the bourbon as a voice said, "That is very expensive."

I forced myself to swallow, my eyes watering as Nox walked towards me, lithe as a wildcat. He wore loose fitting dark pants and a t-shirt that was just tight enough to show off the contours of his chest. His silver hair was unbound for once, the waves framing his face in a way that made me want to punch him but also kiss him. Stupidly pretty king.

He stopped short in front of me, leaning back on the counter behind him. I raised the bottle in the air slightly, my throat still burning.

"Want some?" I ventured.

A small smile flickered for just a second on his face before he said, "You're asking me if I want some of my own liquor, as you're stealing it?"

"I am not stealing it," I scoffed.

He lowered to the ground, sitting across from me with his back leaning against the panels under the counter.

"So, I assume that you're planning on returning it then?"

I shrugged and took another sip. Nox raised a brow and I set the bottle down. We just stared at each other for a moment, me fiddling with a string on the sweatpants I'd somehow ended up in. It seemed he was waiting for me to speak first.

"I really shouldn't be here," I finally said.

His expression was unreadable as he replied, "I know."

"You should've stayed away from me."

"I know," he said again. Then he paused before adding, "It wasn't exactly easy."

I eyed the bottle of bourbon and Nox pointed his head towards it. "You can take some more if you want," he said.

I shrugged. "It's fine."

I wanted to ask what he meant when he said it wasn't easy to keep his distance from me. But I was too afraid the answer was going to be something along the lines of wanting to use me because of my position or my connection to his rival, my uncle.

So, instead, I took a quick breath and said quietly, "I've had the same dream the last few nights. It's a dream I think I've been having for a while but…" I trailed off.

He still didn't say anything, so I continued to ramble, "In the dream, I'm standing on this bridge. There's my side, my—my magic. And then there's another side. On the other side, there's a magic that's not familiar to me, or at least it's not mine. I think," I winced a little at his silence, "I mean, I think it's you."

He continued to stare at me for a moment, before nodding. But still, he didn't speak.

"Are you acknowledging or agreeing?" I said.

"Neither," he replied, his tone neutral.

I rolled my eyes and started to get up, but he gently caught my wrist.

"Asteria," he murmured.

I swear to the goddess, in that moment, my name—my true name—sounded like music on his tongue. I pushed the thought away, but conceded, sitting back down. His hand slid away from me as he sat back again. I missed the warmth of his touch and scolded myself for that.

Finally, I said, "So, you know then. What my magic is."

Something in his eyes sparked as he replied, "What you have is much more powerful than simple magic."

I looked away.

Your destiny lies far beyond the restraints of this place, little star, my mother had once told me.

I shuddered.

Nox furrowed his brow as he asked with a genuine tone, "Why do you fear it so much?"

I forced myself to look at him as I replied, "Because power like that knows no bounds. It doesn't care about who you love or what you stand for. It simply takes…and you take right along with it."

Nox was silent for a minute or two, seeming to contemplate something. Eventually, he asked, "Asteria, have you ever heard of the Evening Star?"

A memory, one from just a few days ago, sparked in my mind. The strange record I'd looked at during my shift at the museum had detailed an account of the Evening Star and the power they held. So, I nodded and stated, "During the Long Night, there was a wielder of starlight. A being… Fae, I think, who supposedly sent the demons back to their realm."

I realized the connection that Nox was making as soon as I said the words.

"No. No way," I said.

He just looked at me.

"Nox, first of all, that is not what I have. Second, even if I did, we definitely don't need or want that kind of power in our world right now."

"What if I told you that you were wrong?"

I furrowed my brow, suddenly itching for another sip of the bourbon next to me.

"What do you mean by that?" I asked.

"I mean," he began, "that we may need a power like that again. Do you remember when I told you I might need your help with something?"

"Yes," I said carefully. "I do."

Nox sighed, cracking his long fingers as he said, "The magic you possess may be the only thing that can stop what's coming."

"What do you mean?" I asked, alarm spiking in me.

Nox looked me dead in the eye as he said solemnly, "I believe someone has been attempting to summon demons. Here, in one of our courts."

I paused, shocked. Then I shook my head and whispered, "That's impossible. The gateways between our realms were sealed off centuries ago."

Nox grimaced. "I wish it was. But all the signs are once again showing up. Obsidian, used for summoning circles, has surfaced again in the black markets and there have been strange disappearances. Members of my court and inner circle have been among those missing, along with their children."

My throat tightened. "Why would they be taking children?"

He held my gaze and replied, "Because demons feed on pure souls and innocent hearts."

My stomach churned and it only became worse as Nox added, "I believe your uncle is gearing up to blame it on me. There are already rumors about the origin of my shadow abilities, so it's an easy cover for him. And it brings me down, and in turn, the entire Unseelie Court, as I have no heir."

"Why?"

"Why what?"

"Why don't you have an heir?"

I regretted the words as soon as they came out of my mouth. But Nox didn't look offended at my intrusive question. Instead, he actually looked a little sad as he said, "My reasons are adequate, as much as they pain me."

"I'm sorry, I didn't mean to…" I trailed off, unsure of what exactly to say.

Had he lost a lover long ago and refused to have another? That was kind of what I assumed.

"No need to apologize, love," he said. "It's nothing you did."

I cleared my throat. "Well, with the demons… it kind of sounded like you think it's my uncle that's summoning them," I said, a question in my tone.

Nox's face was grim as he nodded. "Unfortunately, yes. With what Raven has gathered about his behavior at court it seems very plausible. Not to mention the fact that my spies were able to track a few of the obsidian purchases back to his royal accounts."

"Can we stop him?" I asked, feeling suddenly very naive. I had been around my uncle for years, and though he was cruel, I hadn't noticed him to be any different than he ever was.

Nox slowly shook his head and replied, "I believe it's already begun. In fact, I think he summoned the demon long ago, maybe even before you were born. There had to be a reason your father never trusted him."

"You knew my father?" I asked.

His voice was gentle as he answered, "Yes. He was the first ruler in decades to even consider working together instead of against each other."

I furrowed my brow. "Were you king at that point too?"

Nox shook his head. "Not quite."

The question of *when* hung in the air between us.

When were you born? When did you lose your lover? When did you become king?

But Nox made no move to answer any of the unspoken questions. In fact, he rose to his feet, towering over me. My mouth went a little dry as he stared at me.

"You never really clarified about my dreams," I said. "I mean, does that happen sometimes? I know dream magic exists in your court but I think you're in my dreams a lot…" I trailed off.

I stood too, only coming up just above his shoulders, despite the fact that I was usually considered tall. He reached out, brushing my chin with his fingers as he replied in a murmur, "It doesn't happen often, at least not like that. In fact, these days it's quite rare."

"Why? What does it mean?"

His jaw tightened and the shadow of wings flared behind him, this time unmistakably so.

He didn't answer my question, so I asked another, breathing out, "Why aren't these ever out?"

I reached out to brush my finger down the side of one as they became more and more corporeal. He went utterly still as I dragged the pad of my finger down the smooth plane of the wing. But my Fae hearing detected his heartbeat as it sped up—he knew I could hear it too. I looked at him and I had an intense urge to drag my fingers through his hair. I felt a flush creep up my cheeks and my teeth caught on my bottom lip. His gaze flicked down to my mouth, lingering there for a moment.

"You should go back to bed, Asteria," he said.

Those mighty wings were still there, flared out behind him, the material membranous and thin enough that the light of the moon shining in through the windows illuminated them from behind. A piece of information regarding Fae wings caught in my mind, but floated away before I could pin it down.

He was right, I should go to bed. I should walk away. I had vowed not to care anymore about anyone except for Lil and Raven. Not to mention that, even with all my personal concerns aside, we would never—could never—work. Whether it was my uncle or Nox's duty to his crown or even my duty to mine… it was hopeless and forbidden. We were like two planets circling around each other, doomed to forever remain in this endless orbit. Always looking, always crossing paths, but never entwining.

But, oh goddess, did I want to entwine myself with the man in front of me.

Recklessly, I continued to trail my finger down his wing, smooth under my touch. He sucked in a sharp breath and I shifted my gaze from where it had been lingering on the dark wing, to his face. His jaw was tense and restrained, but his eyes gave it all away. They were edging on wild, black dominating amber and gold as his gaze trailed up my body. One of his hands gripped the edge of the countertop and the other was stiff at his side, long ago lowered from my face.

"Is this… sensitive?" I asked, as I continued to stroke his wing with my finger.

He breathed in slowly through his nose, as if he were

truly barely holding onto his restraint. I lifted my hand from the wing and he relaxed ever so slightly. That is until I reached up and did precisely what I'd been wanting to do again since that night in the club.

His silver hair was soft as I ran my hand through it. I moved closer to him and tangled my fingers deeper into the silky strands. His breathing became uneven, but still, he did not move to touch me. Just as he seemed to master the leash he was holding on himself again; I reached out with my free hand and delicately stroked his other wing. His pupils all but blew out and he groaned softly, clenching his jaw so tightly I was genuinely worried for his teeth.

"What?" I whispered innocently.

"Bed," he gritted out.

I raised a brow. "My, my, you're very forward, aren't you?"

He shut his eyes and muttered, "Your bed. And my bed. Separate beds."

"Mhmm," I murmured sweetly.

"Asteria, please," he said, swallowing another groan.

"Okay," I said with a smile as I stepped back from him.

He opened his eyes, locking onto my gaze. I almost abandoned my resolve then and there, but seconds later, I remembered myself.

"Goodnight, Your Majesty," I whispered with a little curtsy to match.

He opened his mouth to protest at the title, but I was already tiptoeing back to my room.

CHAPTER
TWELVE

THE NEXT MORNING, I awoke to Lil dusting the windowsill.

I groaned against the dim beams of sunlight filtering into the room and asked, "Lil, what the hell are you doing?"

She beamed at me and replied, "Nox gave these to me!"

I raised a brow. "Nox, huh?"

"He told me to call him by his first name," she clarified. "I mean, you do and so does Raven. It would be weird if I was the only one walking around and kissing his magnificent ass—I mean feet."

"Ha, ha," I deadpanned. "But why are you cleaning?"

She adjusted her hair with one hand and said in reply, "I need something to do. With the crap-show going on right now, I can't just sit around."

"Are we just sitting around?" I ventured.

She nodded. "Apparently. Nox told us to just chill here today for now. He's pretty sure your uncle isn't going to just march onto his territory, at least not yet."

"Has he left, then?"

"Nox?"

"Mhm."

She gave me a sly look and questioned, "Why, are you disappointed he's not here to give you a good morning kiss?"

I rolled my eyes and shot back, "No. I just want to figure all this out."

"So... you didn't happen to leave this room in the middle of the night?"

I pushed back the covers and rubbed my eyes as I muttered, "Maybe. It doesn't matter, nothing happened."

"Good," Lil said, though I had the distinct feeling she was a little disappointed.

I glanced at her and said, "Lil, my sweet angel, I cannot fuck that man."

"I hope you're not talking about me?"

I whirled to see Raven leaning against the doorframe. My mouth dropped open in embarrassment and Lil snorted. "You wish, Raven," she said.

He laughed, though it sounded a little hollow. He quickly recovered and asked both of us, "Do you want to watch something? Nox has a pretty sweet media set-up."

"*Siren's Seduction!*" Lil squealed.

Raven raised a brow. "I thought you didn't like that show."

She pouted. "I can change my mind."

I stared at their exchange, an incredulous look on my face. Raven must have noticed it because he said, "I know you want to do something about this all right now, Aster. But the truth of it is, right now we just kind of have to wait and see what card your uncle plays next. We're safe here, for now and we might as well find a way to pass the time. Also," he cleared his throat. "I'm sorry about yesterday."

I pressed my lips in a thin line and replied, "It's fine. Did Nox tell you about the demons?"

Raven's gaze flicked over to Lil as she exclaimed, "The what?"

"Well, that answers my question," I muttered.

Raven turned to Lil and explained, "Nox thinks King Calum has been dealing in some really dark stuff. And that maybe, he's even summoned a demon."

"But… how?" Lil asked, her voice suddenly quiet.

"I think that's what we're trying to figure out, right?" I said, looking at Raven.

He shifted on his feet and said, "That, and then of course figure out how to stop him from doing it again."

The guest bedroom grew quiet until I said, "Let's watch the show."

No one protested. We dragged the comforter from the bed to the living room, because apparently Nox didn't believe in throw blankets, and camped out on the couch. Lil immediately stole the remote and we proceeded to watch four episodes in a row of *Siren's Seduction*. I watched the ditzy girls and hunky guys, with their vendettas and their lust, and I envied them. They had so little to worry about. Yeah, making a fool of yourself on public television was pretty embarrassing but it wasn't going to kill you or anyone else.

Lil made comments and laughed as Raven's face was stoically set. Though I definitely saw him hold back a smile a few times. I snuggled between both of them, enjoying the warmth and the lazy ease of the day. Even if the peace was more of a mirage than reality, I'd take it. We might not get another day like this again for a long time.

By the time the front door of the penthouse clicked open, we'd gotten through the entirety of season five. I was stiff and also hungry, which made me all the more excited to see Nox, because he was carrying takeout bags of what smelled like curry and stir-fry.

"Bless you, Kingly King," Lil breathed, inhaling the smell of the food.

Nox raised one brow and muttered, "Kingly King?" as he set the bags of food down on the glass dining room table. A simple chandelier hung about the table and it illuminated with a flick of his fingers.

"Fancy," I remarked.

"Only the best for my guests," Nox said with a heavy look in my direction.

Okay, he was definitely still thinking about last night. Nothing had really happened and yet... things were different between us now.

Raven walked over to the table and began to unpackage the food, Lil bouncing excitedly on her toes behind him. Nox ventured into the kitchen, presumably to get bowls and silverware. I walked over and then leaned against the counter.

"Need any help?" I asked him.

"I'm good, love," he replied evenly.

He bent over to retrieve something and I'll admit, I might have stared at his ass for a second or two. As he stood back up, Lil caught my eye, a mischievous gleam in her expression. Which probably meant she had seen me ogling at Nox.

"Thanks for the food, King—I mean Nox," Lil chirped.

"It's not a problem, Lilliana," Nox replied as he set down the bowls on the table.

She blushed a little, smiling. It seemed I was not the only one charmed by the Unseelie King. Excluding Raven, whose eyes were narrowed slightly as he looked at Nox. I padded over to the table, realizing at that moment that I was still wearing a pair of old leggings and my sleep shirt, which just happened to be the shirt I'd woken up in the first morning here... meaning, it was Nox's. Then, I remembered Lil's comment about him seeming to like me in his shirt and my neck began to grow hot.

I tried to ignore the mixed feelings coursing through me, instead opening one of the containers. Inside was yellow curry, my favorite. I glanced sidelong at Nox and he cocked his head and said, "What?"

"Did Lil tell you I like this?" I asked, gesturing at the container.

"Nope," Lil spoke for him.

"It's a popular dish," Raven grumbled, digging into his own basil stir-fry.

"Exactly," Nox agreed, though there was a gleam in his eye that told me there was more going on here.

I let it go—for now. I'd ask him later how he knew my favorite kind of food and my favorite dish.

We all began to eat and mostly did so in silence until Nox told us, "It's been pretty quiet on Calum's end."

I nearly choked on a sweet potato and Lil clapped me on the back. Nox paused, then went on, "I'm nearly positive he's planning something." His expression became roguish as added, "We'll just have to see what he comes up with."

Raven nodded seriously. I wasn't sure what I was more concerned about: Raven's grave expression or the gleam in Nox's eye. He almost seemed to be thrilled by the idea of a challenger. Then again, we were faeries after all.

I stared down at my almost finished bowl of food, suddenly not hungry anymore. Nox stood and said, "I'll be in my office if any of you need me. Otherwise, just try and get some more rest. We'll talk more about all of this tomorrow."

Hardly sparing a glance in my direction, he strode over to the door on the other end of the penthouse, presumably his fancy-ass office. He opened it with the flick of his fingers and disappeared inside.

"Well," Lil said. "More sirens?"

"Goddess, no," Raven groaned, though his mood seemed instantly lighter now that Nox was gone.

"How about a movie?" I suggested, my eyes still on Nox's office door. As if I looked at it hard enough, he would reappear.

"Sounds great," Raven said, following the direction of my gaze and adding, "I doubt he'd join us, even if we asked."

Lil smirked. "Maybe if Aster asked, he would."

"Let's watch the movie," Raven muttered, beginning to clear off the table. I moved to help him, but he said, "You two go get it set up. I've got this."

Lil glanced at me but said, "Okay!"

She took my hand and led me back to our crumpled cocoon of blankets. I let her rearrange them a bit, then we snuggled into them together. By the time Raven came over, we'd picked out a movie that was a mix between horror and romance.

Seemed like a pretty good summary of my life.

But I didn't say that. Because Lil would've given me a

sad, puppy-dog pity look and Raven would've stared at me with his longing green eyes. I didn't need to complicate anything right now. Instead, I just sat back and watched the movie, holding Lil's hand through the jump scares.

By the time it was done, both her and Raven looked like they were about to fall asleep on the couch.

"Why don't you two go to bed?" I said.

Lil glanced sleepily at me and asked, "What about you?"

I shrugged and replied, "I think I'm gonna watch some TV. I'm not super tired yet."

"Okay," Lil said through a yawn.

Raven gave me a look and said, "You sure you'll be okay out here?"

I smiled softly. "I'm fine, Raven. Seriously, go to bed."

He patted me on the shoulder.

"Alright. Goodnight, Aster."

"Goodnight."

Once they were both gone I turned on some stupid shifter body-building show. Basically, a chance for air-headed alphas to show the world their big, bad muscles. But, I'll admit, it was kind of funny to hear them grunt as they lifted weights or see them get into fights if their "spot" at the gym was taken.

Just as I was beginning to get into it, I heard a voice say, "Shifters, huh?"

The Unseelie king was standing in the shadows near the kitchen, wearing the darkness like a cloak. Or a cape, though I was pretty sure he was no hero. I didn't know anything about his past, but his display in the alley the other day had been enough to tell me that he'd definitely killed before.

"It's funny," I said.

"Is it?"

"Mhm. Like, right now, the alpha is going off his rocker because that little shrimp is on his usual bench."

"You like the show because of the fighting?"

I reigned in a sharp inhale. Nox was suddenly directly behind me and I could feel his presence like an extra limb, the feeling raising the hairs on the back of my neck.

"Or maybe," he breathed in my ear, "you like to see them sweat. And get angry and flex their muscles. Maybe it reminds you of something... something else."

I swallowed.

Sex. He was talking about sex. And of course, my mind took that exact moment to wander to his body. And to how he would look in certain positions... how he would feel.

I let out a breath I hadn't realized I'd been holding and Nox swept around the side of the couch, his wings fully corporeal. I hadn't even noticed them come out; granted, he'd been behind me.

He curled them in as he sat down on the couch next to me, his expression intent. His hair was unbound again, the silvery strands falling past his chin, fanning out onto the tops of his shoulders. I felt breathless as I looked at him.

"I should probably go to bed," I whispered.

His gaze flicked to my mouth and then back up to my eyes.

"I should too," he finally said.

But neither of us moved. Nox swallowed, his Adam's apple bobbing up and down. I watched it, my stare predatory. He reached out a hand, brushing it down my cheek. I didn't mean to, but I leaned into his touch. Both of our breaths were coming quicker and heavier now. His fingers ghosted my lips and he muttered, "Fucking hell, Asteria."

I met his eyes, the gold specks within them reflecting in the light from the TV screen.

"Why don't you kiss me?"

His jaw tightened and so did his hand on my face. His answer was not what I expected.

"Because I'm trying to maintain a semblance of my morality."

I furrowed my brow. "I'm not some lost maiden. I can decide what I want for myself."

He pulled his hand away and said tightly, "And that should not be me."

"And if it is?"

He closed his eyes briefly and I took the opportunity to move a little closer, just near enough to drag the pad of my thumb down his inner wing. His eyes flew open and he pinned me with his stare.

"Don't do that again," he said roughly, his control clearly slipping.

I liked challenges. I liked winning them. So, I let my lips kick into a slight smile and this time, I brushed all of my knuckles down the sinewy material of his wing.

He was on top of me in an instant, my hands pinned on either side of me. I was crowded with his body, his scent, his stare.

"What did I say, love?"

His voice was different now. Silkier, but in an unhinged sort of way. I'd just let the beast out. And I wanted more.

"Not to touch your wings," I breathed.

His head dipped and his teeth grazed my neck.

"Then do as I say," he hissed against my skin.

I waited for a beat, then whispered, "No."

I tried to free one of my hands but he had me pinned. Lifting his head he muttered, "Up to no good."

And then he kissed me.

Except that "kiss" was a mild way to put it. It was more of a collision, a clash of two forces finally connecting. It felt like much more than a few days of built-up tension. This was *years* of longing and wanting.

But my mind wasn't letting me worry about the logistics of it. Not when he tasted of sin. Not when his hands were running down my body. Not when this felt so damn right.

I pressed my hands against his hard chest, feeling the pounding of his heart beneath my palm.

"You... have no idea," he said between kisses.

I gripped the fabric of his t-shirt and nipped at his lower lip. He pulled back slightly and let out a ragged breath just as I said, "Then tell me."

His entire body stiffened. Both of us were breathing heavily and his hands were resting low on my hips. He pulled them back and then moved away from me completely, sitting on the couch a few feet away.

I wasn't insecure enough about my kissing skills to think he'd stopped and moved away because of something I'd done. But something had startled him and I wanted to know what.

"You were right last night, when you said I should've stayed away from you," he said finally. "This was selfish of me... so incredibly selfish."

"I don't understand. Do you hate me because of my uncle?"

He glanced at me. "No, Asteria. I don't hate you."

"There's something else going on here."

"What do you mean?"

I took a deep breath and whispered, "How long have you been seeing me in my dreams?"

Silence filled the space between us, for what felt like minutes. Finally, Nox said, "Long enough to know that I needed to do everything in my power to keep my distance."

I narrowed my eyes. "What do you mean?"

"I shouldn't…" he trailed off, shaking his head. "You need to forget this happened. And once this is over, you need to forget about me."

"And if I can't?"

His expression became pained. "It's better this way, love."

"Why?" I pushed.

But he didn't answer me. Instead, he cleared his throat and stood as he said, "You should get some sleep. Good-night, Asteria."

And with that, he swept back towards his office. No sleep for him, I guess.

CHAPTER

THIRTEEN

No one visited me in my dreams that night. In fact, I didn't even remember having any.

In the morning, as Lil and I were getting dressed, I asked innocently, "Lil, has a faerie ever shown you his wings?"

She raised a brow and shook her head, scoffing, "Goddess, no, and I hope none ever do."

She must have seen the confusion on my face because she clarified, "Not all Fae have wings, which I know you know. I think the trait is like, really rare these days actually and usually only occurs in the Unseelie Court. But anyways, faeries who have wings tend to show them for a few very specific reasons. I'm surprised you're not aware of them."

I was... sort of. The problem was, I couldn't exactly remember. Wings weren't commonly talked about in the Seelie Court because they were such an Unseelie specific trait. But, in one of the lectures in our intro classes at university, I knew they'd gone over something about them.

It's just that I'd gone out drinking the night before and I think I had been dead asleep through most of the lecture. And no one had talked about it afterward as far as I remembered. They'd had no reason to. None of us had wings.

"Care to explain?" I pressed Lil when she didn't go on.

"Care to tell me why you're asking?"

"Once you explain," I insisted and she rolled her eyes.

"Alright. So, I mean obviously they get used in battle, you know, like life-or-death situations or whatever. But beyond that, there's only two instances that I know of."

She paused, and it was my turn to roll my eyes.

"No need to be dramatic," I said.

She shook her head. "Oh, but it is dramatic."

I was starting to get worried here.

"Faeries show their wings to their enemies, right before they kill them. I think it's some stupid intimidation thing. But the only other time I think it happens is when they've scented their mate."

My world spun.

That was the piece of information that had evaded me? Holy *fucking* shit. This was not happening.

Lil grabbed me as I swayed and demanded, "Aster, are you okay?"

I managed to squeak out, "No," before I sank down onto the bed.

Lil sat down next to me, her eyes wide and horrified as she whispered, "Crap, did Raven show you his wings? I know they kind of half-appear sometimes, but I always thought that was just because he was being a dick or didn't have control over them."

I said nothing, just staring ahead at the wall in disbelief.

Lil grabbed my arm and said, "Aster, baby girl, you're starting to freak me out."

Slowly, I raised my gaze to hers and whispered, "You have to vow not to tell a soul."

She narrowed her eyes scrutinizingly, but said, "I'm good at keeping secrets. You know that."

I nodded, then told her, "Raven didn't show me his wings. Nox did."

Lil looked dumbstruck for a moment, her eyes widening. Finally, she said, quite loudly, "Well, fuck!"

"Lil, shut up," I hissed.

Indeed, a soft knock sounded and from the other side of the door Raven called out, "All good in there?"

"Yup, Lil just stained her favorite underwear with period blood!" I blurted out.

Lil shot me a look, but it was dampened by the shock still lining her features. Raven made a sort of disgruntled sound on the other side of the door and I heard him mutter, "I did not need to know that."

I waited until his steps led him towards the kitchen, where I heard the low rumble of another voice—Nox.

I grabbed Lil's hand and said in a hushed tone, "You're sure there's no other explanation?"

She shook her head. "I mean, unless it seemed like he was going to kill you. Did things seem… tense?"

"Yeah, but not in that way," I heard myself say and Lil clapped a hand over her mouth.

She recovered a bit and whispered, "This is really rare and also super complicated."

"I'm aware."

"You can't just pretend you don't know," she said. When I didn't answer, Lil shook her head. "Uh-uh, Aster.

Absolutely not. I let you ignore lots of shit. But this is a step too far."

She was right. I knew she was. And yet... I couldn't face this. Not now, not ever. Mates were incredibly rare, even more so than they'd once been. Why on earth did the goddess think it would be a good idea to give *me* one? Not to mention the fact that Nox was technically supposed to be my rival, even my enemy, if I ever did rule the Seelie Court.

"I'm hungry," I told her, putting an air of false cheer in my voice.

I made a beeline for the door, flinging it open before Lil could stop me or ask me anymore. Both Raven and Nox's eyes flicked to me as I pranced into the kitchen and snatched a mini muffin that was conveniently perched on a platter in front of me. I stuffed the entire thing in my mouth before either of them could say anything.

Raven, with a furrowed brow, glanced at Lil in question as she entered the kitchen too. She shrugged, also stuffing her face with a muffin. Raven coughed, then said, "Well then... uh, we have news to share."

"Really?" Lil said around her mouthful of muffin and I shot her a warning look.

Nox glanced at Lil for a moment before he said, "I received official word this morning from King Calum that I'm being called to face the Trial of the Goddess, because of my so-called 'crimes.'"

I schooled my face into neutrality even as alarm spiked in me. The Trial was an ancient practice, and I'd only watched one happen once, when I was very small. Essentially, the person tried was hung by a noose from the enormous, gnarled tree that grew in the southernmost hills of the Seelie Court. Legend said the goddess herself was supposed to have been executed there when she had only been the Maiden. But her neck didn't snap as they pulled away the wooden stool beneath her. In fact, she struggled for a long time until they finally pulled her down and declared the ancient Beings of Light wanted her alive.

The Trial went like this: if your neck snapped immediately, then it meant the goddess deemed you unworthy. If not, you'd be spared, the rope would be cut, and you'd be declared innocent of your crime. It was an archaic practice and I remember being sternly told by my father that it was only used in the most extreme of circumstances.

"You're not actually going to accept, are you?" I asked carefully.

Nox avoided my eyes as he said, "I am going to. He did give an alternative, but it's not a viable option."

"What's the alternative?"

"If I return you to him in the Seelie Court 'untouched' he'll forgo the Trial."

A laugh bubbled up in my throat and I said, "Um, are you serious? You're going to let him kill you instead of just returning me to my court?"

"I'm quite aware of what will happen if that bastard gets his hands on you again—"

"I can handle myself!"

"—and I won't subject you to it unnecessarily."

"Unnecessarily? This is your *life* we're talking about?"

"Really, love? I had no idea."

"Nox. No."

He took a step closer to me and out of the corner of my eye I saw Raven stiffen. Nox leaned in, almost close enough that our faces were touching and he said, "This isn't negotiable."

"Yeah, it isn't," I shot back.

"Aster, maybe you should listen," Lil said. "I mean, do you really want to go back there knowing what he'll do to you?"

"No, but—"

"She's right, Aster," Raven cut me off. "They both are. You're not going back to your uncle. He's already taken enough from you."

I flinched.

Nox stepped away from me and continued on, "There will be a gathering the night before the Trial. Raven and Lil, you'll be coming, glamoured as my servants during the trip. Asteria," he paused. "You'll be our spy. The moonstone I gave you will allow me to transfer some of my wraith magic to you, as long as you carry it. That way, you can move freely throughout the palace without anyone seeing you. You know it best, after all."

I was shaking my head, hardly believing the words I was hearing him say. Finally, I managed to say, "Can't someone else take the blame and do the Trial, if this is really the only way?"

No matter how complicated our relationship was, I couldn't let him. The snap of her neck—the Fae girl's trial I'd watched as a child—echoed in my ears now. That couldn't happen to Nox. I wouldn't allow it. But no one answered me.

"Why Lil and I?" Raven asked. "Don't you have members of your circle who'd be more equipped for a mission like this?

Nox, still avoiding my question, replied to Raven, "You've been trained in my court but have also been present in the Seelie Court, Raven. I need someone who knows both. Asteria knows the palace in a way none of us do and Lil, you're there to hold everyone together."

"Moral support," she quipped.

Nox nodded, giving her a small smile that didn't reach his eyes. I didn't fail to notice that he was now speaking about me like I wasn't in the room.

"When do we leave?" Raven asked quietly.

"The Trial is to be held in two days, at dawn. We'll leave tomorrow," Nox answered. "I have business at court to handle before we go. I'll be back this evening."

He turned then, heading purposefully for the front door. I made a move to follow him, but a gentle, broad hand on my shoulder stopped me. Raven smiled tightly and said, "Aster, can I talk to you? In private?"

I swallowed, my attention still on Nox as he swept out of the penthouse. "Yeah, of course."

Raven cleared his throat. "Good. Let's go."

Lil glanced at me and mouthed "good luck." I thinned my lips and followed Raven into the bedroom Lil and I had been sleeping in. I sat down on the bed as he softly closed the door.

He turned to face me and before I could even open my mouth to speak, he said, "Once this is over, you need to stay as far away from Nox as you can."

I fought to keep my expression neutral as I asked, "Why?"

Raven began to pace back and forth across the room as he spoke, "I've seen the way he looks at you, Aster. And I know you look at him too. But that sort of thing cannot, under any circumstance, happen between you two."

I scowled and snapped, "Who are you to suddenly

order me around? I've dated plenty of people and you've never been like this. Does it bother you that he's a king?"

Raven's face was very serious as he shook his head, though he paused before he said, "You know I care for you, Aster. I always have and I think a part of me always will, no matter what you choose to do with your love life. But that's not why I'm telling you any of this."

"I don't understand," I said, unease beginning to creep in.

Raven looked me straight in the eye and said, "Nox cannot care for anyone like that. Not truly. Even he knows it would be selfish to an extreme to do so. Because it would only end in his lover's death."

"What the hell are you talking about?" I demanded.

He sighed. "It's something that's been kept hidden from most Seelie Court citizens, I presume either by your uncle or the kings who came before him. I suppose they think if everyone knew just who Nox was and what he did, it would make the Seelie rulers look too weak in comparison. But most of us in the Unseelie Court know that there's a reason why we don't have a queen, why Nox will never sire heirs. During the last Long Night, he sealed this world's fate along with his own."

Raven must have seen the shock on my face because he laughed humorlessly.

"I know, he's really old. He's probably almost 600 at this point. But he was apparently quite young, barely fully grown when the Long Night ended."

"I thought the Evening Star ended the second Long Night?" I ventured.

Raven nodded and my eyes widened as he said, "Nox *was*

the Evening Star. The story goes that he burned himself out completely, until there was nothing left of his power. But one demon, the Prince of the Abyss, Abaddon, held open the portal. Nox had to make a split-second decision before everything was lost. He was foolish and young and he told the demon he would give it whatever it wanted. Abaddon told him he would leave this world until the Evening Star shone once more. He merely requested the life of whoever held Nox's heart."

For the second time today, the floor felt like it was falling out from under my feet.

If Nox was right and I was the Evening Star *and* his mate, our world might be out of time. Double whammy and the timing couldn't be worse.

Raven waited for me to say something and when I didn't, he urged, "Aster, do you understand what I'm saying?"

I swallowed, looking down at my hands as I said quietly, "If what you say about Nox is true, then... I don't think there's anything I can do to stop the inevitable."

Raven shook his head, striding towards me. He kneeled in front of me, grasping my hands as he insisted, "Aster, you can move on. It'll be okay. I can even help you if you want. I know it might be hard for you but—"

"I think he's my mate," I blurted out.

Raven stilled. His hands went slack in mine and he sank to the carpet, silent. At least a minute passed of him saying nothing. He just stared blankly at the floor.

"Raven," I pleaded. "Say something."

He finally looked at me, his expression pained as he asked, "How long have you known?"

I shook my head, replying, "Not long at all. I only put

two and two together because he showed me his wings the other night when we were talking and I—"

Raven shot up to his feet and shouted, "He did *what?*"

"Raven, calm down," I said in a soothing tone. "It's okay, just take a breath—"

"BASTARD!" he bellowed. He turned, flinging open the door so hard the wood cracked as it hit the wall. I heard Lil shout in alarm as Raven headed for the front door. I rushed after him and managed to block the exit before he could leave.

"Aster," he growled. "Let me go."

"No," I took a breath. "No, you're not going to march into the palace or wherever he is and make a scene that could get you in trouble. We're going to sit here and wait patiently and then, like adults, we're going to have a civil conversation about this."

"Civil?!"

"Yes," I hissed.

Raven was a trembling bundle of anger as he bellowed, "This is your *life*, Aster! This isn't some game or conquest!"

"Oh, really? I had no idea!"

I didn't fail to notice that our argument mirrored the one I'd had with Nox earlier this morning.

Raven made a move to push me aside and Lil shouted, "Raven! What the hell is going on?"

He whirled.

"Ask your friend!"

Lil stared at me wide-eyed in question. I took a deep breath and said, "Raven just told me something about Nox. You know about the Long Nights right?"

Lil furrowed her brow but said, "Yeah, of course."

"Apparently Nox was the one to stop the demon horde

during the second Long Night. But to do so, he made a deal with a demon prince."

Lil looked from Raven to me as I paused. I wasn't sure how to say this next part. Raven took the liberty of explaining it for me.

"Nox cursed himself. The demon agreed to close the portal if he could have the life of Nox's soulmate. And Aster just told me—"

"I know," Lil said, her voice already beginning to tremble. "She told me."

"You knew?" Raven demanded, cornering Lil near the couch.

I stormed over. "Raven, lay off."

He turned, his face still a mask of rage. But it softened as Lil began to cry softly, gasping, "Oh, goddess."

I pushed past Raven and guided her over to the couch. Raven stared at us as I stroked her hair and held her hand. Somewhere in my mind, I knew I should probably be upset too. But I couldn't bring myself to feel anything but numb.

Eventually, Raven sat down at the kitchen table, his leg bouncing up and down. I stayed on the couch with Lil as her crying ebbed away and she dozed off. Around three o'clock, Raven said hoarsely, "You know, I used to think we might be mates."

I glanced up at him.

"I'm sorry, Raven."

He shook his head. "It's not your fault."

I looked away.

Somehow, it felt like it was. Like everything was.

CHAPTER

FOURTEEN

LATER THAT EVENING, just as Lil stirred in my lap, the lock on the front door clicked. Raven had joined us on the couch at some point but now he shot up to his feet.

"Raven," I warned, but he was already heading towards the door.

As soon as it swung open, Raven flung his fist out. Nox barely flinched, in fact, he just snapped back into his shadow form before Raven's blow could touch him. Raven swung again, and again, Nox shifted, avoiding the punch. Lil pushed herself up as the door slammed shut and Raven managed to tackle Nox to the ground.

"Raven!" Lil shrieked. "What the hell is wrong with you?"

He ignored her, continuing his efforts to beat Nox bloody. But each time he got close, Nox would become a shadowy mist and then re-materialize a few feet away. Raven growled in frustration and that was when I realized Nox was toying with him. Raven wouldn't have been able to tackle Nox, not unless he let him.

"Raven. Enough!" I shouted.

Raven glared at me as Nox rematerialized a few feet away from Lil and I, face stony. He stalked towards Nox, this time letting his words land the blows.

"You *knew*. You knew what the curse meant. I don't give a flying fuck about your pathetic feelings."

"Is that any way to talk to your king, bastard?" Nox taunted.

Raven lowered his chin, his expression darkening.

"You're just as much of a bastard as I am, king or not."

That was news. But I didn't dare intervene to ask exactly what Raven meant. It seemed that the Unseelie Court and its king held many secrets.

As they circled each other, Lil gripped my hand and squeezed it so tightly I lost circulation in one of my fingers for a moment.

Raven growled, low and feral, then said, "You should have kept it to yourself. It was all you had to do and she would have never known." Angry tears began to streak down Raven's face as he bellowed, "She could have been happy! All you had to do was keep it to your damned self!"

Raven breathed heavily, his eyes on Nox. And Nox…

Suddenly, the King of the Unseelie Court lost any sense of superiority or swagger. The Evening Star himself lowered his head and said, "You're right. Every word you just spoke."

Raven glared at him. I opened my mouth to speak, but before I could say his name, Nox turned and pivoted into his study, the door drifting closed of its own accord behind him. Lil began to cry again and I held her close to me.

Raven looked at me one last time before muttering, "I'm going out to get a drink. I'll be back tomorrow."

I didn't even incline my head his way as he swept out of the penthouse, slamming the front door behind him.

.✦.

I sat with Lil as she soaked in the bath adjacent to the bedroom we'd slept in. We'd long ago stopped caring about each other's nakedness. I was quiet and so was she, aside from the occasional sniffle or hiccup on her part. When she was done with the bath, I wrapped her in a fluffy white towel like a child and led her back to the bedroom. She pulled on one of my oversized sleep shirts from home and climbed under the sheets. When she looked at me expectantly, I whispered, "I have to talk to him."

She knew very well I didn't mean Raven. She chewed on her lip, but whispered back, "I know. I suppose I should be glad you're not trying to avoid it now."

I snorted softly and she smiled.

"It'll be fine. We'll all be fine," she said.

"Of course."

We both knew that was a lie. But I let her believe it, if only for tonight. She needed to sleep. Maybe I did too, but that wasn't happening, at least not yet.

"I love you, Lil. Till each star blinks out in the sky," I murmured into her hair, hugging her tightly.

Her lips quivered as I pulled back, and a silent tear fell down the side of her face as she replied, "And I love you, Aster. Till the night comes to claim us all."

She would always have my heart. Not in a romantic

sense, but in every other way that mattered. Maybe those ways mattered more anyways.

But she let me leave, and my chest squeezed painfully at her understanding. With one last look her way, I turned and padded out of the room on bare feet. She would let me go, let me follow the path I was meant to follow, even if in the end, it broke her heart.

The penthouse was dark and quiet, reminding me eerily of an empty tomb. But a tiny sliver of dim light filtered under the bottom of the study door where it met the hard-wood. I tried to steady myself as I stopped in front of that door, taking a few calming breaths. But just as I'd managed to slow my heartbeat, the door swung open.

I stared at Nox and he stared back at me for a long moment, before he asked, "Are you going to come in or not?"

I sucked in a breath, gritting my teeth as I said, "You could at least try to be civil about this."

His eyes darkened and he said, "Apologies. I know how much you detest the primal, beastly ways of our kind."

Tears threatened my eyes at his sudden shortness, but I walked into the study, nonetheless. The door shut behind me quietly as I examined the room. It was spacious and filled with a few tall bookshelves. Maps lined the rest of the wall and a mahogany desk sat near the huge window in the center. The sky was dark and starry tonight, the moon just a crescent hanging above us.

Nox stared at me as I walked once around, running my fingers over the spines of a few worn, leather-bound jour-nals and books. When I was done, I perched on the edge of the desk. A muscle in his jaw ticked as he watched me do so. But if my choice of seating bothered him, he didn't tell me to move. So, there I stayed. Surprisingly, he broke the heavy silence first.

"Is Raven coming back?" he asked.

"He said he'd return tomorrow, before we left. So, I assume yes."

Nox nodded. "I don't think he'd compromise our mission because of his feelings towards me. He's a better man than I am. Much better. You'd be happier with him."

I shrugged.

Nox raised a brow. "You don't think so?"

I picked at the nail polish on my thumb as I replied quietly, "I've known Raven's feelings towards me for a long time. I've even entertained taking him up on it before. But every time I tried to imagine myself with him like that, I couldn't. And I couldn't break his heart either, which is what would've happened if I'd used him like everyone else."

Nox seemed to contemplate my words before he muttered, "I always told myself I would never let this happen."

"Wasn't that lonely?" I asked, my voice barely above a whisper.

He looked at me and took one single step closer to me. He was still a couple feet away as he replied, "Of course it was. But it was better than subjecting anyone to the fate that was being with me."

I noticed he stuttered on the words "being with." I wondered if he'd almost said, "loving me."

"Well, what about now?" I dared to question.

He shook his head, running a hand through his hair, releasing the strands still trapped in the remainder of the leather cord. It fell to the ground, but he hardly seemed to notice as he said roughly, "Now I know the goddess has truly cursed me."

I swallowed, my chest tightening.

"Am I really that bad?"

His gaze shot to mine and he choked out a humorless laugh but didn't say anything.

I shook my head and said darkly, "If this is funny to you, then maybe I should just go."

I slid off the desk but was intercepted by Nox. He was breathing a little heavily now and his wings began to take shape behind him as he gripped my waist.

I stared up at him.

"You need to explain everything right now," I said. "The dreams, the bond, the curse. We don't have time to be dancing around the truth anymore."

He let go of me but didn't move away.

"Years ago, when I saw you on that dream bridge for the first time, I suspected what you were to me," he said.

"What does it mean? The bridge?"

His hand twitched but he didn't touch me as he explained, "Unseelie Fae are often gifted with shadow magic, different from shadow walking as I'm sure you know. True shadow magic, separate from demons or even wraiths, deals in whispers, secrets, and sometimes dreams. It is the magic of the thoughts we don't speak, the desires we don't act on, and the dreams that we don't remember. I've stumbled into dreams before, but usually without knowing who it was and without them knowing I was there."

"The first time I found myself in your dreams, I knew something was different. Usually when I'm in someone's dream, it feels as though I am separate from them. There is a wall... a veil of sorts, between me and the dreamer. But with you, there was a bridge, a pathway between us."

"As soon as I saw it, I feared that you were the one I had been trying so hard not to find. And after asking a mated couple in my inner circle about it, my suspicions were confirmed. Dream bridges were unique to Unseelie mates."

"But I'm not Unseelie," I cut in.

This time, Nox lifted a hand and lightly held my chin as he said, "No. But I am, love."

My mouth became dry as he held my gaze. But the moment passed and he let go, continuing, "I stayed away from you because I knew it was the right thing to do. It always would be. And believe me, there were times I wanted to find you. Every time I felt you hurting, I wanted to track down those who were doing it to you and rip their hearts out, just as I did in that alleyway. But staying away kept you alive.

"I didn't mean to run into you at that club. I truly was there for court business, following a lead on a black-market obsidian seller. But when I saw you, I couldn't help but..." he huffed out another laugh. "It was entirely selfish of me to not run the other way the moment I sensed you there. But I couldn't. And now here we are in this mess."

"You don't need to point out that this is my fault," I said, looking away. "I know that much already. Everything has always been my fault."

"That's not what I..." he trailed off, then gripped my chin again, forcing me to meet his eyes as he said, "Why do you think that, love?"

I tried to look away, but he wouldn't let me and I finally choked out, "I killed them."

A heavy silence filled the study and Nox waited for me to continue, to explain. Eventually, I did.

"My parents, they're dead because of me," I whispered.

A tear slipped down my cheek and Nox caught it with his thumb, brushing it away. The truth began to flow out of my mouth, like a raging waterfall I suddenly couldn't stop or slow down, "When I was six, the night before my birthday, something woke me up. I can't explain what it was exactly, it was like a whisper in my head, calling to me. I followed it, all the way down to the palace dungeons. There were so many symbols on the floor and such a strange smell in the air, like decay and acrid smoke. As soon as I got there, my mother intercepted me. She told me I needed to run as fast as I could, to the garden where our orange trees were. She said that I needed to hide."

"But before I could, something rose from the circle of symbols and ripped me from her arms. She screamed and I heard my father shout from down the hall. But it was too late. Whatever had come from the circle was already inside me."

"The next thing I knew, the entire room was filled with a burning, white light. I think I passed out, and when I came to, the presence was gone and so were my parents. When I looked at where they'd stood only moments before, there was nothing but ashes. Just before I lost consciousness again, my uncle found me and was horrified. He was right to be. I knew there would never be any coming back from what I'd done. I was... I am *wrong*. I'm a monster."

I had never told anyone the story quite like that, not even Lil. At some point as I spoke, I'd looked away from Nox's heavy gaze. I forced myself to find it again, expecting to see fear or disgust. Instead, his eyes were soft. He cupped my cheeks with his hands and pressed his lips to my forehead. He barely pulled back as he murmured gently, "You were a child, Asteria. You did what you had to in order to survive. I'm sure your parents would be proud of you if they could see you today."

My breath hitched with a sob and Nox pulled me flush against his chest as I let myself cry. The tears felt like they'd been a long time coming; I'd been holding them in for years.

When I finally quieted and pulled back to look at him again, his expression was contemplative.

"What?" I asked.

He furrowed his brow. "You said the demon went inside you?"

"You're sure it was a demon?"

He nodded. "I'm nearly certain that what you're describing is a summoning circle, meant to break into the cracks of our realm. A sort of one-way portal. If the demon that was summoned tried to possess you, it might have left a mark."

Horror coursed through me at the notion and Nox must have seen it on my face because he said, "Magic like that leaves a permanent mark. It doesn't mean the demon is still in you. I just want to see if I recognize the mark."

"Why would you recognize the mark?"

"Because I have one in me too."

I paused, then said, "Um, okay. Go ahead."

He chuckled softly. "It's not going to hurt, love."

Then he pressed two fingers to my chest, right above my heart. I inhaled sharply and I'll admit, part of it had to do with the magic, sure. But part of it definitely had to do with just where his hand was.

He knew it too. The bastard was smirking slightly as he met my eyes. Though it quickly slid off his face as he seemed to realize something.

"Nox?" I ventured.

His eyes were unfocused and I swore I caught a hint of fear flash across his expression. As soon as he looked back at me, it was gone.

"What was it?" I asked.

He lowered his hand and said one word, one name, that sent an instant chill through my body.

"Abaddon."

CHAPTER

FIFTEEN

I BACKED AWAY FROM NOX, disbelief coursing through me. The demon, the prince of hell he'd sent back to its realm all those centuries ago, was back. He'd been *inside* me. And he was probably really eager to meet me again, for more than just one reason.

I bumped against the desk and Nox took a step towards me.

"Do you think it's true?" I asked. "Do you think I have the same power as you?"

Nox paused, then said, "Are you asking if I think you're the Evening Star? I'm assuming Raven told you."

He stared at me, hand slackened at his sides, and I nodded as I sat back on the desk. His enormous, dark wings manifested then, rustling as he walked over to me, stopping short just before he reached me. He didn't answer my question, but his face said it all.

"When Abaddon returns, do you think you would be able to stop him?" I asked quietly. "I mean, I know the demon wasn't supposed to come back until the Evening

Star 'shone again' or whatever. But there's two of us now, right?"

Nox swallowed and took a breath. "Last time, I burned myself out so completely that I still haven't recovered," he said. "And even then, it almost wasn't enough. I'm not nearly that powerful anymore. Essentially, I'm just a Fae bastard with some wraith-blood at this point. So, to answer your question... I'm not really capable of that anymore. But you are."

"Do you have any starlight left?"

I didn't mean to ask the question so directly, but he didn't scoff. Instead, he folded my hand in his and closed his eyes for a moment. When he opened them, the gold specks in his irises were glowing softly. He raised his hand slightly off my palm and with it a stream of light followed. His starlight was more like pure moonlight, whereas mine was closer to white-hot fire.

I watched the light for a long moment, mesmerized. Once it faded away, Nox murmured, "It started to manifest more strongly after I met you in the club."

"Why?"

"I think my magic recognized yours."

I nodded, at a loss for words. He paused, his hand still holding mine, and I realized just how close we were. I was sitting on the desk and he was standing between my legs. My hand tightened in his as heat began to pool in my core. I knew he could sense the shift in me... just faerie things.

His wings rustled again and I lifted my hand to brush a finger against them. Nox caught my hand, and took a deep breath before whispering, "Careful, love."

"Why?" I murmured in response.

He gripped the desk with his other hand as he leaned in

and breathed in my ear, "Because if you keep doing that, I may not be able to stay in control."

"You managed well enough both times before," I teased, my back arching on instinct at his closeness.

A low rumble escaped his chest and he replied, "The first time you did that, I was about five seconds from taking you right then and there on the kitchen counter. The second time I was even closer to..." he trailed off.

"To what?" I dared.

He leaned in so that his breath fanned against my neck as he said, "To fucking you so hard you forgot your name," his lips brushed my throat, "your title," he made his way up to my earlobe and tugged it between his teeth. "Even the fact that everyone here would have heard us."

My hand was pressed against his chest and I could feel the rapid pounding of his heart. I was breathing unevenly and I knew my heart was beating just as hard as his.

"That's exactly what I wanted you to do to me when you bit my ear in the club," I whispered.

Then I reached my other hand out behind him. My touch was featherlight as I touched the smooth, hard plane of his wing. His hand gripped my waist and his head fell forward onto my shoulder as I continued to circle my finger.

I sucked in a breath as I felt the scrape of his sharp canines on my neck. I should've stopped right there; we both knew he was seconds away from claiming me completely—from maybe even finalizing that bond between us. But still, I didn't stop, my thighs tightening.

"Asteria," he groaned. "Stop, love."

"Stop what?" I murmured.

He pressed forward and every part of me went taut as I felt him push against me, straining through his pants.

Finally, I pulled my hand away from his wing. I was beginning to lose control now too. He lifted his head from my shoulder, brushing featherlight kisses up my neck and jaw. I couldn't help the breathy moan that escaped me, though the sound only seemed to set him off further. He stopped his ascent, inches away from my mouth. Finally, slowly, he brushed his lips to mine. I gasped as he nipped at my bottom lip, gently at first, then harder. I opened my mouth to him and his tongue swept in, claiming me as I claimed him. Once again, I was reminded—he knew how to kiss. I grasped at his shirt, pulling him closer. One of his hands skimmed my neck, his fingers pressing lightly against my pulse point.

He held my life in his hands. And, the scary part was, I trusted him with it completely.

Pulling back slightly, he brushed a finger across my lip. I caught it in my teeth, and his eyes flashed. Both of us were teetering on the edge of our more feral natures. Primal urges that shouted at us; *more, more, more.*

But it was gone from his expression in an instant and he stiffened.

"What?" I asked.

He began to pull away and said quietly, "Raven's back."

Indeed, I could now hear footsteps in the kitchen.

"Do you have your moonstone?" Nox murmured in my ear.

I nodded and he said, "I'll project my magic into it and it'll allow you to shadow walk back to your room."

I raised a brow. "You want me to sneak out of your office?"

The footsteps stopped and there was a knock on the door. Nox stiffened, his wings flaring slightly.

"He'll pick up on my scent whether I leave now or not," I whispered.

"King Nox?" Raven called.

He didn't sound quite as enraged as before. Maybe I should leave...

I plucked the moonstone from my pocket and Nox brushed a kiss to my forehead, before projecting his wraith-born magic into the stone. I became shadow and misty air, the sensation less odd than I'd expected, as Nox strode over to the door. His wings faded away and he quickly tied back his hair. He opened the door and let Raven in. I was suddenly very tempted to stay in the corner and listen to their conversation. But Nox's eyes flicked in my direction, a warning in them. I stuck my shadowy tongue out at him before slipping past Raven and through the open door. It shut behind me and I let go of the moonstone, becoming corporeal just in front of the bedroom door where Lil slept.

Voices raised from the study and I knew Raven must have picked up that I'd been in there. I opened the slightly cracked door to see Lil sitting up in bed.

"Raven's back already?" she whispered in the dark as I sat down on the edge of the mattress.

"Apparently," I murmured.

I climbed under the covers with her, suddenly exhausted.

"How'd it go with Nox?"

Her voice was cautious and small. I found her hand as I muttered, "Interesting."

"What does that mean? Like are you two good?"

I laughed quietly, almost awkwardly. I wasn't usually shy about these things. Lil knew that and she raised a brow.

"What exactly just happened in that office?" she asked.

I cleared my throat and shrugged. From across the penthouse, we both heard a voice shout something angrily. Raven's, presumably.

"Did you two just go at it? Is that why Raven's freaking out in there?"

I rolled my eyes. "We did not 'go at it.' He just… we just kissed. That's all."

Lil peered at me, narrowing her eyes.

"I don't believe you," she said.

"Well, there's more important things to talk about."

"Like what?"

I ran my hand over the comforter, the smooth, soft material calming me as I told Lil, "Nox thinks I'm the Evening Star. And that Abaddon, the demon prince he made the deal with, is already back."

"Wait," Lil said slowly. "If you're the Evening Star *and* Nox's mate… how does that work?"

I shook my head. "I don't know. I guess… if Nox's curse comes true and I die, the world's kind of screwed."

"Okay, first of all, you're not going to die," Lil said. "And secondly, doesn't Nox still have his star power, or whatever it is?"

"Apparently not," I replied. "He told me he burned himself out when he sent the demon horde back to their realm, at the end of the war."

"Oh."

"Yup. We're screwed," I concluded. "And Lil?"

"Yeah?"

"I want you to be prepared for the possibility that I might not be here much longer."

She swallowed audibly and said, "No. I refuse to believe that. I'll fight this demon myself. He is not taking you."

Her voice edged on a snarl as she finished. Lil was as protective of me as any mate was. I felt the same way about her. Which was why I would die before I let her get close to Abaddon, or any demon for that matter.

"Why don't we sleep," I said heavily after a moment had passed.

"Aster—"

"I'm tired," I cut her off. "And we have a long day ahead of us tomorrow."

She sighed and said, "Alright."

We climbed under the covers and both fell silent for a couple minutes. I began to drift off. But just before I did, she said, "I'd take you over Nox. Or the world for that matter. I know that's selfish, but it's true."

In the haze of the half-sleep I replied, "I'd have to disagree. My life has always been cursed. Even before I met him."

It might have been the most honest thing I'd said in a while.

CHAPTER
SIXTEEN

I woke up alone in the guest room. Hazily, I blinked, glancing at the digital clock on the nightstand. As soon as I saw the time I swore loudly. I had nearly slept through the entire morning. Again.

I pushed myself out of bed and hurried to the bathroom to take a quick shower. Steam filled the room once I turned the faucet on and scalding water pounded on my back. I welcomed the sting, the feeling of something other than the fear and uncertainty that were otherwise coursing through me.

Once I was finished with the shower, I mechanically brushed my teeth and ran a comb through my tangle of raven-black hair. I stared at myself in the mirror for a moment. I didn't look like a Seelie princess. In fact, I looked more Unseelie than anything. But I knew I looked like my mother. I still remembered her braiding her dark hair in the mornings, just before she sat down and braided mine too. Her moon-pale skin was mine, and so was her upturned nose. Though my mouth was from my father, as were the smattering of freckles that exploded across my nose and cheeks. And I suppose my power probably came from him, too. My mother had possessed a different sort of power from her family line: kindness.

My mother's parents had passed on long before I'd been born. I'd never met my grandparents on my father's side either... they'd died mere decades ago. Poison, or so I'd been told. No one had ever found out who'd been behind their murders.

Now, I wondered if my uncle had anything to do with it.

I dragged myself out of the bathroom, the notion haunting me. There had been an outfit laid out for me on the loveseat next to the window and I stared at it for a moment. Dark jeans, a tight black turtleneck, and a leather jacket. It seemed my attire would be matching the shadow I would be playing. I sighed and began to pull on the jeans.

Once I was dressed, I swiped on some quick makeup around my eyes and then tugged on my boots. Tentatively, I opened the door and walked out into the kitchen. Lil was perched on the counter, wearing a simple black dress and a crisp white apron. She was also currently stuffing her face with a peanut butter and jelly sandwich. Raven leaned against the fridge, sipping what looked like coffee. He was wearing all black as usual, though the quality of the clothing was cheaper than his normal garb. Plus, his typical leather jacket was gone.

And Nox...

I finally understood his reputation as the feared Unseelie Night King as he emerged from the study. He wore a dark, form-fitting suit, unbuttoned slightly at the top. His hair was loose, framing his face in silver and his amber eyes were lined so they looked shadowed. Atop his head was a crown of black diamonds, each gem seeming to suck the light out of the room.

All three of them turned my way as I stepped into the kitchen.

"Sorry I slept so long," I said, shifting back and forth on my feet.

"That's okay!" Lil chirped, jumping off the counter and prancing over to me.

I looked at Nox, trying and failing not to stare.

"Are we going soon?" I asked.

"As soon as I put the glamours over Raven and Lilliana," he replied evenly.

None of the rawness or hunger of last night remained, and he was almost impassive as he looked at me. Raven, on the other hand, still appeared as though he was about to boil over and rage. I ignored the imploring looks he kept shooting in my direction.

"I've never been under a Fae glamour before, much less one cast by an Unseelie king," Lil said loudly.

Raven glared at her and she glared right back; this was going to be an interesting trip.

"Would you like to go first?" Nox asked her and she shrugged.

"Sure, why not?"

He walked over to her and I and stopped a breath away from me before turning to Lil.

"Close your eyes," he murmured.

She looked genuinely frightened for a moment as Nox towered over her. But she obeyed, her eyes fluttering shut as he pressed his fingers lightly to her forehead with a gentleness that almost made me envious for a moment. Lil would always be easy to love. Uncomplicated and sweet. Whereas me... I was the mess we were currently in.

I was the storm that tore apart my family.

I was rage and recklessness and horror.

I was chaos.

Lil's form began to swirl, then a gentle wave of shadow enveloped her. When it cleared, she was a mousy-looking human girl with dusty brown hair, gray eyes, and a too-big nose.

"How do I look?" she squeaked.

"Plain," Nox replied. "As you should."

Lil made a face at him before he turned to Raven. Just before he pressed his fingers to Raven's forehead, he glanced at me. I wonder if he saw the storm clouds in my eyes. If so, he didn't say anything, just furrowed his brow slightly, before settling the glamour over Raven. When the shadows cleared again, Raven was a touch shorter, his face rounder, and he had the same plain brown hair as Lil, though his eyes were a muddy brown instead of gray.

Finally, Nox turned to me.

"Do you still have the moonstone?" he asked.

I swallowed the last eddies of crackling emotion within me and nodded, pulling out the smooth, white stone. Nox took a deep breath, his cool demeanor seeming to crack for just a moment as his gaze locked onto mine. The break in his facade was smoothed over in seconds though as he told me, "I'll be projecting my magic into the stone the whole time, so as long as you're touching it, you'll be fully hidden. But... if I fail the Trial, know that it will cease almost immediately," he glanced at Lil and Raven, adding, "The same goes for you two, with the glamours."

I could only nod, any words I might have said getting caught in my throat.

Nox stared at me for a few seconds longer before he said, "You're our only chance of finding whatever your uncle is hiding. Be relentless in your search. But Asteria…" he paused for a moment. "Be careful. If you come across a demon, even a lesser one, they will likely be able to sense that you're there, even with the wraith magic cloaking you."

A churning sensation began in my stomach, making me *really* glad I hadn't eaten anything yet. I ignored it, knowing that now was not the time to show fear. We simply couldn't afford to, any of us.

So, I replied coolly, "I'll be fine. We should go."

Nox brushed his knuckles across my cheek and I inhaled sharply. But the moment was short-lived and he stepped back, nodding curtly.

"Agreed," he said. "Lilliana, Raven, hold onto each other and one of you, take my hand. Asteria, cloak yourself with the moonstone now. They'll have eyes on us the moment we arrive."

Raven and Lil joined hands, Lil taking one of Nox's hands. I grasped the moonstone in my pocket, shadows enveloping me. Nox held out his other hand and I took it. Seconds later, we were in the whirling passage of time.

I had never flitted before I'd met Nox—I'd never learned how. The first time had been a few days ago of course, but I'd been barely conscious. Now, I felt every suffocating second of it. I knew I'd be able to breathe soon, but in the cramped, dark wind-tunnel, there was nothing. It was like being void of matter. Like I didn't even exist. Though it was terrifying, I found myself savoring the emptiness—the lack of me.

I wondered if this would be what it felt like to die.

It lasted only a second or two more before we slammed into the ground, a crack resounding in my ears. I held in my gasp, clutching the moonstone tightly. On instinct, I looked up.

The gold-coated gates of the Seelie Court palace loomed ahead. Dread pulsed through me, as I was reminded of my childhood and teenage years. I'd stood outside these gates many times, counting the precious seconds I had before they swung open and I was dragged inside to the horrors that a visit with Uncle Calum held.

But I wasn't going to freak out now. Nope, today I was "badass detective" Aster. Or maybe spy Aster... that sounded cooler. In my invisible, shadowed form, I stuck my tongue out at the gates. I saw Nox catch onto the movement and amusement flashed across his face.

So, he could see me like this. Whoopsie. But it was good to know; I didn't want to do anything too embarrassing, thinking no one could witness it.

Ahead, the gates began to slowly open. The palace that lay behind them was made of stone, worn down and smooth with time. There were three main spires that towered above, coated with ivy, reaching into the cloudless sky. Balconies jutted off in other areas, where once long ago, I had sat with my mother and played in the sunlight. We used to have "tea parties" and I remembered that my mother had often sang as I served her make-believe crumpets and scones made from clay and wildflowers. Once, she'd let me go to a real tea party with the ladies of the court. I still remember their delicate dresses and bell-like laughter.

Now, as we walked past the gates and they began to

close behind us, I was painfully reminded of the stark fact that that life was gone. Along with my mother.

An enormous group of palace guards stood to greet Nox. "Greet" was probably a generous way to put it though. Many of the guards gripped the hilts of their swords tightly, as if they were already gearing up for a fight. Goddess, were they really that afraid of Nox?

I glanced sideways at him as he stared ahead, his mouth lifted slightly to the side in a cocky smirk. He *had* been the Evening Star, long ago. He'd held the power to send an entire legion of demons back to their realm. And when it hadn't been enough, he'd sacrificed his future so that others might have one.

In that moment, I realized, beyond that fateful battle, I knew very little about Nox. He'd said he hadn't been king at the same time as my father, and I had been too young to remember exactly when power shifted in the Unseelie Court. Not to mention that my uncle had nearly forbidden me to even allude to our political rivals, so it wasn't like I'd been able to just ask.

What had happened to his father? His mother? Did he have siblings or even friends? This last week had been spent holed up in his penthouse, but I hadn't even thought to ask about anything beyond the current situation. And now... I might never get to know anything.

The guards were silent as Nox approached, his steps lithe and graceful, like a wildcat approaching its prey. A few of them stiffened as he stopped just in front of them and eyed them with mild interest.

I knew he didn't actually care. This was an intimidation tactic and they all knew it. One guard took a miniscule step back and Nox smiled wide, showing all his teeth. He had won this game, for now.

Finally, a gruff voice cut through the charged silence, asking, "Who are they?"

Nox glanced at the source of the noise, a stocky faerie with sandy blonde hair who stood at the front. He wore a slightly different uniform than the other guards. Dark maroon instead of black and gold, with a phoenix pin on his chest. The symbol of my father's house.

I recognized him as Ewin Wells, the captain of the guard.

Ewin had looked the other way many times as my uncle had dragged me down the hall to his private rooms. Once, he'd even stopped me from running. My resulting punishment had been a hot held iron to my wrist. If we had more time and things weren't so dire, I would've enjoyed terrorizing him in my invisible shadow form.

Nox gave Ewin a flippant half-smile and drawled, "My human servants. I was allowed two, was I not?"

Ewin narrowed his eyes and said, "You were. I suppose they're all slaves in your nightmare court."

Nox ignored the taunt and began to walk up the long, pathed path that led to the grand entrance. The group of guards hesitated for a moment. They were obviously supposed to be escorting Nox, but he had stridden straight off without waiting for them.

"Move, idiots!" Ewin finally bellowed and they unfroze, hurrying after Nox.

I held in a snort. It looked like Nox was leading his own army, rather than being escorted by his enemy's. Just a few feet back from the brigade, I stayed in the long shadows that trailed behind everyone. No one even glanced my way.

When we arrived at the enormous oak doors, the battalion of guards stopped. Ewin whistled shrilly and the doors began to slowly swing open. Nox folded his arms across his chest, waiting. As soon as they were swung wide enough to walk through he said, "Come," to Lil and Raven. They followed him inside.

I held my breath as I slipped into the entrance hall. The white marble floors were spotless as they had been in my memory, the gold and crystal chandelier gleaming above. Sparkling bits of colored light reflected on the chandelier and the floor, from the stained-glass windows beyond. My heart caught in my throat as I gazed at the images that played out on those windows. It was the story of the ruling families of Seelie Court. Familiar tales of betrayal and deceit, of love and heartbreak, of war and epic battles. I'd learned them all in my lessons as a girl. And there, on the last panel that had ever been made…

A Fae man with golden hair stood tall, wielding elemental magic in the form of fire. The phoenix emblem was proudly displayed on his chest, fiery orange and glowing as the sun illuminated the window from behind. Next to him, a beautiful woman with flowing dark locks stood, her face tilted to smile at the man. And in her arm a small bundle was cradled, a halo of brilliant light around its tiny head. I swallowed hard, my swagger dimming considerably.

Nox's eyes traveled to the windows and for a fraction of a second, his body went utterly still as his gaze stopped on the last panel. I wondered if he'd never noticed it. I presumed he'd been here at least once before. A strange feeling in my chest pulled softly. It felt gentle, like the stroke of a hand down my back. It was just enough to keep me from freaking out completely. I clenched my hands into fists and readied to follow again.

It took Nox a few seconds to recover, but once he did, his gaze shifted ahead, back to the group of guards.

Ewin grunted, "Follow," and began to stride ahead.

Nox's eyes narrowed at the disrespect, but he didn't say anything... yet. The other guards flanked on either side of the hall as they led Nox, Lil, and Raven further into the palace. Almost immediately, I realized they were heading towards the throne room. To my uncle, presumably.

Unease pricked at my skin at the notion of seeing him and the shadows around me grew restless, as if sensing how I felt. I bit my lip, hoping they'd quiet. Nox's gaze flicked to my general area and I knew he could probably see, or at least sense the agitated shadows. I could only hope no one else could too. Fortunately, they quieted, just as we stepped under a tall, arched entrance.

The throne room stretched out ahead like the jaws of a great beast ready to devour me. The chasm of my child-hood and teenage years yawned open, threatening to suck me back in time. How many times had my uncle brought me here, dismissing everyone else, and insisting I grovel on my knees before him for hours, until they were aching and bruised?

Once upon a time, my father had pulled me into his lap as he sat on that throne and told me stories of greatness and honor. Now, it was my uncle lounging lazily on it, like he owned the entire world. The ivy and wildflowers that grew up and around the gilded throne seemed to shy away from him, and I noticed they were withered and dying in many spots. That was new.

The silver crown of woven leaves, frozen in time, was

perched atop his head mockingly. I held in the urge to rush ahead and knock it off. I'd tried to do that once when I was very young. It had not been a good call on my part.

Nox approached, still wearing his cockeyed smirk. Lil glanced at Raven and he nodded at her. The two of them stopped a few feet back, dropping to their knees, as was the custom. But Nox did not bend under my uncle's icy stare. He simply strode ahead, stopping a short distance away from the throne. His devious grin grew wider.

I wish I could have taken a picture of the rage on Uncle Calum's face at that moment. It was delicious, the way that Nox made him nearly bend to his will.

"Disrespectful as always, little Nox," my uncle sneered.

"Only the best for you," Nox replied, his expression bored.

"How's daddy's throne?" Uncle Calum said. "I wonder... has it been strange taking the place of someone you stabbed in the back?"

Nox cocked his head and said in a low voice, "I could ask the same, Calum."

Did my uncle mean that Nox literally stabbed his father in the back? Or was it just a political betrayal? Both maybe, I supposed. It would have to be a story for another time though. If we had time.

Meanwhile, my uncle's gaze darkened at Nox's insinuation and a soft growl rippled from his throat.

"Naughty little bastard," my uncle said. "Though I can't say I'm surprised. What else would I expect from the son of a woman who'd spread her legs for any—"

Power rippled through the room, cutting my uncle off. For a moment, it felt as though we were in a bubble, the sound strange and echoing. My uncle's hand rose to his throat just as the bubble broke. It was then that I realized Nox had somehow been holding my uncle's throat without even touching him.

Uncle Calum was cruel, but I knew from years of experience that his magic was powerful. It rivaled my father's. And like most faeries of our status, we had a little more of that "basic" magic that all of our kind did. Being that I grew up away from court, I'd never mastered it nor did I really understand just what it meant.

But I did know that my uncle technically should have been able to fend off an attack like that. Except he hadn't, which meant that Nox was even more powerful than I'd initially given him credit for.

It probably should've scared me. But I won't lie… it kind of turned me on. Which was like, so inappropriate right now. Especially as Uncle Calum rose from this throne, his face a mask of fiery rage. Frost began to form on the dying flowers surrounding the throne—my uncle's typical element of choice. Nox watched the display of my uncle's anger with a continued glazed boredom.

And then, just as he was about to speak, Uncle Calum's gaze landed directly on me.

I froze, my throat tightening in panic. He couldn't see me… it was impossible. I was still cloaked in shadow.

The moment passed quickly and I told myself it had just been a coincidence. Still, a nagging feeling of unease persisted as he sank back down onto the throne.

"I suppose our power displays do not matter," my uncle finally said. "As you are the one who is to be facing the Trial tomorrow. Unless you'd like to refuse of course…?"

He was baiting Nox. Refusing to face a Trial of the Goddess was pretty much another way of saying, *Yeah, I'm guilty but I'm not willing to get my neck snapped under some stupid, ancient tree.*

Nox raised a brow and replied smoothly, "Of course not. I wouldn't miss it for the world."

"And the other alternative?"

Nox's expression sharpened as he said, "Asteria Fairwae isn't returning to you."

"So, you admit you have my niece?"

"I admit that I rescued her from an assassination attempt and gave her sanctuary in my court."

A loud sort of silence rang out in the room following Nox's claim. The implication was very much there that he was proclaiming my uncle was behind the attempt on my life. A few feet from where I stood, Ewin fingered the hilt of his sword, ready to strike should any of the guards believe Nox's words and rebel against their king.

My uncle leaned forward in the throne and hissed, "A clever cover up. But I'm not a fool."

"Really? Neither am I."

Uncle Calum's cheeks reddened, but he simply said to the guards, "Take the bastard king to his rooms."

Nox ignored the insult and bowed mockingly.

"Thank you for your generosity. And when should I be ready for the feast?"

"Someone will retrieve you," Uncle Calum snarled, apparently done talking.

Nox chuckled, though it was void of any humor or joy. "Very well," he said.

He turned on his heel and strode away from the throne, back towards the hallway. Lil and Raven fell into step behind him, their heads slightly bowed. And this time, the guards followed immediately, Ewin at their lead.

I trailed after them again, skirting through the familiar halls. No lords or ladies of court lingered in the alcoves or at the little tables set up along the wall. My uncle's reign was one of fear, and that permeated even here. Only a select few, mostly faeries in his inner circle, walked freely or did as they wished. The others stayed silent for fear of losing their position and wealth all together.

I knew these things, because since I was a child, I'd been good at noticing things.

I noticed how the humans of court slowly lost their places. Then the sirens and the shifters. Until only the Fae lords remained. Their wives grew submissive. Debauchery amongst women became taboo. Laughter died out.

And slowly, slowly, like the dripping of some poisonous honey, that attitude began to spread out into the entire court district. It wasn't bad, not yet. But it was present. It was there in the way that our kind's children played separately from the others and the stuck-up nose of the Fae man I'd seen on the bus, as a shifter crowded his space. The change was gradual enough that I'd hardly noticed it.

But I was reminded now.

The guards led Nox to the northern wing, where guests typically stayed, to a room that I knew was insultingly small for a king. But Nox didn't bat an eye. He only said to Ewin, "And for my companions?"

Ewin balked. He probably hadn't been expecting Nox to treat Raven and Lil with any sort of respect, nor refer to them as his "companions." There were rumors—no doubt spread by my uncle—that humans were kept as slaves in the Unseelie Court. I suppose I didn't know they weren't true for sure; I'd only seen the inside of Nox's penthouse. But I had a very strong hunch it was a falsehood.

170

"I suppose we can set them up—"

"I want them close," Nox cut in.

Ewin cleared his throat, his hand nervously rubbing across the light shadow of stubble on his jaw. Finally, he said, "The room across the hall is unoccupied at the moment."

"Perfect."

"You two," Ewin glanced at Raven and Lil. "There."

He pointed at the door across the hall, as if they were stupid and hadn't heard any of the conversation he'd had with Nox. A lanky-legged guard strode forward and opened the door for Nox. No one moved to assist Raven and Lil, however. Ewin began to leave, but just before Nox entered his room, he said, "Captain."

Ewin paused, and asked, "Yes?"

Nox cocked his head at the captain of the guard and said, "If you insult my servants, or address me without a proper title again, I'll have you choking on your own blood before you can even beg for your life."

Ewin's ruddy face paled and he gritted out, "Yes… Your Majesty."

Nox smiled like a wolf.

"Better," he purred. "I like my dogs on leashes."

Then he disappeared into his room. As soon as the door closed, I watched silently as Ewin swore under his breath and wiped a sheen sweat off his face.

I savored every second of his fear.

SEVENTEEN

I SLIPPED RIGHT through the door into Nox's room, only to find him shirtless. I froze, hardly breathing and hoping he might not notice me quietly invading his privacy.

He chuckled and said, "I know you're there, love."

I unfurled my fingers from the moonstone and dropped it in my pocket. Nox's eyes roved over me as my body became solid and corporeal again.

"You look good in black," he said, almost as if to himself.

"You're not wearing a shirt," I blurted out.

Right, real smooth, Aster.

Nox nodded and said, "This is true." Then, without a pause, asked, "Does that bother you?"

He walked over to me, crowding the space between us with his bare skin and a whole lot of muscle. For a moment, I froze again. And then I remembered I was Aster... Aster Quiin, not Asteria Fairwae. Not the scared little girl, but the sexy, confident woman. Someone who laughed in the face of embarrassment or fear. Someone *I* had chosen.

I flicked my gaze up to Nox's as I reached out and dragged my hand down his chest, savoring the subtle quickening up his heart beneath my palm. I laughed softly, my movements unhurried. I was in control here.

The side of Nox's mouth tilted up and he said, "There you are."

I wasn't two different people, not really. But I was changed, and sometimes I forgot that. Nox seemed to understand that about me, in a way I wasn't sure anyone else ever had. He didn't tell me I needed to suck it up and reclaim myself. He took me as I was and deep down, I knew he cared for me, the me that stood before him right now.

"What are you wearing tonight?" I murmured, letting my hand trail lower, ghosting the waistband of his dress pants. "Traditional court wear?" I slipped my thumb beneath the band. "Or something else?"

"Hmm," he hummed, though it was more of a rumble coming from his chest. "Traditional, but not for here."

His hands found my waist as I said, "I see."

As his grip tightened on my hips and heat pooled in me, a sudden wild idea came to me. Without warning, I began to lower to my knees. But as I did, Nox caught my chin and kneeled down with me.

"Not so fast, my star," he whispered.

That name was new. It made me feel all fuzzy and soft inside, which both terrified and excited me. I was caught in between frustration at his refusal and surprise at the name. And also fear of what the future held for us. Because I knew was becoming attached and he was too. That really couldn't happen, for so many complicated reasons, the simplest of them being that I might die soon.

Slowly, he stroked a finger down my cheek and said, "I

won't allow you to do that until I've pleasured you first. I will not have my mate be unsatisfied."

Mate.

Oh, goddess.

"Nox," I murmured, looking away. "We don't have to… you don't have to call me that."

"It won't change the truth of it if I don't."

"And it won't change the truth of what's going to happen."

Wings flared out behind him, quickly and abruptly. The sight of them dropped some of my defenses and I lifted a hand from his chest and touched his cheek gently. He bowed his head forward and I paused as I realized what he was feeling.

Shame.

I wasn't exactly a stranger to that particular emotion. But this wasn't his shame to take on. It really wasn't anyone's, aside from that demon he'd bargained with. Nox had only done what he'd thought was right. Hundreds of years later, he was facing the reality of it and I knew it weighed heavily on him.

Gently, I dragged a finger across his high cheekbone and said, "This isn't your fault."

He lifted his head to look at me, his expression open.

"I won't let him take you."

"And if you can't stop him?" I dared.

"Then I'll go with you."

My eyes widened and I said, "Nox, don't say that. You have a court to rule. People who look to you and—"

"So do you."

"Not… really," I muttered. "You shouldn't give up your life for me. We barely know each other."

The words felt like a lie on my tongue. Sure, we'd met in person less than a month ago, but we'd been bleeding into each other's lives, each other's dreams and sorrows and desires, long before that. Meeting him had been like meeting someone my soul already knew inside and out. We just had to catch everything else up.

Nox knew it too. And he seemed ready to prove it.

"Do you want me to show you just how little I know you?" he said, the atmosphere between us suddenly changing, becoming charged and warm.

I bit my lip and his gaze flicked to my mouth. We were still kneeling on the floor of the suite and he seemed to decide that wasn't satisfactory anymore, because in a smooth, sudden motion, he scooped me up into his arms, wings still flared behind him. A not so sexy-sounding squeal escaped me as he glanced down at me and muttered, "Cute."

I made a face, though any irritation slid away as he set me down on top of the made bed, leaning over me. His body was warm and hard in all the right places and it took everything in me to avoid immediately writhing against him. I knew he could sense it, just as I could sense the hunger ebbing from him.

"Nox," I ventured as he nipped at my ear.

"Mhm?"

"Is it," I sucked in a breath, "is it maybe not so smart to be doing this?"

He lifted his head, his hair half pulled out of the bun it'd been in, the silvery strands brushing against my shoulders.

"There are many reasons why this is not smart, love," he said. "But I'm quite tired of following the rules."

"The demon won't come quicker because we...?"

Nice mood killer. Ten points to me for knowing just how to dump a bucket of ice water over the moment.

The heat did leave Nox's eyes, but only for a second. It returned, mingling with rage too, as he said, "I have no idea. But I meant what I said. He'll have to kill me first if he wants to take you. That holds true for anyone who dares to lay a hand on you."

"I can take care of myself," I said.

Nox grinned savagely. "I know, love. I'd expect you to do the same for me."

I opened my mouth to retort that, no, I would not. But it was precisely at that moment that I realized... I would. I would do anything to protect him. I would become something I feared. And I believed him when he said he'd do it for me. As with many things related to Nox, I knew that should scare me. But I was realizing again and again that he could never frighten me, not in that way, at least.

He watched me closely, as if reading every thought in my head through my expression. Finally, he asked, "Understood, then?"

I nodded silently.

"Good," he said.

He was still above me, his face inches from mine. I wasn't sure where to look... his eyes, his mouth, his chest. I was drawn to every inch of him. Eventually, I settled on his eyes, watching the gold flecks in them flash as I reached out. I trailed his jaw and then the column of his neck with my fingers. He nudged my legs apart with his knee and brushed his lips against my heated cheek. And that was when someone knocked on the door.

Nox closed his eyes and muttered, "Gods above."

The knocking became more insistent and I whispered, "Now might be a good time to not be on top of me anymore."

He stole a quick kiss and said against my lips, "This isn't finished."

Then he pushed off me, sitting on the edge of the bed. I watched his chest rise and fall slowly and I realized with a smile that he was collecting himself.

"Hello!"

Nox hissed through his teeth as we both heard Raven call out from the other side of the door. But then he rose, striding over to the door. That was when I realized two things: one, he was still not wearing a shirt. And two, he had just said "gods above," not "goddess above."

I wondered if it had just been a slight. But Nox had lived a very long time... maybe he knew something we didn't? Or could it actually be possible he'd lived during a time when the goddess had only been the Maiden? That would make him *really* old.

"As much as I like how you look sprawled out on my bed, love," Nox said, startling from my thoughts, "you might want to get up. Raven likely won't appreciate it and we need him to be calm at the moment."

I blinked and said, "Right, yeah."

I sat up, straightened my hair, and adjusted my slightly untucked shirt.

As soon as Nox opened the door, Raven's eyes immediately went to Nox's half-naked body and then to me, sitting on the bed behind him. I was pretty sure he wasn't ogling at Nox's muscles, though the same couldn't be said for Lil.

Behind Raven, she gave me an enthusiastic thumbs up, her eyes still lingering on Nox's impressive abs.

I saw the corner of Nox's mouth quirk up briefly, but it was gone as soon as Raven walked into the room and began to pace. Lil followed him and Nox quickly shut the door.

"Something isn't right," Raven said immediately.

Lil raised a brow. "No shit."

He ignored her and said to Nox, "This is too casual. It's as if you've been invited for a celebration or a meeting, not to fill out your death sentence."

Nox waved his hand and a dark tunic appeared from thin air and the crown he'd set on the bedside table floated over. He *tsked* at Raven and said, "So little faith in my innocence?"

"You know the Trial is a farce. So does Calum."

"Maybe," Nox said.

The word lingered in the air, leaving me to wonder about it too—could this actually work? I didn't believe in the Trial and I thought it was a barbaric practice. But he was innocent. If there was any way it turned out to be remotely legitimate, Nox could survive it.

"Trial or not, the fact remains that Calum is far too confident," Raven said. "You bested him in his own throne room and aside from getting a little angry, he hardly seemed concerned."

I saw what Raven was saying and yet...

"My uncle has always been overly confident," I said. "He likes to pretend he owns things that aren't this. This is just a part of his game. He's playing his cards and now we have to play ours."

Nox, now dressed in the tunic, glanced at me, his jaw

working. The crown still lingered next to him, waiting. He plucked it out of the air, pulled his hair out of the cord so it tumbled down to his shoulders, then placed it on his head. I probably watched him a little too closely throughout the whole sequence, but I was beginning to be past caring.

Raven cleared his throat. "So, what cards do we have to play?"

Surprisingly, it was Lil who answered.

"We distract them. Play the gracious guests," she looked pointedly at Nox, "while Aster does what she needs to do. Then we go from there."

"Well said, Lilliana," Nox replied.

Her cheeks grew pink and I caught her eye then winked. She rolled her eyes at me, just as Raven asked, "Are we going to talk any more about our other problem?"

Nox's body stiffened and it took me a second to realize that Raven was referring to the mating bond, and the notion of my imminent death tied to it. Though Nox's wings had disappeared before he opened the door, they flickered in and out of existence now, ghostly in their half-appearance.

"What exactly," Nox began, "do you want me to do about it?"

Raven glanced at me, then eyed Nox and said, "There's an alternative and I think you know that."

Lil shot me a questioning look and I shook my head. I had no idea what Raven was talking about. But Nox seemed to because he crowded Raven and said, "You know I can't do that."

"Can't or won't? Unless she's already accepted it, doing so might not even hurt her that much—"

"You don't know a thing about this," Nox snarled. "I've seen what that does to people."

"You'd rather Aster die?"

"Trying that might just kill her."

"You mean it might kill you?" Raven dared, baring his teeth.

"Both of you, shut up!" Lil's voice interrupted. She took a breath, then added, "And an explanation about just what the hell you're talking about would be nice too."

"Stay out of this, Lil," Raven said, hardly looking at her way.

I narrowed my eyes and said, "Don't be a dick, Raven. You know this affects Lil just as much as it affects you. And she's right. You both need to explain to me what's going on."

Nox looked at me, every bit the menacing Night King as he said, "It doesn't matter. I'm not risking it."

"What is the alternative you're suggesting then!" Raven shouted.

Shadows gathered at the edges of the room as Nox said in a low voice, "Stand down, Raven."

Raven opened his mouth, just as there was a knock on the door.

"Sir—I mean, Your Majesty, we've come to escort you to the feast," someone called from the hall.

Nox was already on edge and his expression darkened further as he strode towards the door. Before he could reach it and strangle whoever was on the other side, I grabbed his arm and said, "Gracious guest, remember?"

He held my gaze. "Alright."

"We're not done with this conversation," Raven said under his breath.

Nox ignored him and said to me, "Gear up, love. It's your turn to play now."

And so, it was. I let go of his arm and pulled the moon-stone from my pocket. Immediately, I became shadows and mist as the wraith magic overtook my body. Nox's eyes lingered on me for a moment longer before he opened the door.

The guard on the other side, not Ewin, looked terrified. I had to admit, I might be a little scared if I was him too. Nox looked about ready to rip someone's head off. But the guard managed to say, "Follow me, Your Majesty."

Nox's nostrils flared and then a cruel smile spread across his face. He leaned in close to the guard's face, almost as if he was going to kiss him.

"I'll remember the respect you gave," he breathed in the guard's ear. "Warn the others if you wish. But a reckoning is coming."

Your soul's match will be the reckoning.

A shiver ran through me as I was reminded of the words the little girl, the oracle, had spoken to me. It seemed that everything was coming together, except that I had no idea how.

Nox pulled back from the wide-eyed guard as he nodded silently. Then, Lil and Raven fell into step behind Nox and the battalion of guards, heading off towards the great dining hall. I slipped out of the door behind them, just before it shut. But I didn't follow them, not yet. I had some searching to do.

I knew where I *should* look first, but fear spiked through me as I thought of the dungeons beneath the palace. I would face that place soon. But for now, I decided to start in my uncle's chambers. Just in case, I told myself.

I knew quite well enough where it was. I'd been there many times to receive my "punishments." I glided through the halls and up a few flights of stairs, evading servants and guards alike with the moonstone in my hand. When I arrived at the door of Uncle Calum's chambers, I stopped, listening for the sounds of someone inside. There were none, so I took a deep breath and slipped through the solid door. I was still getting used to the feeling, as if my entire being was scattered about in a cold wind for a moment.

Once I was inside, I paused, an old panic overcoming me.

Here was the place where I was whipped for the first time. Here was the place where I cried for my mother, and my uncle had only hit me harder. Here was the place my innocence had been ripped away from me through unwelcome touch.

Here was where my hope had died.

It took me a moment to tuck away the feelings of despair. By the time I'd cleared my head, I could hear the sounds of the feast beginning, even from inside the room. The musicians were playing faerie music, of course. Though, it was different from what Nox had asked the DJ in the club to play. This music was dissonant and alarming, though at the same time, it was intoxicating. I wondered if this was what it felt like to be glamoured by a siren's song. Lovely, but at the same time, deadly.

After a minute or so, I pulled myself from the thrall of the music and quickly began to peek in drawers, under the bed, and in the armoire. I wasn't even sure what I was looking for.

My uncle's sickly-sweet scent clung to everything,

making me feel panicked all over again. As far as my senses could tell, he was here in this room with me. I ignored them —I was here for a reason. In the end, the only object of note that I found was a small key that I knew unlocked my father's private safe. Though the safe itself was nowhere to be seen. And I knew, I had to go below, just as I'd feared.

I floated out of the room and began to head towards the passage that I knew led to the dungeons and the catacombs beneath the palace. I managed to get down several stairways before I encountered anyone. When I did, I paused. A voice I recognized as Ewin's was speaking to someone else in low tones.

"He says it's almost time," Ewin said.

"And we'll be rewarded?" the other voice asked, then added, "And kept safe?"

"Undoubtedly. Have the remaining Unseelie prisoners been secured?"

There was a pause from the other person before they said, "Yes, the few that remain are ready."

Ewin sighed. "Good. Go enjoy the feast for now. I'll be here."

My hands began to shake as the words I'd overheard sank in. Could "the Unseelie prisoners" be the missing members of Nox's court? If so, I needed to tell him as soon as I could. Or maybe I could try to find them myself. I was heading to the dungeons anyway. And Nox, Raven, and Lil couldn't very well just leave the feast. It would look too suspicious. I would have to go alone.

My decision made, I skirted around a clueless Ewin, who was currently taking a hefty swig from a flask he'd pulled out from beneath his overcoat. I resisted the urge to mess with him and headed for the secret passageway near the servant's hall. Once I reached it, I paused. I knew it was going to be difficult going down here again, but what I hadn't expected was the weird tug I was currently experiencing in my gut. Where my mind was screaming at me to turn around my body was chanting: *Yes, yes, yes!*

Creepy.

Nevertheless, if there were prisoners, maybe even children down there, I needed to suck it up, for them at least. I ghosted through the door and rearranged myself in the dusty, torchlit passage behind it.

Of course, it was torch lit. No need for modern electricity in creepy castle passages.

The shadows were thick, stretching out across the floor as I descended. The stone walls quickly became damp and the air felt heavy. I suddenly was very aware that there was an entire castle above me.

A rat shot across the floor, right near my feet, and I clapped my hand over my mouth to stifle my surprised gasp.

I needed to get a grip. Except that once I reached the bottom of the stairs, it only got worse. I stopped walking as I heard the sound coming from ahead, where I knew the first block of cells were. It was a pained whimper, mixed with the occasional chuckle. As soon as I took a step forward, the laughter heightened, becoming unhinged and wild. Then it cut short. I froze as someone took a rattling breath and whispered, "Come closer, promised princess."

It was almost completely dark down here and I was cloaked by Nox's magic. Not to mention, whoever had spoken was a few cells down. There was no way they could see me and yet, they had.

Before I could think it through, my feet moved towards the voice, nearly on their own accord. They carried me to a cell near the end of the block. Inside was a young girl. I thought I recognized her somehow...

Oh, dear goddess Above.

EIGHTEEN

"Lina?" I whispered.

Inside the cell was the little girl, the oracle who'd come into the museum and had told me of my fate. She was curled up in the corner, wearing a loose, dirty shift dress. Large purple smudges encircled her eyes and her wrists were raw from the crude shackles around them.

Horror rushed through me as I realized Calum had not only been taking Unseelie children, but also children from his own court.

Lina smiled at me eerily and said, "My name no longer concerns me. It is yours you should be asking about."

"Lina, let me help you," I said, pocketing the moon-stone and corporealizing.

She shook her head and whispered, "There is nothing that can be done, princess. He is here, he's always been here and you can try to hide but he already sees you. He's *always* seen you. You have been his target from the beginning."

"You mean the demon?"

She smiled again in reply.

I wrapped a hand around the bar of the cell and asked, "It's because of the curse, isn't it?"

Her eyes were wide as saucers as she said, "The curse is but a wisp of magic. What he wants from you is much more than that. Your mate carries the other half of the promise and the reckoning will be his burden. But you are the bridge between time, the key to the lock that is not to be opened, the breaker of portals, and the keeper of the last light. He cannot find you here! It is not yet time."

She began to rock back and forth, muttering, "Run princess, run. Run, run, run, he will come and take you, run!"

I looked around frantically. I had to get Lina out of here, but I had no idea how. There was no one else in the other cells, so they must be keeping the prisoners from Nox's court somewhere else. I took a steadying breath and knelt down so that I was at her level.

"Lina, how can I help you?" I asked.

She looked me directly in the eye and whispered, "Run."

Then she began to scream shrilly, her hands pressed to her ears. I quickly grabbed the moonstone as the sound of footsteps approached. Two guards turned the corner, and I wondered why they hadn't come earlier, when I'd been talking to Lina.

I stood there, unmoving at first. But then Lina began to screech, "Run, run, run! He is coming! You must run!"

The guards looked around alarmed, their weapons drawn. When it became apparent no one was there, one of them said to Lina, "Stop screaming, human."

Lina's panicked expression froze. Then she slowly lowered her chin, smiled at the guards, and whispered,

"The reckoning is coming for you all. Enjoy your lungs while you can. Taste the air. Savor the beating of your hearts in your chest, because soon they will be torn out."

Nox had ripped a still beating heart from my attacker's body only days ago. Everything seemed to come back to us, which had to be impossible. We were both going to die soon.

Finally, as the guards started to walk away, I took Lina's command to heart and hurried out of the cell block and to the stairs of the passageway. Once I'd made it about halfway up, I doubled over, the moonstone still in my hand. Mr. Rat appeared again, squeaking wildly. I took that as a bad sign and continued up the stairs until I reached the main level again.

Even from my spot near the servants' hall, I could hear the raucous sounds of the feast still floating down the hall. I needed to reconvene with Nox, but I didn't want to risk trying to find him there. My only option was to wait for him, so I headed for his room.

As I floated there, I passed a couple of maids whispering in low tones.

"Something is happening, Mari," the smaller one said. "Something bad. I can feel it."

Mari, put her hands on her curvy hips and replied, "And what do you propose we do?"

"Flee."

The word was barely a puff of terrified breath. But I caught it.

Mari shook her head. "You know we'd be killed. The kitchen boy, you know, the little one, tried to run away last night. His Majesty had his head removed this morning."

"All the more reason to—"

"June, you silly girl, we just have to wait this out."

"Wait for what?"

Mari looked around nervously, then said so quietly I almost didn't hear, "I heard a whisper that the Night King is in league with our princess. Maybe she's finally coming home. Maybe this will be over soon."

I stopped listening after that. How could I? Their hope would be shattered when I inevitably died at the hand of Abaddon and the demons invaded our lands again. My uncle would remain the corrupt ruler and only the goddess knew if Nox would still be here.

I left the maids still whispering in the hall, heading back to Nox's room. Once I reached it and was safely inside, I set the moonstone down on the bedside table and began to pace, thinking over what I'd just heard in the dungeons.

Lina's warning had been freaky as hell, but it didn't make any sense. If I was supposed to be the breaker of portals and keeper of light or whatever, was I not going to die after all? But that didn't line up with what Nox had been telling me and what Abaddon, the demon prince himself, had told Nox. I huffed out a breath in frustration and sat down on the bed.

I just needed to gather the facts, just like if I was at work. Except none of them lined up and they nearly all contradicted each other. Abaddon, the Trial, Lina's omens, my uncle... they all began to meld into one maddening question.

What exactly was coming?

I gave up thinking and had laid back on the bed just as the door opened. My body froze momentarily in alarm, but I relaxed as I saw it was just Nox.

"Asteria," he said, a slight question to his tone as he saw my expression.

I worried my bottom lip, suddenly overwhelmed.

"What is it?" he asked, approaching me, his face lined with concern.

"I just—" but my voice broke before I could continue.

Nox set his crown on the bedside table and walked over to where I sat up on the edge of the bed. My breath was becoming uneven as I tried to blink away the tears burning at my eyes. I wasn't even sure exactly what I was upset about. I had a long list to pick from. But in that moment it felt like nothing and everything, all of it wrong.

Gently, Nox guided me back further onto the bed and then wrapped his arms around me, rocking me as stubborn tears slid down my face. His hand stroked my hair in slow, even motions as I came apart under his touch.

"We don't h-have time for t-t-this," I managed.

"Shh, my star. We have all the time in the world," he said.

I heaved in a breath and without thinking about my words, I said, "It's hard to be here. He..." I trailed off.

I'd never told anyone exactly what had happened inside these walls. Lil knew most of it, but there were things I'd kept from even her, whether out of shame or fear of her reaction. A moment ago, I'd been worrying about the future, but without even realizing it, the past had begun to catch up with me too as I remembered just where I was.

Nox's grip on me tightened slightly and he said, "If you want to say it, do so. If you don't, you do not need to. I'll be here either way."

I swallowed hard. There was a risk in telling him, just as there had been a risk in telling him about what happened to my parents. He could be disgusted with me or look at me with that horrible pity I usually got from Lil or Raven. But I felt a safety in his arms that I hadn't felt in years.

Maybe it was that or the threat of my imminent demise, but I ended up opening my mouth and letting it all come out. I told him about every moment that broke me, yet never defined me. I told him about the lashes on my birthday. About the broken noses and sprained fingers that Lil's mother would repair. About the hidden bruises in places I couldn't let her see. Because then she would know. She would know that I had been used and touched and raped and that I would never be the same.

And I told him how I replaced all that pain, all the unwanted feelings, with my choices. I made my body a canvas so colorful with touch that I had chosen for myself, that it covered up the ugly smudges of bright red hurt beneath.

And when I was finally done speaking, trembling, and ripped wide open, I looked at him. I don't know what I expected to see on Nox's face. But as I stared into his eyes, I saw something I hadn't expected to see after my confession.

Gentleness.

Softness was in his eyes, warming my cold, shaking hands, and slowing the frantic beat of my heart. He could've shown anger or rage, or even sorrow. And I was entirely sure he felt those things. But somehow, he knew that in this moment they were not what I needed. I needed someone to simply listen, understand, and look at me the same, nevertheless.

No one had ever done that for me. Not until now.

"I see you, Asteria," he said.

My lip trembled and I rasped, "Thank you."

"And I know how hard it must be to be here. I know because I walk the halls of a palace that shouldn't be mine by right every day. Walls within which I was shamed and abused too. But know that you are not just a victim, love. You are a fighter. And someday, I'm going to stand by proudly as I watch you rip apart those who hurt you and anyone who stood by and let it happen."

I should've been frightened by his promise of violence and of the violence I could be capable of, but I wasn't. His words made me feel excited and strong. They made me hopeful.

"Was the feast alright?" I asked after a brief lapse of silence.

Nox laughed incredulously. "It was a blatant display of the fucked up way your uncle runs this court."

"Care to elaborate?"

"Let's just say the men in power are at the top of the food chain. The women were either silent or serving, in whatever way the lords deemed necessary."

I got his insinuation. There had been prostitutes at the feast. I wasn't against sex work by any means, but these women likely were not there because they'd chosen to be.

"Lil and Raven aren't still there, right?" I asked.

"No, of course not," he paused, then asked, "Did you find anything?"

I took a heavy breath, then said, "He has prisoners from your court."

Nox's face immediately hardened.

I went on, "I heard Ewin, the captain of the guard, talking to someone about it. And I went down into the dungeons. I only found one person there. It was a little girl, a human oracle. I'd seen her once, not long ago, when her mother brought her into the museum. She'd told me then that my 'soul's mate would be the reckoning.' Just now, she was going on about how some person that she referred to as 'he,' already knew I was here. How he always knew where I was, but that it wasn't time yet."

Nox looked alarmed as he asked, "Did she say anything else?"

"Yes," I said, then recited the phrases: *The bridge between time, the key to the lock that is not to be opened, the breaker of portals, and the keeper of the last light.*

"Then she screamed," I said. "And told me to run. The guards came before I could even try to free her."

"Good," Nox said, his eyes glowing softly. "You should've run."

"She also said that 'the curse' was just a wisp of magic, or something along those lines. Do you think she meant...?"

"Yes," he replied. "My curse."

"What does it mean? Any of it?"

He took a deep breath and began, "There are things you don't know about me, love. About who... what I am. I didn't think any of it would matter, at least not yet. But I'm beginning to wonder—"

A knock cut him off.

Damn that door and everyone who knocked on it.

"Again," he said. "This isn't over. We'll talk more later."

"Later? Nox there might not be a..."

He shushed me with a finger over my mouth.

"Later."

I sighed loudly but he ignored me and walked over to the door. Unsurprisingly, Raven and Lil were waiting behind it. Nox let them in and I recapped what Lina had told me in the dungeons. As I did, Lil kept shooting me concerned looks. I knew my eyes were probably puffy and red, and she could read me like a book on a good day.

Later, I mouthed to her.

"Later" seemed to be a popular excuse for both Nox and I at the moment.

"So, what exactly are we going to do?" Raven asked.

His tone was still icy as he spoke to Nox, the echoes of their weird argument from earlier seeming to cause tension between them.

Nox seemed unconcerned by Raven's cold demeanor towards him. But he did seem more stressed than usual, running a hand through his hair as he said, "I've sent words to my court to be on standby should we need assistance tomorrow. But what you three need to know is—"

"Wait, like your forces would invade?" Lil asked.

Nox glanced at her. "Yes. Asteria has confirmed that King Calum is holding prisoners from my court. It's reason enough to go to war. But"—he looked directly at Raven—"if I should die tomorrow, I'll need you to sound the warning bell. I've informed them that you might be the one to get the message to them. If I fail the Trial, the minute you hear my neck snap, I want Unseelie forces alerted."

I flinched as Nox said the word *snap*. As if it was something so simple.

But Raven just nodded curtly and bit out, "Understood."

Nox went on. "And in that case, get yourselves out as fast as possible. My warriors will be ready to flit out all three of you and my court will be yours for refuge as long as you need it."

Raven suddenly looked a little uncomfortable as he

asked Nox, "Have you… has there been a discussion between you and your council about the line of succession?"

"Yes," Nox replied. "There has."

He didn't elaborate further and Raven didn't push. Lil chose that exact moment to yawn and Nox said, "We should probably all get some sleep."

"I agree," Lil said, yawning again.

Raven glanced at me and I realized I didn't have a room of my own. He and Lil began to head for the door and I stayed where I was.

"You coming, Aster?" Lil asked. "Or…" she trailed off, pausing at the incredulous look I gave her. "Nope, staying. Got it. Have fun."

Raven's jaw was set and the ghost of a smile was on Nox's face. I glared at Lil and she blew me a kiss before prancing out into the hall. Raven turned to face us before following her and said, "I still meant what I said earlier."

Before either Nox or I could reply, he left, shutting the door behind me. Once they were gone, I looked at Nox just as he said, "Would you like to have some fun, love?"

CHAPTER
NINETEEN

"WE SHOULD SLEEP," I said carefully, taking a step back.

His gaze roamed over me, ravenous. And I realized he had meant what he'd said earlier about not being finished. He very much intended to pick up where we'd left off on that bed a few hours ago. I almost told him no but...

He could die tomorrow.

My mate could die tomorrow. And I could too. Anything was in the cards at this point and we might never get another chance like this. I stayed still as he walked over to me.

"You're sure you want this?" I asked.

He traced a finger down my arm, leaving a trail of goosebumps in its wake.

"Love, I've had a very long time to think about the things I want when it comes to you. Our bodies may have just met but your dreams have been mine for years."

I raised my gaze slowly to find his eyes glowing softly again, for the second time this night.

"Show me," I whispered. "I want you to show me just how well you know my dreams… my desires."

"Anything," he said before catching my chin and tilting it up.

Our lips met, slowly at first, but more insistent as I let my mouth open to him, yielding all control. In the make-believe land of *later* I would show him just what I could do to him. But now, I wanted to understand his years of longing. I wanted to resolve the feeling of emptiness in my heart that I knew now had been the absence of him. So close, but untouchable—forbidden.

As we always would be to each other.

The niece of his enemy, heirs of two kingdoms at odds, cursed lovers, the reckoning of what could be the end of an age. There were so many ways I could spell out why we couldn't be together.

But tonight, I didn't care. I let him pick me up, wrapping my legs around his waist. He walked over to the bed unhurriedly and laid me down on top of the covers. His wings flared behind him and then I watched in fascination as they curled around us. They blocked out nearly all the light from the dim lamp on the bedside table, cocooning us in a new kind of darkness.

His hand paused, just a moment, at the edge of my shirt—a final question. But I nipped at his bottom lip in silent encouragement and he lost all semblance of control, nearly ripping the fabric from my body. Once it was gone and my torso was bare before him, he stared at me, his eyes dark.

A breath of a moment passed and then my back arched as his mouth closed over my peaked nipple, sending ripples of pleasure through me. The sensations were already almost too much, but he didn't let up. I gasped as his fingers teased between my legs. The fabric of my jeans was too tight and too rough. I wanted it gone. I wanted to feel him completely.

"Nox… please," I breathed, gripping at his shirt.

He lifted his head from my chest and met my eyes, desire ebbing from them. But his hands tightened on my thighs and I sensed that he was trying to win control back over himself.

I lifted my head slightly, letting my breath rush over the shell of his ear as I whispered, "I don't want you to hold back. Not now, not ever. Give me everything."

He sucked in a breath as I pulled back, laying on the bed. I lifted my hand and let my fingers trail along the edge of his wing. A sound escaped him, something between a strangled groan and a growl. Seconds later, my pants were being tugged off and his tunic was somehow gone too. I'd ask him later how he got it off with the wings. Frankly, right now, I didn't really care.

Once my legs were bare and I wore only my underwear he lowered his head, pressing his mouth between my thighs. The fabric there was so damn annoying and again, I wanted it gone, especially as I felt his tongue drag down, so close.

"Nox," I hissed, wanting more.

"Yes, love?"

He raised his gaze to meet mine and a rush of intensity shivered down my spine at the heavy look in his eyes. He kept his gaze on mine as he pushed the fabric aside with his fingers. The first touch set me aflame and I moaned softly, my back arching again.

"So sensitive," he murmured, just as he began to tease my clit.

"Fucking goddess Above," I said, my voice strangled and he chuckled softly.

But as he slid a finger inside of me, all humor disappeared from his face and he swore softly as another moan escaped me, louder this time. He added another finger and I began to move, grinding against his them. This already somehow felt like nothing I had ever experienced. Abruptly, he pulled his fingers out and I began to protest. But then he pulled my underwear off, flinging them over the side of the bed. And before I could even think, his tongue had replaced his fingers. He teased me at first and I made a disgruntled sound.

"Not what you want?" he murmured and I writhed as his words vibrated across my core. "Hmm," he said. "I like it when you're demanding."

I was just about to protest more when he let his teeth catch ever so slightly on my clit. I gasped and my legs widened. He gripped my thighs tightly as he devoured me. I was already nearing the edge and I bit back a loud cry as he pushed two fingers back into me. He lifted his mouth, ever so slightly as I began to grind against his hand again.

"That's it," he rumbled. "Good girl."

He curled his fingers and my eyes shot wide open.

"I can't," I gasped.

He pulled his fingers out and said, "You can."

His tongue took over again, licking and sucking until I was teetering so close to the edge and—

One last stroke had me shattering, a million stars bursting in my vision. I bit my lip hard, to keep from screaming. He didn't let up, even as I started to come back down to earth.

"Please," I choked out. "I can't—Nox, I—"

My voice cut off as I teetered on the edge of that cliff again. The sensations were almost too much now, but at the same time, I didn't want him to stop. He let up for only a moment, sucking the sensitive skin of my inner thigh between his teeth. But then he flicked a finger over my throbbing clit and I gasped, "Holy shit."

"Look at me, love."

I glanced down at him, at his glistening, swollen mouth and darkened eyes and nearly came just at the sight of it. He looked feral, as if was aware of just what he was doing to me. And then, without breaking my gaze, he curled a finger inside of me and commanded, "Come again."

"Nox…"

"I won't ask twice, love," he said, continuing to work me with his fingers.

This time, I hardly saw it coming. My back arched off the bed and my eyes rolled back, the world tilting and falling from beneath my suddenly weightless body. When I finally returned, limp and panting, he rose back up, kissing my neck softly. No way in hell was I done though.

He seemed to read my thoughts, because he said, "You should try to sleep."

"But I…" I trailed off as he brushed the hair back from my eyes.

"Sleep," he whispered.

Exhaustion was indeed beginning to pull me down, but I fought it, shaking my head.

"We don't get more time than this," I insisted, my voice breaking at the end.

He pressed his lips to my forehead and then said, very softly, "I will find you in the next life, Asteria. I promise you."

"No. It won't be you. It isn't supposed to be you."

He smiled sadly and replied, "The goddess will not find me worthy, my star. I've done too many horrible things in my life for that to happen. I'm just glad I met you. I will always be glad of that, until my spirit is but a whisper in the expanse of time."

I shook my head again, but before I could protest again, he laid down next to me and pulled my head against his chest. I listened to the steady beat of his heart as he stroked my hair. And as we lay there, I silently beseeched the goddess, whoever she was, to take me instead. I begged her to spare Nox, running through every reason why he was needed in this world more than I was. Still, every horrible, damning thing about me still didn't amount to the final plea, the final reason.

I don't want to be here without him.

CHAPTER
TWENTY

WHEN I WOKE up in the early hours of the morning, Nox was still asleep, his arms wrapped protectively around me. I glanced up at his face, nearly boyish in sleep, despite how old I knew he was.

I hadn't dreamed that night, of him or anything else. For some reason, due to our close proximity, I'd thought I might see him even while I was asleep. Though my dreams were the last of my concerns right now. I had somewhere I needed to check, one last time.

I attempted to wriggle out of Nox's arms without waking him, but he opened his eyes almost instantly.

"Asteria," he murmured, his voice still heavy and rough with sleep. He nudged my nose with his and asked, "Where are you trying to run off to?"

"How did you know?"

He brushed his lips against my jaw and said, "You tried to leave without waking me."

"Maybe," I replied coyly.

He glanced at me, his expression soft and open as he

said, "Did you really think I was going to let you run away before I could say goodbye to you?"

My chest tightened and I looked away as I said, "It might've been easier that way."

"I don't do easy."

I forced myself to look at him as I asked, "Out of choice, or because you can't?"

He ran his thumb over my lower lip and asked, "Are you asking if I chose you, or if you were inevitable?"

My cheeks grew warm and I muttered, "Well, not exactly—"

"Because the answer is both. I will choose you every damn time. But you are also a force that I tried very hard to resist, love. Obviously, I failed."

He sounded a little sad as he finished and instinctively I pressed a soft kiss to his cheek. Chaste, compared to what we did last night, but it carried no less weight. As I pulled back, Nox's eyes were wide.

"I have to go now," I whispered. "I'll be back in a little while."

Nox furrowed his brow. "I have a bad feeling about this."

I sat up and snorted softly. "Which part?"

"You should stay."

There was enough true worry in his tone that I paused and glanced back at him.

"I'll be back," I said again.

He reached out, pulling me back to him and kissing me roughly. Something about it was desperate and pained, and it almost made me consider staying here for now. But I forced myself to pull away and say, "I'll see you soon."

I got up off the bed, dressing quickly and then pulling

my hair into a ponytail. Nox watched me, not speaking, at least not until I reached the door.

"Be careful, Asteria."

I forced myself to smile. "Of course."

Then I picked up the moonstone and drifted out of the room. The halls were quiet and empty, and I slipped through them, invisible and in the shadows. It was still early in the morning, the sun just a tinge of brilliant pink hues peeking up from the horizon. Outside, birds chirped a pleasant melody, oblivious to the storm gearing up within the palace walls. I passed a few guards and there wasn't one of them who didn't look nervous, many of them talking amongst themselves in hushed tones.

I entered the royal wing and stopped short in front of my uncle's room, giving myself only a moment before facing what was inside. Because I needed to see him. He wouldn't be able to see me, but this wasn't for him. It was about me facing my fears. And maybe it was reckless, doing this. But I had such a strong feeling that I needed to be here, to see him for just a moment and finally know he couldn't hurt me anymore.

I breezed through the closed door and seemed empty inside at first. But then I heard his voice. I immediately felt a sharp spike of familiar fear. But I forced myself to take a short breath and then head towards the bathroom, just to catch a glimpse of him. As soon as I did though, I knew something was wrong.

He was staring into the mirror above the sink, talking to what seemed to be another person except... there was no one there. And between pauses, the tone and tenor of his voice would change slightly. Almost as if he were possessed by two different people.

Possessed.

Oh, no. Oh, goddess no.

I hoped I was wrong, but if my hunch was right... my uncle hadn't only summoned a demon.

One lived within him.

The moment I realized it, he met my eyes in the mirror. At that moment precisely, I knew I was very unfortunately right. Nox had warned me earlier that demons would be able to see past the wraith magic. And here Uncle Calum was, seeing what he shouldn't be able to see. As he stared at me, the strange pull I'd felt last night near the dungeons flared again. And quite suddenly, I realized just who this demon was.

"Abaddon," I whispered.

My uncle—Abaddon—smiled.

"Clever princess," he said. "Too bad you realized it too late."

"Why?" I breathed, letting the moonstone fall uselessly into the pocket of my pants. "Why are you here?"

"To reclaim what is mine," he said, his voice unnaturally calm. "This realm is ours. We won it twice and twice your kind took it back. No more."

He moved towards me and on instinct, I jerked my hand back into my pocket, pulling out the moonstone again. I pressed it to my lips, but it fell to the ground as I swerved to avoid my uncle's fist. I sprinted towards the door and reached it, just as his arm snagged around my waist.

"Not so fast," he hissed in my ear.

Then he slammed my head into the door and my vision went dark.

I woke up in a rank smelling prison cell. Like *really* rank.

There was something scratchy beneath my face, poking into my cheek and there were shackles around my wrists. Quickly, I figured out I was lying on a bed of straw, which was where the majority of the horrible smell was coming from. I scrunched my nose, trying to crawl away from the pile of who-knew-what soaked hay. It was nearly too dark to see and I bumped into the bars of the cell as I tried to escape the bed… or toilet. Or both.

I squinted, trying to get my vision to adjust. Eventually, I began to be able to make out shapes and little pricks of dim light. As soon as I could finally see more fully, I wished I couldn't.

Just outside my cell, there was a circle of dark stones full of strange, swirling symbols burned onto the ground. With a start, I realized I remembered this place. This was where the demon had entered me and where my parents had died. But now, scattered all around the room, were bones.

I gagged, heaving up nothing. Deep down, I knew—this was where the Unseelie Court members and their children had found their end. This was where *their* hope had died.

Frantically, I tried to stand up. I gasped, falling back down, my wrists burning. That was when I realized the shackles the bastards had put me in were made of iron, repellent to my faerie magic. I tried to wriggle out of them, wincing as I did so, but it was no use.

"Hello!"

My voice echoed around the chamber, but no one

replied. Nox hadn't come for me. No one was coming for me. I was probably going to miss the Trial and miss the last chance to see Nox. Everything went to hell.

I sank down onto the filthy floor, despair clouding my thoughts. There had to be something I could do, but I couldn't think of it. What could have been minutes or hours passed as I dozed off a few times against the wall. Though, I started as I heard footsteps approaching.

Two guards stopped directly in front of my cell, Ewin being one of them. He cleared his throat and began, "Princess Asteria Dianna Fairwae, I, Ewin Wells, Captain of the Guard of His Majesty, King Calum of the Seelie Court—"

"You can skip with the theatrics, Ewin. I'm quite aware of all our titles," I said. I was exhausted and hopeless, but I could still muster a little sass, just for Ewin.

His face twisted into a mix of anger and what I could have sworn was pity as he said, "You've been challenged with the Trial of the Goddess, princess."

"On what charge?"

Ewin cleared his throat. "For plotting against His Majesty, King Calum and his court with members of the Unseelie Court."

Well, I couldn't really deny that one.

"When?" I asked.

"Soon. But first, we've been instructed to take you to… prepare."

If that didn't sound ominous, I didn't know what did.

Ewin reached into his pocket and pulled out a key. He paused, then unlocked my cell. The guard next to him, who I didn't recognize, was staring nervously at the piles of bones.

"Julian!"

The guard jumped as Ewin shouted at him.

"You keep a hold on the princess. If she runs and escapes, it's your head on the line, understand?"

"Y-yes, Captain," Julian stuttered, his eyes still darting from me to the bones.

Ewin stepped into my cell and unlatched the shackles from the chain they'd been attached to. The cell door creaked as Julian opened it wider, stepping inside too.

"Up," Ewin commanded.

I stayed on the ground, smiling sweetly up at him. He growled, then hauled me up and shoved me at Julian, who caught me awkwardly.

"You still have a choice," I said, meeting his gaze. "You always have a choice."

Julian shook his head and whispered, "I'm sorry, princess."

I shifted, feeling for the moonstone in my pocket. It was gone, unsurprisingly.

"Where is King Nox?" I asked Ewin.

Ewin's face was set as he replied, "Awaiting his Trial."

"Where?"

Ewin gave me a strange look and said, "Why on earth do you think I'd tell you that?"

"It was worth a try," I muttered.

Ewin ignored me and strode away from the cursed circle of bones and symbols, leading us out of the cell block. After about a half mile of walking, I realized just how deep down we had been. The cell Lina had been in was much closer to the surface and it was empty when we passed it.

"Where is she?" I demanded.

Ewin glanced at the empty cell. "She's serving her purpose just as you're serving yours."

My stomach churned at his words, but I kept my chin held high and Julian gently tugged me into a passageway of stairs, different from the one I'd come from yesterday. Good to know the secret passageways I knew of were still secret.

All three of us walked in silence all the way up to the main level, the only sound the clanking of my chains. I tried to hide my winces, but the damn iron shackles hurt like bitch. Julian shot me a few apologetic looks, even sliding his fingers between my bare wrists and the iron a few times to give me relief. By the time we emerged from the passage, his fingers were raw and angry red. It made no sense. Why was he helping me, but not *helping* me?

I got my answer before we entered a room in the guest wing. Ewin stepped forward, pulling out another key and fitting into the lock of the door. And Julian leaned forward, so close that his lips brushed my ear as he whispered, "My sister, princess. I'm sorry, he has my sister. He'll kill her—"

"Julian!" Ewin bellowed. "Move away from the princess."

"Yes, Captain," Julian said quickly, releasing me and taking a step back.

I glanced back at Julian and blinked once.

It's okay, I tried to tell him silently.

He blinked back and I interpreted it as: *Thank you.*

Then, Ewin shoved me roughly inside the bedroom. It was like any of the guest rooms in this wing. A large bed, a vanity table, and an armoire in the corner. At the doorway to the bathroom, two maids waited, their faces taut and their hands clasped tightly in front of them.

"You have thirty minutes," Ewin barked at the maids.

"If one of you tries to help her escape or give her a weapon, I'll kill you on sight. Understood?"

"Yes, Captain," both of them murmured.

Surprisingly, Ewin pulled out yet another key and unlocked my iron shackles, jerking them off my wrists roughly enough that I couldn't hold in the hiss of pain. He tossed them on top of the bed carelessly.

One of the maids, a young faerie girl with kind brown eyes, said quietly, "Come, princess."

I walked over to them, noticing Ewin didn't follow, but remained inside the room, in front of the door. The young faerie took my hand and led me into the bathroom. The other, an older faerie who was visibly trembling, said to me, "We're to help you bathe, princess."

"I don't think I need—"

"Let us help you, princess," the younger one said.

Both of their expressions were earnest enough that I conceded, nodding, and saying, "Alright."

There was already a warm bath waiting, flower petals floating atop the water. I undressed quickly and the maids averted their eyes until I sank into the bathwater, which smelled of rose oil. The maids poured shampoo into my hair and gently massaged my scalp before rinsing it and repeating the process with conditioner. Their touches were gentle and kind and I knew that they were as blameless as Julian. They were both probably trying to protect their families or friends, or even just themselves. In any sense, I didn't blame them.

Once they were done helping me with the bath, the young girl handed me a soft towel. The maids turned respectfully as I stepped out of the bath and toweled off.

The older one disappeared into the bedroom, making sure to keep the door mostly closed for my privacy.

"Princess," the young faerie whispered, hardly looking at me.

I glanced at her. "What is it?"

"Can I... may I say the parting rite for you?"

I swallowed. Faeries had ancient, traditional words of farewell for honored deaths; soldiers, monarchs, mothers lost to childbirth. And this girl very much thought I was going to die if she was offering them to me. But her voice was gentle and I knew her intentions were good, so I replied, "Just be quick, so you don't get in trouble."

She nodded, closing the distance between us, and pressing two fingers to my forward and then whispering rapidly, "Daughter of the sky, sister to the sun, cherished child of the moon, may the goddess hold you gently. May you rest easy in the stars with those who came before and may your soul find its home in the Light."

She stepped away just as the older maid reappeared with a bundle of fabric in her arms. She looked from the girl to me but said nothing of what had just occurred. Instead, she set the fabric, a dress, down on the counter. Silently, they dressed me in a set of strange undergarments, what I assumed to be something the ladies at court wore beneath their dresses. Then I stepped into a soft, navy-colored dress, the fabric so dark it was nearly black.

"Five minutes!" I heard Ewin shout.

The maids ignored him, instead focusing on brushing my hair, swabbing my wrists with perfume, and then, as a finishing touch, clasping a delicate chain of diamonds around my neck.

"There," the older maid said. "Now you're ready to meet your sweet mother again."

I looked at her sharply but she only curtsied and stepped away. The younger one opened the door and led me back to Ewin, who looked impatient as he said, "That was nearly ten minutes."

"My apologies, Captain," the girl said, bowing her head.

"And why is she wearing a necklace?"

The girl swallowed and replied, "It was her mother's."

"Then it belongs to the crown. It will only be wasted today."

Right... because a noose was about to be the only necklace I would wear again. The girl seemed to realize that too, paling and then gently unclasping the necklace and setting it to the side.

Ewin grabbed my arm and said, "They're waiting for you, princess. Let's go."

We stepped out into the hall, and without warning, Ewin flitted us out of the palace.

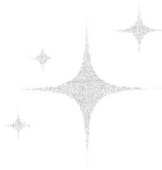

CHAPTER
TWENTY-ONE

WE LANDED ABRUPTLY on the top of a grassy hill. Ewin didn't let go of my arm, clasping it so tightly I knew his fingers would leave bruises in their wake. Not that it mattered, not anymore.

It was early morning, which meant I must have spent the entirety of the night in that cell. Ewin had said Nox was still awaiting his Trial, so they must have pushed it back, just for me. How kind of them.

A cool spring breeze blew through my loose hair as I looked out across the landscape. We were atop one of the many rolling hills in the southern corner of the Seelie Court. Almost immediately, my gaze snagged on a familiar gnarled tree at the bottom of the hill we stood on. I was transported back to my childhood, on a different morning, when my father had sentenced someone else to the Trial.

This time, my uncle stood at the head of the small crowd surrounding the tree, the silver crown of ivy shining atop his head. He looked back as Ewin dragged me down the hill and towards the hanging tree. Nox was nowhere to be seen, but I quickly found Raven and Lil in the crowd, still glamoured. My eyes met Lil's, her expression frantic. Next to her Raven mouthed, *Hold on.*

Someone was coming. We just needed to stall until they did. But where the hell was Nox?

"The Night King of the Unseelie Court has betrayed us all!" my uncle shouted. "His offense: summoning demons back into our world, is so great that not even I can decide upon his fate! Only the goddess sees."

"Only the goddess sees," the crowd murmured.

"Additionally, my niece, the princess of the Seelie Court, has been found to be conspiring against my throne and my council! She will also stand Trial today for this grievance. Only the goddess sees."

The crowd was a little quieter this time as they murmured the phrase back to him and a few people even looked shocked. It looked like the knowledge of my coming execution hadn't been widely known until now. My heart sank a little as I saw Lil's parents in the crowd, lingering near the back. Her mother looked like she was about to cry. I didn't doubt that my uncle had required her to be here.

Ewin led me forward, past the gathered crowd and to where a small wooden platform sat just below the noose.

"Nice setup," I said to my uncle or the demon, or both —I didn't know anymore. "Upgraded from the wooden stool, I mean."

My uncle smiled and said, "So cocky, even when facing your death."

I simply returned his smile and replied, "If not now, then when?"

He narrowed his eyes at me, just a crack sounded through the air and Nox materialized a few feet away, in front of us. His wrists were bound in iron and two guards were flanking him, holding onto him tightly. His jaw was set and his eyes were glowing again as they met mine. And like me, it looked like they'd had him dress up for the occasion. He wore a pristine suit, complete with shining dress shoes, though his crown was missing.

My uncle—or Abaddon—leaned in and whispered in my ear, "You can thank your mate for the fact that you're still alive. Your execution would've occurred last night in the depths of the dungeons, but dear little Nox made quite a fuss. Killed nearly fifteen of my guards trying to get to you before he finally agreed that he would stop, as long as you went free. Well, here you are. You're free, as long as the goddess finds you worthy."

Nox fought against the guards, snarling, "Bastard."

There had to be another plan. Nox wouldn't have been stupid enough to make a deal like that with my uncle, even without knowing he was possessed by a demon. I also knew he could easily escape the hold of those two guards if he really wanted to. Something else was going on here.

I was led up onto the crudely cut platform, the breeze swirling around my ankles. Nox struggled against the guards restraining him, true rage flashing in his eyes, especially as the noose was placed around my neck. It was rough and scratchy and I squirmed a little. As if my comfort mattered in this situation.

I looked out at the crowd, a mixture of shock, pity, and anger on their faces. Between that moment and the next, I made a decision I'd been avoiding for most of my life.

I held my head up high and proclaimed, "I am Princess Asteria Dianna Fairwae, daughter of Theodore and

Dianna Fairwae. I am the rightful heir to the throne. I am your true queen."

It was the first time I'd ever claimed my title as my own.

I figured that if I was going to die, I should at least do it being exactly who I was. And I had to tell them the truth. All of them, including Nox.

"King Calum was the one who summoned the demon!" I shouted over the wind that was picking up. "He did it many years ago when I was merely a child. He lies to you every day, in order to keep his hold on a throne that is mine by right!" I paused, meeting Nox's eyes. And I said, almost too quietly for the crowd to hear, "Your king is no longer truly of our world. The demon prince, Abaddon, possesses his body."

Nox's eyes widened and my uncle's face twisted into an ugly display of rage.

"Lies!" he hissed. "The traitor lies!"

The crowd began to shift and murmur, just as I heard several loud cracks split through the air. Someone was flitting into the area, just behind me. My uncle turned and the rage he wore sharpened.

"Drop the platform!" he screamed at the guards, spit flying from his mouth.

Faeries wearing dark leather battle suits emerged from my periphery. They all carried a mixture of sharp swords, loaded bows and arrows, and even a few firearms. The man leading them carried a flag bearing the sigil of the Unseelie Court: a half-moon covered by a cloud of shadowed night. Relief pulsed through me as I realized Nox's forces were here.

In the crowd before us, I saw Raven pushing Lil ahead just as Nox dropped their glamours. Their mother shouted in alarm as her children appeared. Lil shouted my name frantically, her eyes wide with fear. A group of nearly ten of my uncle's guards flanked the platform I was on and Unseelie warriors fought to get past them. Blood sprayed at my feet, splattering over the fabric of my dress. Nox freed himself from the guards who had been restraining him. The faerie who was leading the Unseelie forces reached Nox, bending his shackles apart and pulling them off, as if they were made of cardboard and not iron.

To my left, my uncle screamed, "Do it, you idiots!"

One guard, a young looking faerie with auburn hair and brilliant green eyes, stared at the lever that controlled the platform. He looked up at me for half a second. Then he reached for the lever.

Nox's eyes widened as he roared, "STOP!"

My uncle just smiled, nodding at the guard, who paused for only a second more before pulling the lever. The platform beneath me fell away just as Nox began to rush towards me. The last thing I saw were his glowing amber eyes. Then, the deafening sound of my neck cracking filled my ears as my world went dark forever.

CHAPTER
TWENTY-TWO

I WAS MADE OF STARLIGHT.

Or maybe I was starlight. I didn't think I had a body here. Wherever the "here" was. It was dark, but also glowing softly, almost fuzzy around the edges. It was as if my vision couldn't quite focus on anything. I reached my hand out, the strange, heavy air swirling between my fingers.

"Asteria Fairwae."

I turned as a familiar-sounding voice said my name. Standing before me was a woman who looked very much like me. In fact, for a moment, I wondered if she somehow was me. Our faces were a mirror and our eyes were matching blue portals. Her irises were softly glowing and I knew mine had to be too. We were one in the same... that much I knew.

"Who are you?" I asked, my voice just a whisper on the wind of time.

She smiled, though it wasn't quite a warm smile. It was guarded and her expression was closed off. Looking at her expression, I felt as if someone had not only painted my features, but also personality, my essence, and quirks, onto another identical body. She was me and yet she was not.

"Before, they called me the Maiden," the woman began. "Then, I was the chosen wielder of starlight. In time I became much more than that. But that was after they tried to kill me, just as they tried to kill you."

"Aren't I dead?" I asked.

She chuckled and reached out her hand, stroking a featherlight touch down my very essence. It was a strange feeling, as if she was touching both my mind and my body at the same time.

"My dear," she said. "You are much more than a fragile life force. You *are* life. You are light."

I shook my head. "I don't understand."

The goddess standing before me sighed loudly in a way that really made me think she was me, or at least my twisted twin.

"There is much you are unaware of," she said.

"Care to explain?"

She gave me a look and said, "I was getting to it, my dear."

"Sorry, sorry, go on."

She looked a little irritated and began to pace as she explained, "Long ago, during the first Long Night, when Hell's kin crawled up onto the earth, I was simply a young Fae girl. But everything changed, on the eve of my twenty-first birthday, when I was visited by a young man with silver hair and fiery golden eyes."

Surprise lit me up—wait, *actually* lit me up—and the goddess must have noticed because she smiled slyly and said, "Yes, I will get to that part of the story soon."

I could only nod.

Continuing her back-and-forth walk, she went on, "The young man told me his name was Sameul and that he was from Above, where the gods and their kin dwelt, along with a warrior class known as the Nephilim, which he belonged to. He couldn't stay long, as his form was not compatible with our world and he would soon fall to Hell if he remained. But he told me I was to be a conduit of pure starlight. I was to be the first 'goddess on earth' as he put it, the only being of our realm to possess this kind of power. He touched my forehead," she pushed back her dark bangs, and my eyes widened as I saw the four-pointed star glowing there, "and he marked me as a being of Above."

"At first, I was feared by my own people for the power I suddenly possessed and the mark I wore. They tried to hang me on a tree in the southern hills of my court. But I would not die. When they asked what I was, I told them I was a goddess who came to shield them from what was coming. And Hell's creatures did come. But with my newfound power, and the aid of both faerie courts, I cast them back to their realm. I thought the nightmare was finally over. And it was, in a way. Except that Sameul had made a grave mistake when he came to our world."

She paused for dramatic effect. I would have laughed at it if I hadn't been so shocked at everything she was saying.

"He gave his heart to a Fae woman. As I said before, he could not stay long in our realm and he was long, long gone by the time his son was born. The situation was complicated, as the woman was already married, and to a king, nonetheless. And as her son grew, her husband began to realize his heir looked absolutely nothing like him, nor did he carry his scent."

Holy *fuck*.

I must have said the words aloud because the goddess smiled and chuckled softly before continuing, "Your mate is far older than he lets on. But in a way, so are you."

"I defeated Hell during that first Long Night. But Nox's presence in your world caused an imbalance. He was two halves of two separate realms and it caused a rift in the energy that holds worlds together and keeps them separate. The demon prince, Abaddon, used this imbalance of energy to manipulate and widen a small crack in the closed portal between Hell and your realm. When I realized the demon horde was returning, I knew I would not have enough strength to defeat them again. But I thought that Sameul's son, the offspring of a creature of Light from Above, might be able to take my place. My body passed on, and I became as you see me now. I met Sameul once more and though I was tired, he claimed that there was more to be done."

"Another Long Night, a final one, would come someday and starlight would once again be needed. His son would not be enough, not a second time, as his power was partially diluted, whereas mine was pure. But I was tired and I did not want to return to your world. Sameul proposed a solution—my core self, my memories, my emotions, my conscious mind, would stay with him. I could live out my days as an overseer of your world. But my spirit and the power I once held would be projected far ahead in time, into the body of a Fae babe who shared my bloodline. You, Asteria."

A loud, whirling wind filled the space. I wondered if it was somehow a manifestation of my own shock and confusion. Once it died down, I asked, "So, I'm the only one who can prevent the demons from coming back?"

She shook her head. "No, my dear. The final Long Night has already begun. You are the only one who will be able to *end* it, for good this time. If you return, your mate can train you, as he is the only one who understands the power you have. And then—"

"If I return?" I asked, cutting her off. "Do you mean I have a choice?"

She smiled, more warmly this time and replied, "Of course. You always have a choice, even in death."

I thought about it for a moment. I knew the path ahead would be difficult and painful if I went back. And if I stayed here, maybe I could see my parents. Finally have some peace. But then, an image flashed through my memory; Lil laughing so hard she spit out her wine. Then another; Raven, grinning as we danced in the backseat of his car. And there was Nox, my mate. Nox, who had given everything and lost it all too. He couldn't do this on his own.

And with that, I had my answer.

I had to go back. But more importantly, I wanted to. I wanted life and love, even if it brought more pain. So, I looked at the goddess whose spirit I held, and said, "Send me back. Now, before it's too late."

She glanced around at the wind as it began to pick up again and sighed.

"You're right, we are running short on time. One last thing, Asteria. Remember that your mate is not merely a creature of your world. You need him, but sometimes, his actions will not make sense. They will feel like betrayal, because it is not in your nature to understand that they are right or good. Sometimes, good wears a mask of evil so that the monsters will not find it."

Confusion rushed through me at her words, and I began to ask, "What do you mean?"

But she was already fading away into the whirling chasm of wind.

"Good luck," she whispered just before she disappeared completely.

But I was still here. Why was I still here?

Suddenly, the ground beneath my feet disappeared and I was falling, falling, falling...

When I opened my eyes, I was watching a scene unfold in front of me. My body felt smaller than normal and someone had a death grip on my hand. I figured out very quickly that I had no control over the body I was in. The feelings and emotions that rushed through me felt foreign, yet familiar. Whoever this was, was sad, so deeply sad, and terrified too.

Though my attention was quickly pulled away from those feelings as I heard the agonized, guttural sounds that were coming from ahead. The body I was in looked up and so I did too, meeting Raven's bright green eyes. That was when I realized I was seeing the world through Lil's eyes.

And ahead, just below the gnarled hanging tree, Nox held the limp form of someone in his arms—me, I realized. The Unseelie warriors encircled him, their faces set into snarls that warned anyone who might try to approach to stay back. A few feet away, my uncle was standing very still, surrounded by his own group of guards. No one in the crowd spoke a single word or dared move as Nox slowly looked up from my body, pure, undiluted rage lighting a fire in his eyes as he stared at my uncle. The guards closed in tighter around my uncle, many of their faces twisted in fear.

Then, there was a shift in the air.

The pleasant spring breeze became cooler and the shadows grew longer. A prickle crept up the back of Lil's neck and a few faeries looked up at the sky as it darkened with swirling clouds. My uncle rolled his neck and a smirk grew wide across his face. And I knew that Calum, cruel, cruel Calum, was now entirely gone. In his place was pure evil.

Abaddon.

"What did you think would happen?" Abaddon said, sneering at Nox. "You made a deal with me and I simply claimed my prize when you failed."

"I will kill you for this," Nox snarled, still not letting go of my lifeless body. "I will turn you to ash and I will scatter your remains so deep in the pits of Hell that you will never be whole again."

Abaddon rolled his eyes. "How valiant of you. Spoken like the true son of a Light warrior. But you are not your father, Nox. You are weak, like your poor, dead Fae mother."

Nox growled; the sound unhinged. Lil began to shake as she—we—watched Nox's eyes start to glow brighter than I'd ever seen them before. I knew what was about to happen. He was trying to dredge up his power and he would burn himself out completely trying to destroy Abaddon. He would fail and I would lose him. I needed to return to my body *now*.

I began to push, far, far away from Lil. It felt like clawing through thick, churning water as I crawled back to my body. For a moment there was darkness and I was afraid that I'd somehow gotten lost in some in between. But finally, I opened my eyes.

I knew there would likely be pain when I woke up, but this was worse than I expected. My throat was on fire and my limbs felt like they'd been torn off and stuck back on at odd angles. Still, somehow found the strength to rasp, "Nox."

He didn't look down, still staring at Abaddon in rage.

Again, I said his name, louder this time, "Nox."

I think Abaddon noticed my miraculous return to life first, because the smirk slid right off his face as his eyes flicked down to meet mine. I winked at him and he took a step back in shock. I took great satisfaction in the fact that I'd surprised a prince of Hell.

Finally, Nox looked down at me, his body becoming unnaturally still.

"Asteria?" he said, his voice breaking.

I took a deep breath and said, "You didn't really think they could kill me that easily? There are no tequila shots in the afterlife."

He let out a strangled sound that was somewhere between a sob and a laugh. Behind, someone shouted, "Is she alive?"

I lifted a hand and waved awkwardly from my spot in Nox's lap. A hushed murmur rushed through the crowd. The last time this had happened was when the Maiden became the goddess. Which, I supposed was me now since I had her spirit.

As I dropped my hand, Calum—Abaddon—began to advance towards Nox and I, shadows swirling around him. His blue eyes were gone, instead replaced by pits of endless, swirling black. It looked like the game was up. The demon was no longer hiding from my uncle's court.

Ewin backed up away from him, his eyes wide and his face sheet white.

I struggled to sit up and muttered under my breath, "You knew what he was, you idiot. What did you expect a demon to look like?"

Nox must have heard me because let out a small, strained chuckle.

The other guards followed Ewin's lead, stepping away from Abaddon. One even tried to flit away before a shadow flowing from the demon grabbed the guard by the throat and shoved him to the ground. His body was still after that.

The shadow limbs began to creep towards us and someone in the crowd screamed. But before it could touch Nox, me, or his Unseelie warriors, a wall of concentrated, solid light cocooned us.

I stared at the blindingly bright shield for a moment and said to Nox, "Nice trick."

He nodded wordlessly, staring at me as if I was the sun and the moon in one.

"They need our help," I said, sitting up and wincing at the screaming of my muscles and my lungs.

Nox didn't move or let me go, his jaw tight. I touched his face momentarily, staring into amber eyes that were still aglow with that otherworldly light.

"Coddle me later," I whispered. "Right now, I need you to help me stand, so we can save everyone on this hill."

He swallowed, catching my hand as I pulled it away.

"I have questions, love," he said.

"And I'll answer them," I replied. "Later."

Someone screamed again beyond our shield, the sound

echoing shrilly around us. Nox helped me stand upright before dropping the shield, one hand wrapped around my waist to steady me. The pure light faded away to reveal that the world around us had nearly gone dark and the storm clouds that had been brewing on the horizon were now circling eerily above us.

My eyes widened in horror as I realized that the scream a moment ago had come from Lil. Raven lay unconscious on the ground a few feet away, as if he'd tried to protect her and Abaddon had thrown him aside. There were no other demons here yet, which was a relief, but was also confusing. The goddess had said the Long Night had already begun. Wouldn't they all be coming to Abaddon's aid now? Or maybe he didn't think he needed their help....?

Every thought flew out of my head as I watched Abaddon advance towards Lil.

"No!" I cried.

He glanced back at me with a devious grin and then picked Lil up as easily as if she was a doll. Her mother cried out, lunging forward. But Lil's dad caught her before she could run at the demon holding her daughter. She screamed as Lil's eyes rolled back in her head.

I grabbed onto Nox's hand, still wrapped around my waist, and said, "I need you to try to stop me if I go too far."

I knew he understood my meaning as he squeezed my hip. I took a deep breath and then I closed my eyes.

When I opened them, pure light was flowing from me, snaking across the grassy earth just as Abaddon's shadows did. I focused on concentrating it all towards the demon standing at the head of the crowd of terrified faeries. Lil's mom was sobbing openly as her daughter's body lifted into the air, swirling shadows surrounding her.

"Enough," I snarled.

Abaddon glanced at me, as if I were nothing but a nuisance. But as my light reached him, it began to permeate through his shadows, like beams of sun casting holes in a cloudy sky. His magic grip on Lil weakened, the shadows dissipating. She fell to the ground next to Raven, her small body crumpled. As much as I wanted to rush to her, I knew I wasn't done. I tugged harder on that well of power inside of me. Abaddon laughed as it began to consume me.

"Are you going to kill them, Aster?" he said. "Are you going to kill them just like you killed your—"

My scream of rage cut through the air as my magic exploded across the hillside. More and more, it took and my mind became blank in its grasp. Still, Nox did not let go of my hand. His other was outstretched, holding a luminescent shield over everyone else. I burned and burned, channeling every bit of anger towards the demon inside of my uncle. Vaguely, I felt my grasp on the power begin to slip.

More, more, more!

It tugged sharply, demanding for me to give into its thrall. And I was slipping fast. Soon, I would not be Asteria Fairwae anymore and everyone on this hillside would be reduced to nothing but ash. This was otherworldly magic, and though it was mine, I was not accustomed to its endless magnitude.

My vision flashed red and I gasped out in clipped words, "I'm losing control."

I felt the arm around my waist tighten and Nox said in my ear, "You're alright."

"No, I can't—"

"Come back, love. Come back to me."

He didn't sound alarmed or angry and the gentle notes of his voice soothed the magic within me. As always, he seemed to know exactly what I needed and slowly, slowly, the power ebbed back into me, my eyes fluttering shut. When the light finally died down completely, I opened them. Nox's shield was still up, but he dropped it to reveal the scene around us. Faeries were quivering, many of them cowering on the ground with their hands covering their heads.

"Let go of me," I said softly to Nox. "Just for now."

He looked reluctant but released his grip on my waist. I saw Lil begin to stir, just as I began to advance towards my uncle. As I strode past them, many of the faeries bowed their heads in respect, some of them murmuring, "Blessed goddess."

When I reached my uncle's body, it was curled up on the earth, blackened by powdery ash. When he lifted his head to look up at me, I froze.

His blue eyes, my blue eyes, were unclouded and bright as my father's had been. As his eyes had once been too. Deep down, I knew the demon was gone. And I didn't know what that meant. Was he just as evil, or would he be different? And how would I separate out his actions from the actions of the demon. Who had abused me all those years?

I stayed still as he struggled to lift his head. Seconds later, Nox was at my side.

"Don't move," he commanded icily.

My uncle obeyed. I wasn't sure he even had the strength to stand as he said weakly to me, "So, your father wasn't lying about the magnitude of his heir's power. What you did that night all those years ago was magnificent. But this was... unprecedented."

I flinched and his answering smile was cruel.

"He always knew what you were, your father. He held so many secrets in that head of his, as did your mother. It was a mistake on his part, trusting me with the knowledge. Because once he told me just what you were, I knew I'd never take the throne, not while you were living."

"So, you summoned a demon?" I asked, unable to hide the quiver in my voice.

"I was young," my uncle said, as if that atoned for everything. "The demon claimed he would take your father's magic and in turn make him unfit to rule. And then he would kill you. I didn't know he would overtake my body."

"Was it you or him? All those years... hurting me."

I wasn't exactly sure why I asked the question. But I needed to know. I needed to see if I could separate the man from the monster that had lived within him. I was sorely disappointed as my uncle replied, "Both of us," as if it were a simple, easy thing to say.

"Where is the demon prince now?" Nox demanded from beside me.

My uncle grinned weakly and said, "He likely took over another body. It's what he's been helping others of his kind do for years, ever since I summoned him. They are all around you, in the bodies of those you once cared for and trusted. No one can be trusted now, not even..." he took a heaving breath.

But he never finished the sentence as his blue eyes fixed on the horizon.

230

CHAPTER
TWENTY-THREE

I STARED at my uncle's still, lifeless body and felt nothing. How many times had I pictured this moment... pictured finally defeating him? Now, it was bittersweet, with the acrid taste of the parting knowledge he'd given us sitting on my tongue. Beside me, Nox was stiff, though his hand grasped mine, entwining our fingers.

"King Nox?"

We both turned to see a man, one of the faeries that had come to our aid from the Unseelie Court. I let my gaze slide over him as he approached us. His short crop of hair was dark and so were his eyes; such a deep shade of brown that they were nearly black. He was built with cords of muscle that moved under the tight battle leathers he wore as he stopped in front of us. And right under his left eye, a jagged scar cut his face in half, creating a deep rift in his cheek, barely missing his mouth. Though he looked generally intimidating, his expression wasn't cruel. In fact, it was familiar in a way I couldn't quite place.

Nox raised a brow at him and said, "How many times do I have to tell you, Griffin? Just Nox."

Griffin smiled tightly and replied, "I know, my friend. But we're among... interesting company."

Indeed, the crowd of Seelie Fae were beginning to recover, standing up shakily and staring warily at Nox and me. I started to pull my hand away from Nox's, but he held fast.

"I need to speak to them," I said, indicating my head towards the crowd.

He held my gaze and I saw fear shining in his eyes. Not fear of me, I realized, but fear *for* me.

"I just watched you die," he said, his voice breaking off slightly on the last word.

I swallowed and, damn, did it hurt. Stupid, haughty goddess couldn't have taken away all of the pain when I woke up? But I ignored it for now, gently pulling my hand from Nox's as I said, "I'm here now. I promise, we'll talk about this later and I'll explain everything. But they need me right now."

Griffin was watching our interaction quite closely, his expression a mix of wariness and curiosity. I realized he was probably very keen to know more about me—the lost Seelie princess and his king's mate, who had been sequestered away without his knowledge for nearly a week in his own court.

"Go," Nox said, glancing up at the still-dark sky. "But be quick, love. We need to get off this hill."

I squeezed his hand then let go. But just as I turned to move closer to the crowd, I was intercepted by a small body crashing into me.

Lil's arms wrapped around me as she sobbed, "Aster, oh goddess."

I hugged her tightly, despite the fact that it kind of hurt, and said, "I'm okay. I promise, I'm okay. Are you?"

She looked up at me, her face tearstained and said, "I'm fine."

"You're sure?"

She touched my cheek and assured me, "Really, I am. But Raven won't wake up."

A stone dropped in my stomach at her words. In the blur of my power and then my uncle dying, I had nearly forgotten about Raven, thrown aside by the demon.

"Where is he?"

"My parents are with him. But Aster... you might want to address the rest of the crowd before you do anything else."

I pursed my lips and said, "I know. Then we all need to get out of here."

Lil nodded, glancing at the darkened horizon. She let me go, standing just behind me as I turned to the group that had gathered to watch my death. I paused for a moment, nerves making my heart race. Then I began.

"The third Long Night of our world has begun. Demons walk among us. Now is no longer the time for court divides and political feuds. We will all need to work together if we are going to survive this. Go home. Prepare yourselves. Talk to your children and warn them that dark times are coming. And know that should you need refuge; your queen will provide it within the palace walls."

No one moved. Not at first. But then, to my surprise, Lil's father met my eyes, bowed his head, and took to his knee. Lil's mother, who was leaning over Raven, bowed her head and then, one by one, the entire crowd followed suit.

"Long live the queen," Lil proclaimed, sinking down right in front of me.

The crowd followed her lead, repeating the words, some in hushed whispers, others louder and more surely. Fear rushed through me as I stood before them all. I never thought I'd take my crown. But now people were kneeling before me.

"Rise," I said, just as my father had once told his court. I tried to hide the uneven tremble in my voice as I uttered the word.

Everyone scrambled to their feet. A few gave me final nods of respect before promptly flitting off the hill, the cracks cutting through the charged air. Eventually, of all the Seelie Fae, only Lil and her family remained. I rushed over to them, kneeling down in front of Raven.

His face was pale and a trickle of blood had begun to dry on his forehead. His mother was gently stroking his hair, guilt and sorrow etched into her soft face. My senses pricked and I turned to see Nox standing behind me.

Lil's mother's eyes widened and she said, "King Nox."

"We can take him to the palace," Nox said. "He needs a healer."

"Mom, can't you wake him up?" Lil asked, her voice wobbly.

Her mother pursed her lips and shook her head as she said, "I've tried to… but maybe my skills aren't adequate enough for this kind of injury."

"What do you mean?" I asked her.

Her eyes were glassy with tears as she said, "He's in some kind of coma. I can't detect what exactly is keeping him from waking, but it's some sort of magic. I can feel it permeating into him and... it's not natural, or at least not something I recognize."

Fear gripped at me as I glanced back down at Raven. On the horizon, the storm clouds were darkening. Nox looked at them again for the umpteenth time and said quietly, "We need to go."

Lil glanced at her mother and father and asked, "Are you coming with us?"

Her mother glanced up at her husband, then shook her head and replied tearfully, "You go, my darling. But please send word as soon as you have any news."

Lil's expression fell but she nodded, murmuring, "Alright."

Her mother took my hand and said to me, "You're going to make a wonderful queen, Aster."

I smiled tightly and said, "Go. We'll let you know as soon as we know what's going on."

She sniffled, let go of my hand, and stood, giving Lil a tight hug, and murmuring something in her ear. I tried not to listen to whatever it was, wanting to give them some privacy. Then she pulled away and both her and Lil's father bowed their heads one last time before disappearing with a crack.

A droplet of water hit my nose and I looked up at the sky. When I looked back around me, Nox's Unseelie warriors were circling around us. Griffin approached me and knelt down next to Raven.

"I can carry him. I'll flit directly to the healers," he said.

I narrowed my eyes at him, scrutinizing. There was something about him that was nagging at me... something oddly familiar. It made me trust him instantly, which was more unsettling than anything.

"You hurt him and it'll be the last thing you do," I said.

A smile slowly spread across Griffin's face, softening the hard lines of it. He glanced up at Nox and said, "Now I believe you."

Nox's mouth lifted only slightly and he said, "Go, Griffin. We'll see you there."

Griffin nodded, scooping Raven's limp body gently into his arms. Something shuttered in the warrior's expression as he glanced down at Lil's brother. But before I could place what he was feeling, they were gone.

Finally, I stood up and returned to Nox's side. He took my hand again immediately and asked, "Ready to see my court, love?"

"Haven't I already?"

He shook his head. "Not truly."

"Then I'm ready, I suppose."

His grip on my hand tightened. After a moment's pause, Lil warily let one of the other Unseelie warriors take hers. And then we left the gnarled hanging tree behind. My uncle's body remained, crumpled on the dampening earth.

Not one of us suggested taking it with us.

·✦·

The first thing I noticed about the Unseelie Court were the people.

Nearly as soon as we flitted into the entry hall of the palace (which, mind you, *was* pretty intimidating, with shining black marble floors and a ceiling painted like the night sky) several faeries and an aged siren greeted Nox, all wearing expressions of concern. A few of them bowed to me and I realized that Nox must have told his court about me. The thought both alarmed me and warmed me in a weird, fuzzy way.

Nox assured them that he was fine and the faeries and the siren cleared away. Once they were gone, I took the chance to drink in the palace. Aside from the starry ceiling and impressively clean floors, there was a grand staircase just ahead that swept up to a balcony on the second level. Richly dark purple roses twisted around the banister, their thorns almost daring you to touch the rail. A chandelier hung above, just like in the Seelie palace, but it was made of spears and swords instead of crystals.

Charming.

I kind of loved it.

I didn't have a chance to look around for very long though, because just as the initial group left, a very friendly human woman arrived. In fact, she was cozy enough with Nox that warning bells went off in my head as I watched her rub her bare arm against his.

She was beautiful, in the most annoyingly conventional of ways. Long, golden-blonde tresses cascaded down her back and the deep maroon dress she wore dipped low in the front, putting her impressive cleavage on display. A full, red mouth whispered something in Nox's ear and he nodded his head. She laughed girlishly and smiled widely, looking up at him with heavily lined doe-eyes. All while I was basically hanging onto his other arm.

I wanted to punch her in her pretty little face.

Lil picked up on my irritation right away and shot me a

look that said something along the lines of, *We're new here. Let's keep the fighting to a minimum for now.*

I ignored her, flicking my gaze to that of the blonde woman, who had finally decided to notice me.

"Oh my," she gushed. "You must be—"

"Aster."

I didn't try to warm my tone as I cut her off. In fact, I made sure that it was coated in just enough ice to make her balk a little.

"Not Princess Asteria?" she ventured.

I surveyed her slowly, from the tips of her painted toes to the top of her perfect head. And then said, "I believe 'Your Majesty' would be the appropriate title."

Her eyes rounded and she glanced at Nox, who said distractedly, "Wista, please escort Ms. Hephaste to the guest wing."

"And the princess—I mean, Her Majesty?"

"My mate stays with me."

The words were final and feral, edged enough for me to know that Nox was still reeling from what had just happened. And as his wings flared behind him, I knew his control was slipping quickly.

A few other court members arrived, some gawking and whispering. Wista's gaze skirted across my neck, as if finally noticing the bruises I knew had to be blooming there. Nox's grip on my hand tightened, his wings curling around me protectively. And that was when the reality of precisely what had just happened suddenly hit me like a speeding bus.

I had died.

I had died and he had watched. Lil had watched. And I was kind of acting like it hadn't happened.

"Ms. Hephaste, you can follow me," Wista said carefully, her eyes not quite leaving me.

Lil moved to follow her, but then stopped, turned, and said to Nox, "When can I see my brother?"

Nox's face softened only a fraction and he said, "I'm certain that Griffin has already transported him to the healers. They should have a report for me within the next few hours and I'll send word right away once I receive it."

Lil took a deep breath and replied. "Okay. And Nox, I mean, Your Majesty—"

"Just Nox, as always, Lilliana," he said.

She sighed. "Nox. Can I please hug my friend?"

Nox smiled, though it was strained as he replied, "Of course."

He released me from his death grip and Lil and I stepped forward at the same time, nearly toppling each other over. She wrapped her arms around my middle and held me tight.

"I love you, asshole," she whispered. "Please don't ever fucking do that again."

I smiled and replied, "I'll make note of it."

She choked out a laugh and muttered, "Not funny."

"I love you too, Lil."

She peered up at me and said, "This is all going to be messy as hell."

I raised a brow. "Sounds just like me."

She snorted, though her expression quickly sobered as she glanced at my neck.

"He'd better get you to a healer right away, or I'll have to hunt him down in his own palace and cut off his—"

"Don't finish that sentence, Lil," I said, half-serious, half-joking.

I felt Nox brush up against behind me and every nerve ending in me went on high alert.

"Don't worry. I was planning on it," he said, adding, "A real healer. I'm not quite equipped enough for this."

I could feel his hands lingering on my back and I knew it was probably taking a lot of effort on his part not to wrap both his arms around my waist.

Lil shot me a questioning look and I realized she didn't know Nox had healing magic. But before I had a chance to explain, Wista asked loudly, "Ms. Hephaste, are you ready?"

She was clasping and unclasping her hands as she eyed Nox's continued proximity to me. I gave her a sickly-sweet smile as she briefly met my gaze.

Lil rolled her eyes at my territorial behavior.

"Cool it, baby girl," she whispered, pecking me on the cheek. She faced Wista and said, "I'm ready."

Then, she glanced at me one last time as she said, "Don't abandon me in this creepy castle."

"I wouldn't dream of it," I replied with a raised brow.

Lil gave me one more small smile before following Wista down the hall. I glanced at Nox and asked, "She won't try to murder Lil because she's my friend, right?"

It was meant to be a joke, but his expression darkened and he said, "You and your friends are safe in this palace. If anyone so much as looks at you in the wrong way I won't hesitate to remove their head from their body."

There was real violence in his spoken promise and it sent a thrill up my spine, igniting a strange, soft tug just below my heart.

Nox furrowed his brow and stared at me for a long, long

moment before clearing his throat and saying, "She's right. You need to see a healer."

Instinctively, I raised a hand up to my neck. Nox followed the movement like a hawk, rage flashing in his eyes.

"I will destroy that bastard and then scatter his essence to the deepest pits of the Abyss, along with every one of his kin," he vowed, his hands clenched tightly at his sides. His wings curled around me again, this time nearly blocking out the entrance hall completely.

"What exactly are we going to do about this... the demons?" I asked.

Nox shut his eyes briefly before opening them and replying, "This is different than the last time. If what your uncle said is true, we're fighting the enemy from within our own courts. We'll need to find a way to detect them and destroy them without murdering innocents..."

He trailed off and I suddenly noticed how exhausted he looked. I bit my lip and said, "Should I return to the Seelie Court tonight? What if people need me or——"

"No."

The word cut through space between us like a bolt of white-hot lightning, harsh and charged with desperate, angry energy.

"Nox," I said softly, touching his arm. "I will have to return soon."

He huffed out a breath and said, "I know. Just... not tonight."

I held his gaze and then replied, "Okay."

He pulled back his wings and held out a hand to me. I took it and he led me down a hall that led away from the grand entrance. The marble floors continued, though the ceilings were lower here and art tastefully lined the walls, along with what I thought might be fae-lights, glowing with soft iridescence.

After walking the length of just one hallway, I began to slow my pace, hardly able to keep up with Nox. Exhaustion was overcoming me like a heavy, warm blanket and my knees felt wobbly and weak.

Nox stopped walking and began, "Asteria…"

"I'm fine."

My voice was thin and raspy—not very convincing. Nox huffed out a breath and the next thing I knew he was scooping me off my feet and into his arms.

"This is not necessary," I grumbled as he cradled me against his chest.

He sighed. "I won't have you passing out on me, love."

"You just wanted an excuse to carry me through your palace."

"Mm, maybe."

I snorted, then we both fell silent. I drifted in and out, the soft glow of the faelights flashing behind my drooping eyelids. By the time we reached what I assumed was the healer's wing, I was nearly asleep. Voices floated past me, Nox's rumbling through his chest as he held me close.

"—anything else besides the bruises?" someone was asking.

"I'm not sure."

"My king, forgive me, there are rumors. And for me to adequately diagnose and heal her, I need to know…" the voice trailed off.

My eyes fluttered open and I vaguely saw a young man in front of us, his dark hair pulled back in braids from his sharp face. His gaze flicked down to me as I stared at him, probably a little creepily. But I was too tired to care.

"The rumors are true," Nox replied. "I… I'm not sure what was healed and what wasn't."

It wasn't like Nox to stutter or trip over his words and even in my half-awake state, my heart clenched a little. Braid-dude's eyes widened at Nox's statement, but to his credit he quickly recovered at the news of my miraculous return from death.

"You can bring her here, my king, and I'll just start by running a detailed diagnostic to ensure we don't miss anything," he said.

Nox began to walk again and I was set down on something soft. The next thing I knew, my vision tunneled and everything went dark.

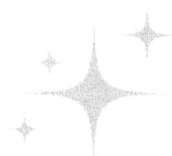

CHAPTER
TWENTY-FOUR

I STRETCHED my hand out into the familiar webs of light and shadow that encompassed the dream bridge. Just across the way, the shadows were restless, swirling and shifting. I knew Nox would appear soon, as he always did. I waited for what seemed like an eternity before he finally took shape. I reached out my hand, but like always, the shadows shied away from my shimmering luminescence.

"Why can't I ever reach you here?" I asked.

"You can always reach me," his voice echoed back.

I shook my head, insistent. I *needed* to know why. It suddenly felt urgent and important. I tried to force my way into the shadows, but to no avail. Nox stayed where he was, the shadows flowing from him just barely skirting past and around me.

Nox ignored them as well as my question, and instead said, "I need you to wake up now, love. Come back."

"Has it been long?"

He paused, long enough to worry me.

"Try to wake now, my star. It's time."

He took a step back, beginning to fade away into wisps of shadows and blinking stars. I lunged for him, but I couldn't quite reach him in time. For a moment, I stood on that bridge alone. I felt empty, void of something I didn't know I was even missing.

And then, blinding moonlight filled the bridge. Just before it blocked everything out, I realized the stars had been from me.

Our magic had finally begun to merge.

.✦

I gasped, my eyes flying open.

There was light in the room and it hurt my head. I blinked against it and said, "Fucking siren's tits, someone turn off the lights."

Someone let out a breath and said, "Yeah, I'm pretty sure that's Aster."

I blinked a few more times, trying to clear my vision as I muttered, "Of course it's me."

When my view of the world finally unblurred and focused, I saw Lil standing over me, her brow furrowed in concern.

"Hey," she said carefully.

"Shut up… trying to give me a migraine," I hissed.

My mouth was uncomfortably dry and Lil quickly handed me a cup of water with a straw in it. I sucked it down until she pulled it away and said, "Slow down, girl. I don't want you to puke on me."

I squinted at her, then looked around the room. I was in

what appeared to be an infirmary or hospital of sorts, with two rows of neatly made, empty beds and cabinets lining one side of the wall. Dim fae-lights illuminated the space, not nearly as brightly as I'd initially thought.

I turned back to Lil, who was still scrutinizing me.

"What?" I asked.

"You're Aster, right? Not…"

I winced as I tried to move my head to the side, then said, "I'm not possessed, Lil. Where's Nox?"

Lil tilted her head forward. I waited, staring at her in confusion, and she did it again.

"Sorry, I don't speak head," I said.

She snorted, seeming to relax as she replied, "I dunno, Aster, I'm fairly sure you speak some pretty good head."

Someone to the left of me chuckled and said, "I'll be the judge of that."

Lil made a face. "I did not need to hear you of all people say that."

I shifted, turning to see Nox sitting on the edge of the bed directly next to me, wearing a half-smirk. His hair was falling out of a loose bun, caressing the hard planes of his slightly flushed cheekbones and jaw.

"Were you just *sleeping*?" I asked.

He raised a brow. "How else was I supposed to reach you?"

I furrowed my brow. "Reach me?"

A wave of shadow fell over his features, instantly wiping away the humor from his face. "You've been asleep for… a while, love."

"How long?"

"Eight days," Lil replied instantly.

Shock rippled through me, replaced quickly by unease.

Nox shot Lil an irritated look and she shot one back as she said, "She can handle it. All of it. She deserves to know right away."

"Know what?" I asked sharply, sitting up and ignoring the pounding in my head.

Nox rubbed at his eyes and said, "Why don't you rest for a while first?"

"No," I replied immediately, glancing back at Lil. "I want to know."

Nox sighed, standing as he said to Lil, "This is a bad idea. She just woke up."

"She needs to deal with all of it. We're running out of time."

"And if it sends her over the edge and she falls back into a coma? Do you really want to risk her not waking up ever again?"

"Of course, not but——"

"There is no but."

"There is when——"

"Hello," I cut in. "I am fully awake and currently present in the room."

Both of them paused and looked down at me.

"Sorry," Lil said, looking away from me and back to Nox as she added, "You tell her then, if you're so concerned."

I looked up at him expectantly and he sat down on the edge of my bed, taking my hand. He began to rub circles in my palm and tap against my fingers in enough of a rhythm that I wondered if it was some sort of healing technique.

"Raven woke up two days ago," he finally said. I felt relieved for a moment, but it was short-lived as Nox went on, explaining, "He's not himself."

"What do you mean 'not himself?'" I asked slowly.

"Do you remember what your uncle said before he died? About the demons possessing bodies?"

It took me a few seconds to realize what he was insinuating. Once it clicked, I whispered, "No."

"We don't know what exactly it is. There are many classes of demons and he... it... doesn't seem to want to speak to us beyond insults and threats," Nox said.

I closed my eyes as the world crashed around me once again. It only got worse when Lil said, "And your uncle's former small council sent us a message."

I opened my eyes and asked flatly, "What do they want?"

Nox answered, "They're demanding you make an appearance at court so they can discuss the... validity of your claim to the throne."

"By tomorrow," Lil added.

"Anything else?" I asked, already exhausted.

Nox's hand stilled and he answered quietly, "The members of my court that were still alive in the dungeons are in the same condition as Raven. The demons possessing them killed the little girl, the oracle, before we were able to get them out."

I felt sick. Actually sick. Lil smoothly grabbed a basin of sorts just in time for me to vomit into it. Nox's hands caught my hair, gently pulled it back. Once I'd finished vomiting up a whole lot of nothing, Nox waved his hand and the basin disappeared.

I reached for the glass of water, sucked some down, then said, "Okay. Well, I need to get out of this bed if I'm going to appear at court tomorrow."

Nox stiffened and said, "I don't think that's a good

idea."

I shook my head. "I have to go. They'll see me as weak otherwise."

"She's not wrong," Lil said, her voice quiet.

Warring emotions crossed Nox's face before he finally said, "I won't keep you here against your will. But let me come with you."

"I think that's a very bad idea," I said. "At least for the first time I appear before them."

"Unfortunately for you, love, I don't really care," he said shortly.

"Okaaay, I'm going to let you two sort this out," Lil said. "I'll assume we'll be going back home tomorrow but let me know if that changes."

"It won't," I replied.

She raised a brow, but leaned over and gave me a quick kiss on my forehead before walking away, past the row of beds and out the front entrance of the infirmary.

Once she was gone, I met Nox's gaze and said, "I can't compromise my crown. And believe me, I never thought I'd hear myself say that but…" I trailed off.

"I know."

I bit my lip, then said, "This is going to be complicated. Us, I mean."

He nodded and said softly, "I know."

I looked at him, really looked at him then. I let my gaze travel over his body, studying every inch of him. And in that moment, it *hurt* how beautiful he was. It hurt how much I cared and it hurt to realize how impossible this was. Not just because of our separate courts, but because of the inevitable chaos that was coming. No one could be trusted and nothing was real anymore. Anyone could be a demon in hiding.

A flutter of something I couldn't quite identify pulled a cord just below my heart. It felt like... like exactly what I was feeling. A combination of pain and adoration. And something else, a reality that I was not yet willing to face.

I was falling in love with Nox.

I had been for some time and now, as everything slipped between our fingers, the danger that I would lose my heart completely to him was becoming a nearer and nearer reality. I was afraid, terrified even, of that prospect. The last person who I'd loved like this had shattered my heart into a million pieces and never looked back. And even I knew that what I'd felt for Jude paled in comparison to my feelings for Nox. It wasn't simply emotion between us; it was a force of nature itself.

"What is that?" I asked, my voice barely above a whisper. "The pull?"

Nox looked at me and there was something oddly cautious in his expression as he asked, "You feel it then?"

I nodded, reaching out and touching his chest in the same spot that the pull had manifested for me. He looked down at my hand before placing his palm over it, warm and calloused.

I felt the steady, resounding beat of his heart and he said, "When your neck snapped," he sucked in a breath. "When you died, this was gone. Only for a minute or two but I still remember how I felt without it. I never want to feel that again."

"But what *is* it? I only feel it sometimes like when..." I trailed off, suddenly bashful about just what I felt in moments like this.

Nox let go of my hand, though I didn't move it from his chest as he reached out and touched his fingers to my heart. His eyes were molten amber-gold as he said, "It's the mating bond, love. And you don't always feel it because you haven't accepted it yet."

I furrowed my brow and asked, "Can mates actually reject their bonds?"

Nox looked a little stricken as he said, "They can."

I knew so little about mating bonds because of just how rare they were. My mother and father had been mated; I knew that. But I'd never known anyone else, whether faerie or otherwise, who'd shared one with another. The notion of it had begun to die out since the last Long Night.

"Do demons have anything to do with this being less common?" I ventured.

Nox sighed heavily and nodded. I waited for him to explain, slowly lowering my hand from his chest. He dropped his hand too and he said, "There were a few instances during the war, what you know as the Long Night, in which very, very powerful demons broke bonds and essentially absorbed their essence for their own power. During the remainder of the war, there was a movement of sorts amongst those who discovered mating bonds. They rejected them out of fear of what could happen to them. Even rejected bonds never truly disappear, but the demons couldn't feed off them in the same way."

A cold feeling spread through my limbs and I asked, "What happened to the people whose bonds were broken by the demons?"

Nox looked away for a moment and replied, "A few of them died in the process. The ones who lived were... lost. The bond is a living thing, a magic all on its own. When one's mate dies, the remaining soul is essentially ripped in two, one half of it forever gone."

So, that's what he'd meant about the feeling disappearing when I had died. That's what he felt in those few minutes I was gone.

"I'm sorry," I whispered.

He shook his head. "Don't. You have nothing to apologize for."

A heavy silence followed and I knew he wanted to say more. I wanted to say more too. But neither of us did. We were toeing a line that we couldn't turn back from once crossed. For now, for today, I simply said, "Come with me tomorrow. And then we'll figure it all out from there."

"Alright," he said. "You should rest now."

I *was* tired. Really, really tired. But I was kind of sick of this rickety hospital bed.

"Can we leave the—what is this? An infirmary?" I ventured.

"It's an infirmary. And yes, you can leave," he replied.

"You won't come with me?"

He cocked his head to the side. "I will if you want me to."

"I do."

And that was that. A second later, before I could even protest, he scooped me up in his arms and we flitted out of the infirmary, landing on a much softer, much bigger bed. The room we were in was large and lit by more glowing fae-lights. The doors to the attached balcony were open, letting in a gentle evening breeze. The rest of the room was sparsely furnished, though it wasn't necessarily cold or impersonal, as small trinkets were scattered around on the tables. There were even a few crumpled shirts thrown over the armchair near the window.

"Is this your room?" I asked after looking around for a moment.

He nodded. "It is."

"It's not very fancy."

Chuckling softly, he explained, "I don't stay here very often."

Then he adjusted me so that I was propped up against a mountain of plush pillows. I rolled my eyes at his coddling. He ignored it, mostly, just flashing that incessantly annoying smirk at me. Though I stopped complaining once he pulled the blankets over us and my exhaustion caught up with me.

"Sleep," he murmured. "I'll be right here."

I began to drift off, but before I did, I mumbled, "She told me your father was an angel."

I'm not sure why I picked that exact moment to disclose to Nox my strange conversation with the goddess. But as I said it, his body stiffened, before he relaxed again and sighed, "Tricky goddess. We'll talk about that sometime soon, I promise. But for now, try to rest."

I did let it go for the moment, allowing myself to relax against his chest and listening to the beat of his heart. The gentle sounds of an owl hooting and crickets chirping drifted in through the open balcony door, melding into a soft lullaby of sorts as I shut my eyes. Nox stroked my hair, his motions slow and unhurried.

A long while later, just before I drifted off completely, I heard him whisper, very softly, "I love you as the stars love the night sky. Endlessly."

Hours later, when I awoke in his arms, I wasn't sure if what I'd heard was real or imagined.

CHAPTER
TWENTY-FIVE

LATER THAT MORNING, I stood with Lil and Nox in the entrance hall of the Unseelie Palace. Lil wore a sundress and heels, and Nox, his usual dark suit. I wore a specially made dress of autumn orange accented with winter silver. The orange being the color of my father's house. Silver; the exact hues of my mother's family crest.

Nox had apparently requested the dress be made as soon as he received word that the small council wanted to meet with me. He already knew me too well and it hurt my heart in a sort of pleasant, but also scary, way that he'd even thought I would want to wear such a garment. But I did, truly, because, for the first time since I was six years old, I would walk into the gilded gates of that palace, proud to be my parent's daughter.

Nox glanced sidelong at me as he took my hand to flit out out of the Unseelie Court. I'd learned he was the only one who could actively flit in and out of the palace walls. Well, and apparently me once I learned how.

It had been a part of our quick, hushed conversation

this morning. I'd wanted to ask about his whispered words from last night, but I had been too much of a coward. And, in truth, I had enough to face today.

"Ready?" he asked me and Lil.

"Ugh, do we really have to flit everywhere?" Lil complained.

Nox raised a brow. "How would you prefer we travel?"

She rolled her eyes. "Oh, I don't know… a bus or a car like everyone else?"

"It's easier to flit when traveling between the borders," Nox replied, equally as prickly.

Their relationship was turning out to be interesting. But I was glad Lil felt comfortable enough around Nox to be snarky and that he didn't seem to mind her attitude.

As funny as it was to see them bicker, I was mostly distracted by the fact that my stomach was currently doing nervous somersaults. Lil seemed to notice and peered at me from the other side of Nox as she said, "You'll be great, Aster."

I took a shuddering breath. "Thanks."

"Walk in like you already wear the crown," Nox added. "They don't matter, not to someone like you. They should be bowing and begging for mercy. Make that known."

I searched his gaze and nodded. In truth, I wanted to rip apart every member of my uncle's council and inner circle. They had stood by for years while I was abused, knowing full well what was happening. But for now, I needed their support and our court needed steadiness as we moved into the unknown. The time for revenge would come later.

But it would come for them. I would make sure of that.

"Let's go," I said heavily.

"Hold on," Nox said.

Lil sucked in a readying breath and then we were swept up into the chasm of time. I was pretty sure I heard Lil squeak just before we landed directly outside the palace gates, though I couldn't be entirely sure. I knew that Nox didn't have the ability to flit directly inside the Seelie palace, something I was thinking about changing once I took my throne. But apparently for now, there were shields of a sort preventing it, just like in his court's palace. Another kind of magic for the more powerful of our kind that I was somehow just learning of.

We were immediately greeted by a small group of guards, wearing familiar dark uniforms.

"Princess," one said and they bowed their heads, many of them wearing wary expressions. I recognized the guard who'd spoken as one of the ones who'd been there when I faced the Trial.

"King Nox," another said. "Are you... joining us today?"

Nox surveyed the guard. "Obviously," he drawled. "And I believe your queen would appreciate appropriate titles."

The guard muttered something along the lines of "Right, sorry," and after a quick whistle from one of the guards, the gates opened to let us in. I led the way, Nox and Lil following a short distance behind me. That was when I noticed things I had not noticed when we'd been here only days ago. Things I must have been too terrified or distracted to see.

The greenery, the flowers, even a few of the trees, were dying. Some of them were even rotted and curled or crumbling in decay. I lifted a hand and ordered, "Stop."

The guards halted.

256

"What is it prin—my queen?" the one who seemed to be the tentative leader asked. He was a little scrawny for a guard, but he seemed to be the most confident. Ewin's replacement, no doubt, as he was wearing the maroon uniform, a little large for his shoulders. I wondered what had happened to the previous captain of the guard.

He'd probably fled like a coward. One day, I'd hunt him down. But today was not that day. Today, I walked into my mother's flower garden and knelt in front of the dying beds. As I ran my hand across the soil, a keen sorrow made my chest feel heavy. She had adored this garden. I had no doubt that Abaddon's presence here for so many years had caused the decay.

After spending a few minutes with my mother's dying garden, I rose, smoothing my silky skirt and walking back to Nox and Lil, who were both still surrounded by the guards. Lil gave me a short nod in encouragement. Nox was staring at the wilting garden thoughtfully.

"Alright. Let's continue," I said.

The guards exchanged nervous looks, but bowed their heads and led us up the small set up stone stairs into the grand entrance hall. My uncle's small council was assembled in the hall, awaiting us. Several of them scowled or turned their noses up as they saw Nox at my side.

One of them, a faerie lord I vaguely knew of named Jasper, said, "Princess, I must inform you immediately that the Night King is indefinitely unwelcome in our small council chamber."

I gave him a cold smile, surveying the finery he wore and the sigil pinned to his chest. Maybe someday I'd shove that pin right into his throat.

"As your queen, I'd have to disagree," I said. "Given the

current situation, it is in our best interest to join forces with the Unseelie Court. A united front is the only way to face what is amongst us."

I'd bet a large, large sum of money that one of them was possessed. But one thing at a time.

"You are not queen yet, Asteria," Jasper said, narrowing his mossy-green eyes. "Do not assume we will grant you the crown."

I took a step closer to him, relishing the fact that I was quite a few inches taller than him, and asked sweetly, "And who else would you grant it to? Yourself, perhaps?"

Jasper scoffed. "Well, we have yet to discuss it. We've been in disarray since the loss of our king—"

"Your king was possessed by a prince of Hell. I'd hardly call his death a loss," Nox said.

Jasper's nose twitched in irritation and he replied, "We've yet to establish the validity of this claim."

"I was there," Lil said, her voice quivering. "King Calum admitted it all before he died. And he told us that there were already demons among us, possessing the bodies of our court members."

Jasper chuckled, his gaze shifting to her. "My, my. Lilliana Hepheste, is it? Your mother is the one with the Unseelie bastard, isn't she?"

"Something wrong with being Unseelie?" Nox asked silkily. I noticed that the shadows at the edges of the room began to creep closer as he spoke, some of them gathering at the council member's feet. A few of them paled, shifting uncomfortably, including Jasper.

"Shadow Walker," he hissed. "Princess, this magic is—"

"You remember my mother, Lord Jasper?" Nox asked, cutting Jasper off.

There was an edge to his voice that told me Nox knew him outside of just today's encounter. I'd ask him about it later. But for now, I was enjoying the way Jasper's face continued to drain of color, both in rage and fear.

"Yes," Nox said, circling him. "Of course, you do. I'm sure you remember; she was half-wraith."

"Tricky Unseelie queen," Jasper said, though his bravado was beginning to wear away.

Nox cocked his head to the side. "Tricky Unseelie Queen who nearly lost you your title. We faeries with wraith magic have a way of seeing things others don't, wouldn't you agree?"

Jasper's face was twisted into an ugly scowl and he said, "This is not why we're here."

"No," I said. "It's not. Though I'm sure it's a story I'd be intrigued to hear someday soon. But for now, I'm all ears as to why you think I'm incapable of claiming the crown that is rightfully mine."

"We should continue this conversation in a private space," Jasper said. "Come."

He turned before I could correct him for his continued lack of respect. Nox's gaze darkened considerably as he watched Jasper walk away. I glanced at him and shook my head slightly.

This is my fight, I tried to convey to him. *Let me fight it.*

He nodded back, as if to say, *I know. I'm trying.*

We wove through familiar halls, reaching the small council room within a few short minutes. I'd actually never been here but was un-surprised to find it was dripping with finery; gold goblets on the table, richly woven tapestries hanging on the stone walls, a polished mahogany table, and numerous plush rugs on the floor.

When we filed in, Jasper took the head seat, where the king or queen leading the council typically sat. He smirked as he did so, looking at me so directly it was almost pathetic. As if I needed him to point his disrespect out for me to notice it.

"Interesting seating arrangement, Lord Jasper," I said dryly.

Though he'd been silently gloating about his seating choice only seconds ago, the asshole pretty much ignored my comment and said, "Princess Asteria, you asked why we think you are incapable of claiming the throne. We've prepared a... proposal. Or rather, a—"

"Laundry list of petty reasons," I cut in, adding, "But please, continue."

Jasper's nostrils flared and he went right into it, before all the small council members were even all seated.

"You were not raised in the palace and therefore have little idea of our customs," he began. "You have no political or leadership experience. Your education is inadequate, given your choice of study. You spent your teenage and adult years gallivanting around the court district, engaging in activities unfit for a female of your status."

Ugh... *female.*

He went on, a thick layer of distaste coating his words, "We will not have an irresponsible child lead our court. We will not have a defiled woman, who had degraded herself so fully that she would not be acceptable in a marriage proposition, we will not—"

"Enough."

My voice was like ice as it cut through the room, sharp as the edge of a sword. And as I prepared to speak, I let just a fraction of my power shine through. A few council members murmured nervously as the starlight illuminated my eyes.

"Each and every one of you who sit at this table before me watched on for years as your regent king abused a child, no less your princess and the chosen heir to the throne. I dare you to deny it. I dare you to claim that you did not see the bruises or hear the screams. I cried out for help and not one of you came. And then I stopped crying. I stopped screaming. Because I knew, there was not a worthy soul amongst any of you. As far as your insults regarding my worth as a woman and my "usefulness" on the marriage market." I laughed. "I am not an animal to be sold off. And I will have it known that my *mate* finds no issue with my past nor my present."

Jasper's eyes widened as those magnificent wings flared from Nox's back.

"This is… you can't…" he gasped.

"Oh, but she can," Nox said, leaning forward, his palms braced on the table. "And be aware that if another one of you spineless bastards insults Asteria again, I will not hesitate to rip your throats out."

His threat echoed across the now silent room. I let it sit for nearly a minute, watching the council members squirm under both of our cold stares.

"The third Long Night of our world is upon us," I finally said. "We need a strategy. Citizens have already become victims of possession. We have to find a way to destroy the demons without destroying their hosts, or there will be a massive, unnecessary loss of life. And we have to find a way to seek them out, and a way to keep our citizen's calm. In order for this all to happen successfully, we need a united front across the faerie courts and the mixed districts that surround us. If you are interested in aiding the war effort, please keep your seats. If you are only here to threaten me or turn a blind eye to our current reality, I invite you to take your leave."

Jasper stared me down and I stared right back at him. Apparently he was a fan of staring contests because he kept glaring at me until his eyes watered and he was forced to blink.

Ten points to me, Lord Asshat.

"My queen," an older faerie with graying hair began tentatively. "Given the current atmosphere of the room and the… confusion that began this meeting, I suggest we reconvene in a day or two. I understand the dire circumstances, but I think some of us would like time to, ah, settle first. Then we can begin a war council with clearer heads."

I sighed. "Very well. I concur with Lord…?"

"Thestle," he finished for me in a quivering voice.

I nodded. "We'll meet again in two days, at the same time as today. If you are not present, I will assume your leave from my council."

Most of the council members stood respectively in their chairs as I turned to leave. A few stayed seated and continued to scowl at me. I ignored them as I headed for the door. Once Lil, Nox, and I were out in the hall, I made a beeline for the entrance hall.

"Aster," Lil said breathlessly. "You were amazing. You sounded so regal and official."

"Didn't think I had it in me, but apparently…" I mumbled, my feet carrying me faster than Lil could properly keep up with.

As soon as we stepped outside, Nox put a hand on my shoulder and I whirled, breathing heavily. It was all very suddenly too much and my breath came out in quick gasps as I said, "I need to... I need to leave, I can't be here, not now, I'm sorry, I just——"

"Asteria, love," Nox said, gently grasping my chin so I was forced to meet his gaze. "It's alright. We can go back to my court for now. Take a deep breath."

I felt my lower lip tremble and I rambled, "I'm fine, I'm fine. It's just that I..." I gasped. "I miss them. I miss my parents. I never let myself miss them because I pretended I wasn't their daughter. I pretended to be Aster Quiin and now I can't anymore."

I inhaled sharply and Nox pulled me to his chest.

"Breathe," he said. "Feel the rise and fall of my chest. Just try to breathe with me. That's all you need to worry about right now. I promise."

My mind was whirling but I focused on his words. His breaths were steady and deep and as I copied them, the buzzing panic in my chest began to subside.

Finally, when I pulled back, and wiped at my face, Lil said, "I'm proud of you, Aster. No matter who you are."

"Thank you," I whispered.

She smiled gently. "I'm going to go home for now, to my mom. She's probably worried about Raven and I still haven't told her..." she trailed off.

"I know," I said. "Go. It's fine, I'll be alright."

"You're sure?"

I stepped back from Nox and held out my hand to Lil. She took it and I said, "I'll be okay. I'll contact you right away if anything happens with Raven. Tell your mom I love her and I'll be by as soon as I can."

"Okay," she whispered.

"And Lil?"

"Yeah?"

"You're still my best friend. Even if…" my voice trailed off and a grin broke across Lil's face.

"Even if you have a sexy, macho, half-wraith mate?" she finished for me.

Not exactly what I was going to say, but she wasn't wrong either. Behind me, Nox choked out a laugh and I smiled slightly and replied, "Even then."

I hugged her and once we pulled away from each other, Nox said, "I can flit you to your mother's house if you'd like?"

Lil raised a brow and said, "Um, no. I think Evelyn would have a heart attack if you put one foot near her doorstep. I'll take a bus. And before you warn me, yes, yes I will look out for killer demons roaming the streets and try my best to avoid them."

"Text or call me when you're there, at the least," Nox said.

"Speaking of, I've been meaning to ask you, can I have my phone back?" Lil asked.

"You'll have to borrow one, yours is gone. I destroyed all of your devices when you were staying at my penthouse. Security, remember?" Nox replied.

Lil rolled her eyes. "Fine, fancy-pants, but I expect a new one. And Aster, make him buy you one too."

"Planning on it," I said.

She sighed. "Alright. Girl-boss the council, check. Post girl-boss panic attack, check. Phone request, check. I'm heading out."

And with that, she turned on her heel and pranced towards the gates. A few of the guards who had been awkwardly standing around during my "post girl-boss panic attack" let her out. I swear one even checked out her ass as she sauntered away.

"Let's go," Nox said, glancing back at the palace. "I want to kidnap you for the night."

The guard nearest to us shot me an alarmed look. I ignored him and said to Nox, "Fair enough."

I smiled at the guards and they bowed their heads, avoiding my eyes. The gates and we walked out of the courtyard and past them. Within seconds of taking my hand, Nox flitted us out of the Seelie Court.

CHAPTER
TWENTY-SIX

Once we'd returned to the Unseelie Palace, a random thought came into my head and I asked Nox, "Why do you have the penthouse?"

He shrugged and replied, "It's more... normal. And I have a TV there."

"You don't have TVs in your palace?"

"Do you?"

I thought about it and eventually answered, "No. I don't think we do."

"No TV, no *Siren's Seduction*. And no sweaty shifters, or whatever the hell it's called."

I glared at him. "*Pack*."

He raised a brow. "It's just called 'pack?' Kind of lame."

"I'll show you just how lame it is."

"Hmm, a fan of wolves I see?'

"Maybe."

He narrowed his eyes and leaned in, murmuring into

my ear, "Why don't we put on the show and see just how much you… enjoy it."

He pulled back as heat began to course through me.

Throughout our entire exchange, neither of us had noticed that Wista was apparently lingering nearby. She coughed slightly and we both whipped our heads around.

"Your Majesty," she said, glancing at Nox. "Do you need anything tonight?"

Something ugly and territorial rose up immediately in me, along with a sort of irrational anger at Nox. I suspected he and Wista had… history. It was stupid for me to be angry given my own past, but what could I say? This bond was weird.

"Just inform Griffin we've returned," Nox replied. "Otherwise, no."

The *no* was final and short enough that Wista shrank back a little, bowing her head and saying quickly, "Very well, my king."

She left promptly and Nox asked me, "Fancy a bath, love?"

.✦·

Half an hour later, I stood in Nox's private chambers, in the royal wing of the palace, as he tested the temperature of the water. He was already shirtless, though his wings were currently away, presumably because they wouldn't fit in the bath along with me.

Because I was about to get naked and climb into a bath with him—also naked.

He glanced back at me, raising a cocky brow at my obvious, lingering stare. Though the expression slid right off his face as I let the entirety of the dress I was wearing fall to the ground. The only thing I wore underneath were thin, lacy underwear slung low on my hips. The cut of the dress hadn't really allowed for a bra, though I hadn't minded. I didn't always wear them anyways. My breasts were nothing to write home about.

Except that Nox didn't seem to think so.

His gaze trailed my body slowly enough that I felt as though I was being undressed all over again. Shadows curled around my ankles, reaching up my legs and teasing my thighs.

"Are these… sentient?" I asked.

Nox's gaze snapped back to mine and he replied roughly, "No. They're essentially just an extension of me, of my magic."

I swallowed. "I see."

He continued to drink me in as I padded over to the bathroom.

"Your turn," I murmured.

He was still kneeling on the ground and I pressed my palm against his bare shoulder as his hands skimmed my legs. His hair was still pulled back in a bun, though a few silvery strands fell loose in his face. I wanted nothing more than to run my hands through it, but I needed to ask him something first.

"Wista," I stated.

He nodded, seeming to understand my question immediately. "She is… quite attached to me," he said.

"Did you and her ever…?"

"I kissed her. Once. Not my finest moment."

268

I rolled my eyes. "I'm not judging you, Nox."

He sighed softly, his hands tightening on my thighs as he said, "I was… in a compromised state when it happened."

I waited.

His finger stroked my bare skin, raising goose bumps along it as he said, "You did not know about me before we met, at least not in your waking memory. But as you know, I did, and I occasionally would catch glimpses of your life in your dreams. There was a man a few years ago who you used to dream about quite a lot."

"Jude," I said instantly.

Nox nodded.

"I got drunk one morning, after a few nights in a row of constantly seeing him. Believe me, love, I don't judge you in any way for your past partners. Of course, a part of me wants to hunt each of them down and rip off their heads, but that's only natural. The difference for me was, you loved this man."

"I did," I whispered.

"The story goes, I was drunk and sad, Wista knocked on my door, and…" he trailed off, the insinuation of what had happened clear as day. "Like I said, not my finest moment. But she hasn't let it go since."

I paused, then said quietly, "The water's going to get cold."

He nodded silently, not breaking my gaze as he rose to his full height. He trailed a finger over my lips before pulling his hand away and stripping down to nothing. Just as he had done with me, I let my stare travel down his body, taking in every contour and dip and…

Yeah, he was really into me. And I was going to have a *hugely* phenomenal night.

"Bath," he said, his thumbs hooking around my underwear and dragging them down. He knelt again, kissing my inner thigh, and sending a pleasure shiver through me. But he stopped there for now, standing and taking my hand, helping me into the enormous bath. Though, "pool" was probably a better description for the porcelain and marble monstrosity before us.

Frankly, I stopped thinking about it as soon as I sank into the warm water. I sighed softly, though it turned into a sharp inhale as Nox pulled my back flush against his front. He nuzzled my neck, sliding his teeth along the column up it. My body became taut and loose all at the same time. His tongue swirled over my pulse point and I sucked in a breath.

Though he paused as I asked breathily, "What do I have to do to accept the bond?"

"You just have to accept it," he said.

I rolled my eyes, turning to face him. "No ceremony? We don't have to frolic and fornicate under the full moon or something like that?"

A smile tugged at his mouth and he replied, "No, though I wouldn't turn that offer down."

"So... what?"

He furrowed his brow and asked, "You're sure?"

"I pretty much already accepted it by declaring you my mate in front of my entire small council."

He cupped my cheek and said, "I know, love. But you'll feel it when it truly locks into place, or so I'm told. And as far as how it's done, it can be simply an exchange of words or a thought. But you have to mean it."

"I know," I said, quietly.

He had once lived in a time where mates had been

common as lovers. A time before demons ruined the sacred nature of them and instead replaced it with fear. I hadn't even realized that fear still permeated today, nearly woven into the magic of bonds themselves.

Mulling over it all, I reached for the soap and lathered it before running my hands down my arms. Nox watched me carefully. I knew he was aware that I was thinking. He probably thought I was deciding. The truth of it was, I already had days ago. I was just afraid that he'd reject me all of the sudden, or worse, something catastrophic would happen and I'd lose him. Which at this point, was actually very possible. But I was sick of being afraid. I was tired of running from my feelings. And I was done with denying myself of good things.

So, after rinsing the soap from my body, I waded back to him, climbing in his lap as I said, "I'm a messy person," I whispered, shaking my head. "And I'm still figuring a lot out. I know that. But—"

He kissed me, cutting off my doubts and tossing them straight into the wind. His arms wrapped around me, pulling me close so that our chests pressed together. I gently tugged the leather cord from his hair, so that it fell over his damp shoulders, a canvas of silver fanning across his tanned skin.

As soon as I began to grind against him, he groaned.

"Not here," he hissed.

He rose up out of the bath, carrying me with him. My legs wrapped around him and water streamed off our slick bodies, dampening the floor. He ignored it, walking straight to the bed and laying me down on top of the covers. He leaned over me, one hand tangling in my hair, the other braced on one side of me.

He kissed me fiercely, though I pulled back for a second to say firmly, "I accept the bond."

He froze, his eyes searching mine. I meant it, truly and completely. And just as I finished saying the words, something eternal and sacred locked into place between us. My breath came in shaky inhales and exhales and I swore I found eternity in his gaze as a rush of feelings barreled through me, both his and mine. At that still, quiet moment, I hardly knew where he ended and I began. I felt a flare of white-hot emotion rush down that newly solidified bond and he kissed me again. My stupid eyes began to burn and a few stubborn tears fell down my cheeks.

"I'm sorry," I rasped. "I'm not sad, it's just…"

"I know," he whispered. "I know, love."

And he did. He was fully aware of just how much this meant coming from me. Becoming close to someone in a way I'd never thought I would, aside from Lil. I had cracked myself open for him and he had done the same for me. And now, as we stared at each other, bleeding and bruised, I realized this feeling between us was beyond words.

I wrapped my legs around his hips, arching my back into him. He groaned as my core brushed up against his cock.

"Need to be inside you," he said roughly.

I felt it too. The urgent need to *claim, claim, claim*, overtaking my body and my mind. This wasn't just sex, or fucking, or even making love. It was carnal need. I needed him now just as I needed air to breathe.

His hand drifted between us and at the first stroke of his fingers, I was writhing beneath him. He hardly wasted time —now was not the time for teasing or waiting—and he found exactly the right spot just as his teeth scraped against my neck.

Fae teeth. Sharp teeth.

"Do it," I gasped. "Please."

He plunged a finger inside of me and just as he curled it, he sunk his teeth into my neck. I was caught between a mad rush of pain and pleasure, all melding into a frenzy that was turning my vision into stars. He swirled his tongue over the hurt and brushed his thumb over my clit.

I fell off the cliff I'd been edging since I stepped into that bath, practically screaming his name. As I came back down, he kissed me roughly and I tasted my blood on his lips. It was fucked up and strange and messy. Just like me. Just like him.

He didn't break the kiss as he thrust into me for the first time. I gasped against his mouth and he groaned loudly, hissing, "*Fuck.*"

His hands grasped both of mine, pinning them to either side of my head as he pounded into me. Already, I began to near the edge again and I knew he sensed it, because he let go of one of my hands and moved my leg up to get a deeper angle.

"Come again, love," he growled.

I met his wild eyes, black with desire and said, "You're mine."

"I'm yours," he affirmed, just as I began to feel myself fall.

I started to look away, but he moved a hand to grasp my chin. And through ragged breaths he commanded, "Look at me."

I forced myself to keep my eyes open while the light blasted through my vision. Even before it was over and I was fully back, he began to move again, going at a slower pace for a moment.

"Don't want this… to end," he rasped.

I kissed him and he lost any scraps of control that remained, thrusting into me fast and hard. He shouted my name as he came, and my breath hitched even as he slowed and then stilled inside of me. He kissed me slowly and then pulled out and laid down on his side next to me.

We were both still breathing heavily and his hand was visibly shaking as he reached out and stroked it down my cheek.

"No matter what comes, you're mine," he whispered.

I held his gaze. "I'm yours."

He kissed me and then I said, "We're all wet."

He smiled slightly. "True."

Then, with a flick of his hand the water soaking the covers and the mattress beneath us disappeared, leaving the bed clean and warm.

"Showoff," I said, rolling my eyes.

He chuckled, rolling off the bed and striding over the bathroom, emerging a moment later with two towels. And yeah, I stared at his ass the entire time, no shame.

Once we'd dried off, I quickly used the bathroom—no UTIs for me, thank you very much. When I emerged back into the bedroom, I found him sprawled across the mattress, his head buried in the pillow.

"Damn," I said. "What'd I do to you?"

He lifted his head, a slightly loopy grin on his face and he replied, "You made me happy." I froze where I was and he did too. Eventually, he said quietly, "Come here."

Without hesitation, I made my way over to the bed. He pulled me under the covers and against his warm body.

"Things are about to get bad," I whispered.

"You're right," he said, his voice solemn.

He didn't deny it or tell me that things were going to be fine. Because they weren't. We were about to enter a freaking war against an army our world had barely defeated before—a narrow victory that Nox had sacrificed everything for. And now there was so much more at stake. The question was, what were we willing to sacrifice now?

I couldn't find an answer, not as I fell asleep in his arms.

CHAPTER
TWENTY-SEVEN

IN THE MORNING, I awoke pulled tight against Nox, his arm slung over my waist. Seconds after I opened my eyes and stirred, his lips brushed against my shoulder.

"Awake, love?"

I rolled over to face him. "Mhmm."

His eyes were luminescent as they roved over me.

"Did you know you're the first person, other than Lil, who I've let sleep with me?"

My voice was barely above a whisper as I said it and his gaze slid to mine, holding there.

"No one," he finally said.

I furrowed my brow. "No one, what?"

"No one has ever shared my bed. Not like this... not sleeping."

I narrowed my eyes. "I didn't just deflower you, did I?"

He chuckled, stroking a finger down my cheek as he replied, "No. When I was much younger I was quite... promiscuous. That was, until being so could have consequences."

"Wait," I said. "How long has it been since you've had sex?"

"Hmm, maybe eight hours…"

I rolled my eyes. "You know what I mean."

His expression grew a little more solemn as he admitted, "A long while."

"Why? You can have sex without falling in love."

"That depends. I didn't want to risk stumbling upon the wrong person," he replied, his voice low as he stroked his knuckles over my lips.

I stared at him as I took in the weight of his words, desire already beginning to set me aflame. I curled my hand on his chest and his eyes flashed. He leaned forward, his nose brushing mine. And then he whispered, "The way I see it, you have two options. Either you keep doing what you're doing and I won't let you leave this room for a long, long while. Or…" he paused, "or we can stop now and attend to the current situation outside the door."

I could sense the reluctance in his tone as he said it. Because the truth of it was we did have things that we needed to deal with. The demon in Raven, for one, and how to get it out without hurting him. The thought immediately sobered me and I sighed.

"I'm sorry, love," Nox said, sounding a little resigned.

I propped myself up, rubbing at my eyes as I said, "It's fine. You're right, we have stuff to deal with."

"We do."

He sat up and before I knew what was happening, he'd scooped me up into his arms and was walking both of us towards the bathroom.

"You have a thing about carrying me," I muttered.

He strode over to the shower that was housed next to

the enormous bath and turned on the hot water before saying, "Is that a problem?"

"I'm not a damsel in distress," I quipped as he set me down.

He stepped into the shower and I admit, pretty much every thought flew out of my head as I stared at his water-slick body like a creep. His mouth quirked up into a half-grin.

"Coming in, love? Or do you prefer to watch?"

I closed my mouth and as I joined him under the water, I muttered, "You're an asshole."

He reached past me to grab a bottle of shampoo and said, "Such gallant declarations of love for me this morning."

My body froze up as he said "love." But he didn't balk or get angry at my sudden discomfort. Instead, he simply poured shampoo onto my hair and said, "Don't worry, I'm not going anywhere."

He could read me so well it was a little scary. Because I *was* worried, just a tad. I'd never taken this much of a risk on someone and come out unscathed. Nox let his words sink in, rubbing the shampoo into my wet hair.

"I can do that," I said, turning.

He *tsked* and said, "Ah, but I want to."

"Then I get to wash yours too."

"Not a chance, love," he said, turning me back around so I was staring at the tiled wall.

I let out a sigh but allowed him to finish. Once I rinsed the soap out of my hair, he went for the conditioner too, but I snarled, snatching it from him. He lowered his chin at the challenge, before lunging at me. I ended up pinned between him and the wall, his hand holding my wrists, the conditioner bottle falling to the floor.

We were both breathing heavily, more heavily than was probably warranted for our little scuffle. His gaze lowered to my mouth for a split second before he kissed me roughly.

"I thought—we had things to do," I muttered.

He let out what sounded like a mix between an exasperated sigh and a growl. I knew exactly what he felt. It seemed that being freshly mated drove a lot of those innate faerie instincts harder than normal. Meaning, we both just wanted to fuck. A lot. All the time. Now.

The world had a funny way of creating horrible timing for me.

"Later," I breathed.

He nodded, but leaned in further, tugging on my earlobe with his teeth just as he had in the club the first night we met. Then he whispered in my ear, "Later… I'm going to fuck you senseless. That's a promise, my star."

He pulled back, his gaze lingering.

The rest of the shower was pretty torturous. He kept stealing covert glances at me and I kept ogling at him. By the time he turned off the water and we stepped out, the rough friction of the towel he handed me was nearly too much against my skin.

But we made it out of the bathroom without incident. My resolve nearly shattered though, as Nox walked into the bedroom wearing only a towel slung low on his narrow hips. He strode over to a set of drawers and began pulling out clothes.

"Nox?"

"Yes, love?"

I cleared my throat slightly and said, "I don't have any extra clothes here."

He glanced back at me, looking very pleased at the notion. But he sighed and flicked his fingers and a pair of jeans, underwear, and a lacy-looking bra appeared on the bed. I walked over, letting the towel drop from around me and starting to get dressed.

It took me longer than it should have to realize he hadn't given me a shirt. I turned to ask him why and he was already right in front of me, wearing dark pants and a tight black shirt that probably should've been illegal given the way it showed off his muscled chest and abdomen.

"Need a shirt?"

I scrutinized him and said slowly, "Yes, I do."

He smirked, flicking his wrist. A t-shirt from his drawer flung itself at me and I caught it just before it hit me in the face. As I looked down at it, I realized it was a band shirt, proudly sporting the name of my favorite punk band. I had a nearly identical shirt back at home.

"How did you... how much did you spy on me?"

He raised a brow. "I didn't spy. You simply tended to dream about things you liked."

"So, the curry..."

"You must've been hungry that particular night."

I rolled my eyes as I pulled the shirt on, muttering, "Is there *anything* you don't already know about me?"

He stepped forward, tucking a strand of damp hair behind my ear as he said, "A great many things. But I intend to learn them all."

A knock sounded on the door and I jumped. Nox brushed a kiss against my forehead and strode over to the door. He opened it partially and someone spoke in low tones from the other side. I tried to get a view of who they were, but Nox's body was blocking the way. Whoever it was, they were gone by the time Nox turned back to face me, his face more serious than it had been a moment ago.

"What is it?" I asked, my stomach fluttering nervously.

He furrowed his brow. "The demons have finally begun to talk."

.✦.

I stood in the chilled cell block beneath Unseelie palace, my arms wrapped around myself. This was where most of the possessed faeries, aside from Raven, were being kept. He was still upstairs in the infirmary, as his physical injuries were still healing. A concussion, I'd been told.

I approached one of the cells tentatively, Nox lingering close behind me. All of the cells had been furnished and made as comfortable as possible and warmth emitting lanterns burned all down the hall, just out of reach of the possessed faeries. At first they were all quiet, but soon, they looked up at me and began to speak in eerie tones.

"Bridge," one of them, a woman with sunken gray eyes, hissed.

"Key!" a man in the cell next to her shouted.

"Breaker," a little boy whispered.

"Keeper," murmured a girl who looked about my age.

"They've been doing this all morning."

I whirled to see Griffin standing a few feet away, his face

set. He looked solemn as he stared at the members of his court who were no longer themselves. I wondered if he had friends or family among them.

Nox looked highly disturbed as he turned to face me and recited the words I'd told him the night before I'd died. The words Lina had told me.

"The bridge between time, the key to the lock that is not to be opened, the breaker of portals, and the keeper of the last light... they're talking about you."

Griffin furrowed his brow. "Care to explain, Nox?"

Without looking away from me, Nox said, "The oracle, the little girl they killed, spoke those phrases to Asteria less than two weeks ago."

"Well, shit," Griffin said.

I huffed out a breath and muttered, "Well, shit is right."

Abruptly, one by one, the possessed faeries began to chant, "Run, princess, run. Promised princess, he's come. Run you better run... RUN YOU BETTER RUN."

They were nearly screaming now, clawing at the bars of their cells. I felt Nox's hand close around my arm and he began to pull me back.

"Let's go," he said into my ear.

"But..."

"Asteria, we need to leave."

I felt strangely entranced by the possessed faeries. Which was definitely not a good sign, but my brain was having a really hard time reminding me of that at the moment. A cold wave washed over me and I met Nox's eyes.

"There's something here that I need to—"

"We're leaving," Nox cut me off sharply as the faeries in the cells began to laugh hysterically.

"Promised princess!" they screeched in between cackles. "Down, down, down!"

Finally, I gave up trying to stay and let Nox lead me up the worn stone passageway and back onto the main level of the palace. Griffin followed closely behind and all three of us were silent as we walked.

Once we emerged into a hall off the main entrance hall, Nox finally let go of my arm.

"What the hell was that?" Griffin asked no one in particular.

"They wanted something from me," I muttered. Then I shook my head, clearing it, and said, "I want to see Raven."

Nox looked wary and he said, "I don't know if that's a good idea."

"Nox," I said, my voice imploring.

He swallowed visibly and relented. "Alright."

"I'll come with you," Griffin said immediately.

Nox nodded curtly at him. I was *super* interested to know just what the heck their history was. But at the moment, I was more interested in seeing Raven.

We walked the short distance to the royal infirmary. When we arrived at the entrance, I stopped short.

"He's really not himself, is he?" I asked quietly.

Nox's jaw tightened and he shook his head. "No, love. He's not."

I took a deep, steadying breath and said, "It's fine. I just... I just need to see him for myself."

"I understand," Griffin answered quietly. There was enough emotion in his voice that I paused and glanced at him. But he was already looking the other way, dutifully posted just outside the door.

With one last scrutinizing look at him, I stepped inside the infirmary.

It was empty, aside from a bed all the way at the end of the row on the left side of the room. The fae-lights were softer and dimmer than I remembered them. It made the mood feel even more somber as I walked slowly towards the bed where Raven lay.

His wrists and ankles were encircled in heavily padded chains and his eyes were closed. For a moment, he looked just like he always did. My second-best friend in the entire world. The big brother I'd never had. And then he opened his eyes and I knew… that person was nowhere to be found.

His eyes were the same green but dulled somehow. And there was a wicked gleam in them, along with a cruel curl of his mouth as he saw me standing there.

"Promised one," he whispered, though it was more of a hissing rasp.

I clenched my hands into fists, so tightly that my nails cut into my palms as I asked, "Who are you?"

The demon cocked its head and replied, "Who I am does not matter. I am but a piece in their plans. But you…" it trailed off.

"How can we get rid of you? Of any of the demons possessing bodies?"

It was a long shot that the damn thing would tell me, but it was worth a try.

The demon raised a brow. "You cannot. It will kill the host."

I flared my nostrils and shot back, "I don't believe you."

"Then why don't you try? Use that magnificent power on me and see if your friend survives it?"

The demon was taunting me, I knew that. Yet still, a

part of me, a dangerous part of me, wanted to give in and show it just how "magnificent" my magic was.

"Asteria," Nox said quietly, probably sensing the shift in me.

The demon's gaze flicked to where Nox stood behind me and it snarled, "Cursed bastard."

Nox took a step forward and said, "Funnily enough, I heard you the first ten times you called me that. What is your name?"

The demon wearing Raven's body only shrank back, hissing.

"We should go," I whispered.

Nox glanced at me and nodded, then took my hand. As we walked towards the entrance, the demon began to murmur, in the same creepy, singsong-like way as the other demons, "Run, run, run, princess, run…"

Griffin straightened as we walked out of the infirmary and into the hall.

"How was he?"

"The same," Nox replied.

Griffin seemed to deflate a little. I glanced at him, my brow furrowed, but he avoided my scrutinizing gaze.

"The demon doesn't like you," I said, turning my attention toNox.

He rolled his shoulders and replied, "No, it doesn't. I imagine it's old enough or intelligent enough to remember the last Long Night."

"Does its dislike also have anything to do with your… heritage?" I asked carefully, unsure how much Griffin knew.

Nox didn't seem bothered by my question though, he simply answered, "Yes, I imagine it does."

Griffin cleared his throat and said, "I should be going.

Let me know if you need anything." He glanced at me and added, "Either of you."

He bowed and Nox bowed back. I gave an awkward little wave and Griffin chuckled before striding away without another word, leaving us in the hall outside the infirmary.

"Who is Griffin?" I asked.

"An old friend," Nox replied. "He has always supported my claim, even when it was... dangerous to do so."

I still wasn't sure what I was trying to figure out about Griffin, so I just asked, "How did you two meet?"

Nox's answering smile was a little devious. "I met Griffin in a place much less refined than this, when we were both in rather interesting positions in life."

"Sounds like an interesting story."

He met my eyes. "It is. And sometime soon, I'll tell it to you."

But not right now... were his unspoken words.

There was still so much I didn't know about Nox, about his past and his family. He was very good at avoiding telling anyone about it all. Even me. Yet, I knew, even if he was hiding anything horrible or dark, I wouldn't care. I was past that point now. The line between caring about morals when it came to Nox and his actions had been crossed the minute I accepted the bond between us.

"Soon, love," he affirmed, brushing a hand over my cheek. "I promise."

"Soon we could be dead," I muttered.

His hand froze and his gaze locked onto mine. His expression slowly ebbed into something sharp and feral. And then he grabbed my hand and began to drag me down the hall.

"Where are we——"

But I was cut off as he pulled me into one of the shadowed alcoves that lined the palace halls. His mouth lined up roughly with mine and his hand closed around my breast, his finger flicking against my nipple.

"Nox," I gasped. "Anyone could see us."

He ground against me and growled, "Does that bother you?"

"I——"

"Because I don't care. You're mine and they can all see it."

His sharp teeth scraped against my neck and a spark in me ignited. I understood his insistence, the need for *now*. Going forward, nothing was a guarantee, not even our lives. So, *now*, he would show me just how alive I was and just how much he possessed me.

My back scraped against the rough stone wall in the back of the alcove as he hiked me up. I braced my legs around him as he abruptly pushed into me. It was rough and unhinged, feral in a way that fed our innate natures. Someone could have passed the alcove and I would have had no idea nor care.

Our breath came in heavy, shared gasps and his hand drifted lower, between us.

"You don't have to——"

"No," he cut me off, his voice rough. "I do."

The position shouldn't have been great for what he was doing, but he somehow managed it, his fingers working me quickly and efficiently. I shattered under his touch within a minute, just as his wings flared out from behind him.

Then, all caution went to the wind and he pounded into me, my hands gripping his shoulders to keep steady. I felt a prick in my mouth and I realized my sharp Fae teeth had finally decided to come out and play.

He must've caught sight of them because in between one moment and the next, he flitted us out of the alcove and into his bedroom. He hardly paused his thrusts as we landed on the bed, ordering, "Do it, love."

At the first scrape of my teeth against his neck, he slowed and his hands grasped mine, pinned them to the bed on either side of me. I wasn't really sure what I was doing, but this felt right enough that I didn't really care. I teased him for a few seconds more before letting my teeth sink into his skin, leaving two shallow marks. His blood was rich on my tongue and as I pulled back, I wrapped my legs around his hips.

"Fucking hell, love," he groaned. "Never thought…"

He trailed off, kissing me instead as he began to move faster. His hands tightened in mine and he let his head drop to my shoulder as a shudder wracked his body and he came, muttering my name over and over against my skin.

We didn't leave the bedroom for the rest of the day. I knew it had been a while for Nox, but he was *insatiable*.

By the time evening rolled around, I was thoroughly sated and hungry. Like actually hungry, for lots and lots of food. He didn't disappoint, flicking his fingers and summoning a spread of cheese and crackers and then vinegary subs, and finally chocolate cake. An odd assortment of some of my other favorite foods.

Once the food was cleared away, we fell back into the bed, me leaning against his chest, his arms around me. I had questions for him—questions about his past, about our magic, about what was going to happen next. But for now, I kept them to myself. We had time. We had to have time.

That night, on the dream bridge, Nox wasn't looking at me.

He was looking straight past me.

And he looked afraid.

CHAPTER
TWENTY-EIGHT

I JERKED awake to the sound of someone screaming. Screaming and wailing, like the world was ending. My gaze locked with Nox's as the sounds of terror escalated. We were both momentarily frozen, then he pushed himself up out of the bed. He snatched pants and black t-shirt from the dresser and quickly pulled them on. Then I watched as he flicked wrist and a set of the same battle leathers his Unseelie warriors had worn that day under the tree appeared in the air next to him.

Just as he was finally finishing up with the leathers, my mind unfroze and I ventured, "Nox?"

"Stay here, love," he said.

I rose from the bed, still naked from last night. I crossed my arms over my chest and said, "There is no way in hell that I'm staying here and letting you go out there alone."

His gaze snagged on my body and he huffed out a breath, muttering, "Damn bastards couldn't have waited a little longer."

But he didn't hesitate before flicking his wrist again.

Another set of leathers appeared, along with leggings and t-shirt to wear underneath them, as well as lace-up boots. I plucked them out of the air one by one and dressed quickly, not failing to notice that each piece of clothing fit me perfectly.

"When did you have these——"

"Not too long ago," he replied shortly as another voice joined in the chorus of screaming. "We need to go."

A long, curved sword materialized at his side, along with a slim dagger. He handed the dagger to me and said, "Just in case."

"Nox, I don't know how to use this."

"And I'll teach you very soon. For now, just hold onto it. For my sanity, at least."

"Okay," I relented.

He stared at me, then kissed me quick and hard, muttering against mouth, "Do not leave my side. Please."

I don't think I'd ever heard him say that—*please*. That was when I realized how afraid he was. He had just lost me, less than a few weeks ago. But we'd both known what we were getting into when we solidified our bond. The road ahead wasn't going to be safe or easy and I wasn't one to be coddled or sequestered away. We were going to be in danger, today on. And who knew how long this fight would last?

"I won't," I assured him as he pulled back.

He took my hand and we headed for the door. When we emerged out into the hallway, the screaming stopped, the palace falling eerily quiet. Our steps echoed as we slowly crept closer to the entrance hall. We passed a maid cowering in a shallow alcove. Nox paused, keeping his hold on my hand as she gently asked the girl, "Violetta, can you tell me what happened?"

The maid, Violetta, shook her head, her eyes wide as tears fell down her face.

"He came," was all she managed to say.

Nox looked highly disturbed at Violetta's words. My ears pricked and all three of us froze as we heard the sound of someone running towards us. Nox raised his sword, his expression cold as stone. Though surprise and alarm lit up his face as Griffin burst into the hall, a sickly stream of dark blood running down his face.

"Nox," he said frantically, through heaving breaths. "He took him. I tried to stop him but he started killing the healers and I panicked. But he took him, he took him and I don't know where… I failed and—"

"Griffin," Nox said sharply. "I need you to take a breath and tell me what's going on."

Griffin shook his head and said, "The demon prince is back. He was in his original form, without a host, just like last time. I don't know how but," his breath caught, "he took Raven."

A weight dropped in my belly as Griffin said the words. Words that couldn't possibly be true. When I had killed my uncle, I had forced Abaddon from his body. I thought that meant the demon had been sent back to Hell, at least for now.

"Was he alone?" I asked, gripping Nox's hand with a death vice.

"I didn't see any others," Griffin said. "But, Nox, I…"

The Unseelie Fae warrior's shoulders bowed forward and his head dropped. Nox squeezed my hand once before letting it go and walking over to Griffin. He gripped his shoulder and said, "We'll get him back."

"He doesn't even know. I was a coward and now he might never know," Griffin choked out.

I fisted my trembling hands at my sides and said, "What's going on? What does he mean, Nox?"

Nox turned his head to look at me, one hand still on Griffin's trembling shoulder.

"Griffin is Raven's father," he said simply.

As if it were as simple as that. As if the world was not falling out from beneath my feet.

"We need to tell Lil," I said, my mind whirring. "We need to tell his mom. And we need... we need to get him back."

"I know," Nox replied. "And we will."

Tears were starting to sting my eyes. But this time, I was not sad and I was not scared.

I was angry.

Griffin stared at me, at the starlight I knew was glowing from behind my eyes. He didn't look afraid of my power. Instead, cold determination was surfacing across his features too.

Nox released Griffin's shoulder and faced me once more. He trailed his gaze from my toes to the top of my head, those mighty wings appearing behind him. And then he said, "Let's show them just how brightly you can burn, love."

And burn I would.

To be continued...

ACKNOWLEDGMENTS

The first chapter of this book had many attempts and many versions. And with each attempt, I became more and more comfortable with being vulnerable and showcasing what I consider to be the messier side of healing. I wanted to find a way to tell people that there is no *wrong* way to heal and no correct way to overcome trauma. Asteria is a result of that message. So, perhaps vainly, I want to first give credit to myself for being brave enough to explore a piece of my past that I usually would shy away from or try to hide.

Next, to Kayla Hill, the editor of this book. Calling you to discuss chapters was the highlight of my last semester of college. Thank you for helping me shape this book into its final form and for giving me the encouragement and support I needed along the way. And sorry for the slow burn. I hope it was worth it in the end (LOL).

As always, thank you to my parents Brian and Sara for constantly being my biggest supporters and cheerleaders. Thanks especially to Mom for the final proofread... apologies for the smut.

Thank you to my partner, Ryan, for listening to me relay the plots of many books yet to come and for reminding me to attend to basic human needs when I'm in goblin-writing-mode. You're right, I *probably* shouldn't sit on my feet so much and I definitely need to stretch more.

Finally, to you, the reader: thank you for sticking through here until the end. There's plenty more to come, so if you enjoyed this first one, I invite you to hang around for the rest of the saga! There'll be more healing, more magic, and of course, more smut.

BONUS CHAPTER

Chapter One: Nox

THE BASSY BEAT of club music was a drumbeat in my chest, distracting me from even the task at hand. Flashing lights reflected the revelry around me; scantily clad bodies danced and engaged in *more*. More, which I had not thought about in some time. I hadn't let myself—and I didn't know why tonight of all nights, as I trailed the alleged obsidian seller, sex was on my mind. Or, perhaps it wasn't really sex at all, but the allure of sharing myself with someone in a way I haven't in decades.

Shaking my head slightly, I attempted to clear it. In all my foolish, wandering thoughts, I had lost the faerie I've been following. Swearing under my breath, I brushed past a couple, intertwined and swaying in one of the further corners of the club. They didn't look my way. No one did, thanks to the glamour I'd put over myself. It was unlikely that most Seelie Court citizens would recognize the king of the Unseelie Court, especially in the dim, hazy light of the night club, but I didn't want to take too many chances.

Cloaking myself subtly with shadow, I strode towards one of the dim alcoves that lined the back of the space. I was sure the seller must have slipped into one of them. But just before I flicked back the curtain of the closest one, I paused.

There was something catching in my chest, a feeling I couldn't quite place.

Without really thinking, I began to walk back towards the throng of dancing and drinking near the center of the club. Light flickered in my vision and I wasn't sure if it was simply from the strobe lights above or something else entirely.

A few paces away, a girl was dancing, the violet streaks in her hair aglow under the neon lights. But she wasn't—

"Aster!"

A body stumbled into me and the light in my eyes exploded into a blinding supernova. The catching in my chest became near painful and my whole damn world suddenly narrowed as the girl turned and met my gaze.

Her eyes were a striking shade of blue, bright and ice-cold, clouded only by what I assumed was one too many drinks. Dark hair tumbled down her back and full lips parted as she looked at me. It wasn't until a laugh escaped her and she reached up did I realize that my glamour had all but slipped away from the shock of what I was seeing. Of *who* I was seeing.

Sure, I recognized those eyes. I had seen them on another, on the few occasions I'd met Calum Fairwae, regent king of the Seelie Court. And yes, there was that unmistakable hum of a powerful bloodline surrounding her.

But neither of those things were what caused me to nearly flit away on the spot.

I *knew* this girl. I knew her like I knew myself. She was a spector in my dreams and had been for many years. But as I looked at her now, I knew she had no memory of me in her waking. Which was good because I needed to leave now. I had to save Asteria Fairwae in the only possible way I could—by walking away and never returning.

But my resolve cracked in two as her fingers touched my hair, just barely brushing my cheek. I was suddenly rooted to the spot, powerless under her hazy, drunken stare. She started to move closer but then a voice chirped loudly, "Hey, woah, woah, Aster! Let's not just go petting random strangers."

I flicked my gaze momentarily to the girl with the violet in her hair, stumbling over. I thought I recognized something about her too, but I was too distracted to ponder why further.

Asteria gave her friend a blank look and an invisible string urged me closer to her. Before I even realized I was speaking, I heard myself say, "Is that what you were trying to do? *Pet* me?"

Her attention swung back in my direction, her gaze trailing the slant of my ears, her head tilting just slightly, as if she was trying to decide precisely what I was.

A soft laugh slipped from my lips before I could stop it and my hand lifted, guided by that pull. I brushed back a strand of her silky, dark hair, the movement feeling oddly natural, as if I'd done it a thousand times before.

"Yes, love, I'm just like you," I murmured as I slid my finger up the point of her ear too.

Even though I just meant to assure her I was Fae too,

the words felt deeper than that, as if a hidden meaning even I was unaware of laid behind them. I didn't let myself think too much about it, not as her eyes brightened and her cheeks flushed.

The heated look she was giving me nearly brought me to my knees and I forced myself to drag my hand back, to step away, slipping into the crowd again.

My breath was coming in quick gasps, my vision tilting. Gods, I *needed* to leave. I would just...

I had to see her one last time before I let her go forever.

Slipping up to the elevated platform where the DJ was, I appeared in a flurry of shadow behind him. He stiffened, sensing my presence before he saw me.

"Play something else," I murmured in his ear. "Something a little more... traditional."

He didn't look at me but said tightly, "I don't play faerie music here."

"Hmm," I hummed, letting a shadow slip between his fingers. "I think you do."

The idiot actually began to tremble slightly as he saw the wisp of darkness, but to his credit, he replied quickly, "Right, yeah. I'll play it next."

"Good," I breathed before returning to the dance floor.

It wasn't hard to find Asteria and her friend again; I simply followed that feeling in my chest. Her friend glanced around nervously as they both heard the odd, uneven rhythm of faerie music begin to play over the speakers. Only our bodies were naturally equipped to keep up with music like this. Once upon a time, I had danced in ballrooms to this kind of music with faeries who were long-dead, lost to a war I didn't want to remember. But I remembered it now, especially as Asteria saw me again. She had no idea the price she might pay if I continued to be any more selfish than I already was.

But her breath, her heartbeat, her damn laugh… They were all a thrumming rhythm, matching the one in my chest. I couldn't walk away now.

"If the ears didn't convince you, maybe this will," I said in her ear before sweeping her into my arms.

She stumbled only slightly before matching my movements and the beat of the song. I let my hands trail the soft curve of her hips as she moved, the sway of her body intoxicating. Her teeth caught her lip as she lifted her gaze to mine and a spark ignited in me. The flame burst into an inferno as she reached up and ran her hand through the loose strands of my hair again. I resisted the urge to downright purr and I wonder if she sensed it because she laughed again, the sound a delicious rasp.

"What's that?" I murmured, close to her.

Her reply was breathless. "I didn't say anything."

A feeling deep inside of me stirred as I heard her voice for the first time. It reminded me both simultaneously of falling and settling into place. And perhaps that would be what having her—and *being* had by her—would feel like. Because I was certain she was one to take as well as be taken.

The song faded out, replaced by the pounding bass from earlier, but neither of us moved to disentangle from one another. She stared up at me, eyes wide and shining with sharp interest… and something else. A deep thread of feeling I could not let her discover more fully if I wanted to keep her safe.

But as she looked at me with that unflinching stare, I think I knew what I had always known but had been

301

running from ever since I saw her for the first time on that dream bridge. Asteria Fairwae was my rival, as heir to the Seelie Court. She could also very well be what brought back a powerful demon into this world if the curse on me still remained. And yet…

She was the other half to a sacred bond so few of our kind experienced since the last war.

Mate.

I exhaled, my hands trailing up her back. She let out a soft sigh at my touch and for just a moment, under the flashing lights and in the midst of a pulsing crowd, I let my hands tighten. It was as close to holding her as I would ever get.

And then, I let her go.

She stumbled and I resisted the urge to catch her, instead giving her one last half-smile,an expression I hoped was merely the silent goodbye of a stranger. But as I turned and began to walk away, she called, "Wait!"

I froze for a split second and instinct had me turning to face her again.

"What's your name?" she asked.

A shadow curled at my ear, whispers urging me on.

Tell her…. Tell her.

For once, I ignored them, though, judging by her expression, not before she caught a glimpse of the wisp of darkness. Good. It would likely make her afraid, as she should be of me.

I moved close to her once more and murmured in her ear, "You don't want to know my name, love."

I meant it, and I meant to move away once I said it. But then, she shivered as my breath ghosted the shell of her ear and keen senses told me the shiver was not one of fear.

Some part of me that was less logical and more primal had a low sound dragging its way up from my chest. Gods, I wanted to claim her right here and now, to damn the consequences and graze my teeth along the column of her neck. I wanted to bite her, to taste her blood and the homecoming I knew it would be.

Instead, I tugged her earlobe between my teeth, earning a gasp from her. She didn't hear the sound I made seconds later, because the last shreds of my morality had me flitting away in a flurry of shadows. I landed with an ungraceful thud in the middle of my penthouse, panting.

"What the hell happened to you?"

I looked up to see Griffin looking down at me, dark brows furrowed and arms crossed over his chest. I barely remembered that I had told him to wait here for me, so we could go over what I'd discovered about the obsidian seller.

But now…

I looked up at him, shaking my head. "I saw her."

It took Griffin a moment to understand what I was saying. But I saw it, the moment the realization washed over his features. His lips parted and his brows raised further before he stated, "Your mate."

I nodded, feeling numb. Griffin sank to the floor with me, sighing and then saying, "I assume you had the wherewithal to leave before—"

"Yes."

We sat there in silence for a while after that, me absorbing the force of what had just happened, him trying to buffer some of it. Eventually, I said roughly, "I don't… I don't know if I can stay away."

He glanced sidelong at me. "No one would blame you if you couldn't."

A shaky laugh left me. "I would. And she eventually would too."

"Perhaps."

I took a heavy breath, standing and walking to the window, staring at the moon, high in the sky. When I glanced back at Griffin, still sitting on the floor, he shook his head.

"Even you, my friend, may not be able to stop this from playing out now."

And as the moonlight was blocked out by the pair of magnificent wings stretching out on my back, I feared I might agree with him.